Bruce Beckham

Murder in Adland

Detective Inspector Skelgill
Investigates

LUCiUS

Text copyright 2021 Bruce Beckham

Kindle edition first published by Lucius 2012
Second edition published by Lucius 2015
Third edition published by Lucius 2021

Paperback edition first published by Lucius 2015

For more details and rights enquiries contact:
Lucius-ebooks@live.com

Cover design by Moira Kay Nicol

EDITOR'S NOTE

Murder in Adland is a stand-alone whodunit, the first in the series 'Detective Inspector Skelgill Investigates'. It is set in the English Lake District, London and the Scottish capital, Edinburgh.

Absolutely no AI (Artificial Intelligence) is used in the writing of the DI Skelgill novels.

THE DI SKELGILL SERIES

Main characters in order of appearance

DI Daniel Skelgill, 37
Detective Inspector, Cumbria Police

DS Emma Jones, 26
Detective Sergeant, Cumbria Police

Dermott Lord Goldsmith, 32
Joint-principal of Tregilgis & Goldsmith

Miriam Tregilgis, 33
Widow of Ivan Tregilgis, 33

Julia Rubicon, 27
Head of Edinburgh office

Elspeth Goldsmith, 31
Wife of Dermott Goldsmith

Krista Morocco, 32
Head of London office

Melanie Stark, 29
Employee in London office

Grendon Smith, 23
Sacked employee of London office

Ron Bunce, 62
Media supplier to Tregilgis & Goldsmith

Glossary

SOME of the Cumbrian dialect words, abbreviations, British and Irish slang and local usage appearing in *Murder in Adland* are as follows:

Alreet – alright (often a greeting)
Aye – yes
Barney – argument
Batter, on the – drinking heavily (Irish)
Brae – hill (Scots)
Burn – stream (Scots)
Cuddy – donkey
Deek – look
Donnat – idiot, good for nothing
Fae – for (Scots)
Frae – from (Scots)
Gattered – drunk (inebriated)
Ginnel – alley
Grubber – cricket delivery that does not bounce
Happen – maybe
Heid bummer – queen bee (Scots)
Hey up – hello, look out
How! – cry used for driving cattle
Howay – come on
Irn Bru – a Scots brand of soda, made from girders
Int' – in the
Ken – know, you know
Ladgeful – embarrassing
Lass – girl, young woman
Lassie – ditto (Scots)
Marra – mate (friend)
Mesen – myself
Mithering – bothering

Nay – no
Offcomer – outsider, tourist
Ont' – on the
Ower – over
Pike – peak
Reet – right
T' – the (often silent)
Tek – take
Thou/thee – you, your
Thysen – yourself
Us – me
While – until
Yin – one/man (Scots)
Yon – that
Yonder – there
Yowe – ewe

1. BASSENTHWAITE LAKE

Late May – dawn

'Wakey wakey, Skelly – 4 a.m. alarm call.'

'George – I'm in the middle of Bass Lake. It's Sunday. Tell me you're just bored.'

'Sorry, lad.' The Desk Sergeant's disembodied voice softens: as a fellow fisherman, there is a note of compassion in his tone. 'You've got a murder on your patch. Body's still warm by all accounts.'

'You're pulling my leg, George.'

'Fraid not, lad.'

'Where?'

'Know Bewaldeth Hall – the hotel?'

'Aye, it's ower yonder.' Skelgill stares pensively across the stern of his small craft to a distant cluster of grey rooftops and chimney stacks that blend with the dawn shadows. 'Look – I'll call you from the motor. I need to get these lines in. Then I'm a ten-minute row from Peel Wyke, and I'll have to chain the boat up. I'll be there in half an hour max.'

'Okay, I'll pass it on. Caught owt?'

'Nay. Not a tickle. It's a cracking morning though.'

'Ah well, bigger fish to fry now, lad.'

*

Daniel Skelgill, 37, dedicated pike-angler and Inspector, Cumbria CID, reels in his last dead-bait with practised aplomb. He

8

unhooks the slender sprat and lets its lifeless form slip through the mirrored surface of Bassenthwaite Lake, "The only *lake* in the Lake District," as he enjoys telling bemused visitors.

The A66 trunk road bordering the wooded western bank is empty and silent, though the ponderous chug of a distant tractor drifts across the still water, a contrast to the soft rhythmical swish and splash of Skelgill's oars. In his wake the imposing bulk of Skiddaw seems pumped up like a body builder, as the sun's first rays raise into relief the sculpted musculature of its upper slopes. Another of Skelgill's nuggets of information, cheerfully dispensed to groaning stretcher-borne casualties in his voluntary role in the North Fells Mountain Rescue, it is England's fourth-highest mountain. Its perfect reflection, slowly receding, begins to ripple as the boat's wash creeps towards the opposite shore.

2. BEWALDETH HALL

Sunday 4.30 a.m.

'*J*ones?'

Having slewed his car to an extravagant halt that has scoured his signature into Bewaldeth Hall's neat gravel drive, from the open driver's window he regards the girl with some uncertainty. At first sight her informal and scanty outfit would suggest a hotel guest, eager to intercept him – but now he identifies her as Detective Sergeant Emma Jones. A twenty-six-year-old product of the graduate programme, she is a local lass with a degree in English Literature from London. Competent and confident, she is quickly making a name for herself, and is referred to by some as 'Fast-track' – while others covet her affections. However, perhaps Skelgill's gun-slinging reputation precedes him, for she seems a little star struck beneath his reproachful glare.

'Yes, Sir – that's correct, Sir.'

'Didn't recognise you.'

'No, Sir – there's a rave in a hangar over near Cockermouth.' She gestures with a downward sweep of the hand, indicating her party wear. 'I was on duty – undercover, Sir.'

Skelgill makes a cursory nod. His features remain taciturn. A man's man – a touch chauvinistic, he would admit – he prefers male company when it comes to the cut and thrust of police work. But his regular DS is on annual leave, and his Chief's rota has dealt him an unfamiliar hand. This – allied with the annoying curtailment of his fishing trip – is more likely the source of his dismay than what she wears. He pushes open the door in a careless manner, causing her to take a sudden step backward.

'Call us Guv, will you? I'm more used to it from that Cockney layabout Leyton.'

'Yes, Sir – *Guv.*'

He shoots her a sideways glance and sees that her gaze has been drawn to his attire. He has revealed himself to be sporting threadbare brown corduroys, a faded olive-green t-shirt, and a scale-spangled taupe gilet hanging with jangling angling paraphernalia; these are lived-in favourites, owned for best part of a decade and laundered only slightly more often.

'Aye?'

'Er – you came in a bit of a hurry, too – Guv?'

Though her tone is sympathetic, he remains defensive.

'This is professional fishing gear. Cost a packet.'

*

Bewaldeth Hall is typical of the many small Victorian hotels scattered throughout the Lake District. Dressed grey slate stone, a modern bedroom-block added at the back, lots of jutting eaves and mossy tiles, and mature grounds where rhododendrons strain like ravenous tethered goats, eager to gobble up what remains of the gardens. A portly middle-aged constable stands yawning to attention on the stone steps. He seems to salute the two detectives, but in fact is just shielding his eyes from the early-morning sunlight, now slanting over the eastern fells. He stares quizzically as he notices their unconventional apparel.

'Hey up, Art.' Skelgill acknowledges the older man, the long-time local bobby for Bewaldeth and Snittlegarth, then adds, pointing by way of explanation:

'Me fishing – her dancing. What's the story here?'

'Young Dodd's guarding Room 10, where the body is. The Doc's in there, too. Just arrived. Lot of blood. Knife-job, I reckon. The owner's back in her cottage behind the hotel. Advertising agency's booked out the whole place for the weekend.

Dead lad's one of the two business partners.' He consults his notebook. 'Name of Tregilgis, Ivan. Thirty-three. His wife's int' bar with t'other partner – Lord Goldsmith (also thirty-three), and his missus. WPC on the way. SOCO on the way. I've told all the rest to stay int' residents' lounge. Most of 'em are still gattered.' He makes a drinking motion, and then purses his lips. 'Some fit lasses, Skelly, lad.'

Skelgill steals a sidelong glance in the direction of his assistant, but she has not reacted to this latter remark.

'Behave, Arthur.'

Skelgill nods his appreciation and leads the way into a square entrance hall, heavily beamed and adorned with paintings of African battle-scenes with red-coated soldiers; staring stuffed animals; antique rifles and various tribal artefacts, feathered spears and great machete-like knives. DS Jones hesitates, as if to comment on the frightening arsenal, but Skelgill instinctively bangs through a swing door guarded by two suits of armour. It opens on a corridor with windows on the right-hand side and a row of doors on the left. At the far end the aforementioned PC Dodd jumps to attention from a sitting position at the foot of a staircase. Then he sways, and drops back down with a thump.

'Alreet, lad?' Skelgill approaches and puts a hand on his shoulder.

'Sorry, Sir. I'll be fine.'

'Tell us what you know, then.'

The young PC swallows.

'Sir. No sign of the weapon. Alarm was raised by Mrs Tregilgis about three-fifteen a.m. – she'd got into bed in the dark, thinking her husband was asleep. Felt the damp, thought he'd been sick and switched on the light. Saw it was blood – then all hell broke loose – and the whole lot of them came crowding into the room. It's a private party and it was still going strong. According to the wife he'd gone to bed first, maybe about two a.m., taking the room key. He'd left this door to the corridor unlocked so she could get in. No sign of a forced entry or a struggle, but the French door onto the terrace was unlocked and the small top window was open. Jewellery and a wallet lying in full view on the dresser. Couple of empty beer bottles. I had a quick look round outside – nothing obvious and nobody about. No thefts reported from other rooms, Sir.'

Skelgill, listening intently, nods his approval.

'Good work, Dodd.' He indicates back along the corridor. 'Are these all the bedrooms?'

'Not all, Sir. There's ten on this floor and ten more if you go up these stairs.' He gestures over his shoulder.

DS Jones is pushing at an unyielding fire-escape door that faces the staircase.

'How about this, was it closed?'

'Exactly as you see it, Ma'am – at least, when we arrived at about three forty-five.'

DS Jones tries to conceal her discomfort at being called *Ma'am*. PC Dodd and she are erstwhile classmates.

'Go and get some fresh air. We'll take over here.'

'Yes, Ma'am.'

3. ROOM 10

Sunday 4.35 a.m.

Skelgill taps a knuckle beneath the Roman numeral *X* and gently pushes open the door.

'Right then, Herdwick – what have you got for us, you old cuddy?'

From his left materialises a dark, slender woman of Mediterranean appearance. Skelgill evidently does not recognise her, nor she him. With a look of alarm she tries to press shut the door, trapping him against the jamb.

'No, no! You may not enter!'

'We're the police!'

Skelgill yanks his Cumbrian Water fishing permit from the breast pocket of his gilet and flashes it briefly. The woman's startled demeanour relaxes, and she steps away, raising her hands in a flamboyant gesture, one that might owe something to flamenco.

'Ah – *perdone* – accept my apologies. I did not recognise – I mean, you English detectives, you are so – eccentric in your dress.'

She peels off a blue nitrile glove and holds out a firm hand to each of them in turn.

'You are Inspector Skelgill – *y Signorita* – ?'

'DS Jones, my Sergeant. Doctor –?'

'Maria Garcia Gonzalez. I am locum for Doctor 'erdwick.'

Skelgill might wish to pull a disapproving face at his colleague, but the intelligent black Spanish eyes never leave his own, even as the woman moves aside to reveal the double bed against the left-hand wall. There follows a few moments' silence while they gaze, not breathing, on the scene. Frowning, Skelgill is reminded that one can never cease to be amazed by the amount of blood that fits inside a person. Ivan Tregilgis lies naked, quite peacefully; face down, in a sea of crimson among waves of crisp white linen.

'A matador, it is you seek.'

The two detectives exhale in tandem and turn abruptly to Dr Garcia Gonzalez as her unintentionally melodramatic words break the spell.

'What do you mean?'

'Inspector – 'e was killed by a single violent blow to the back of the neck from a knife or sword. It severed the carotid artery and probably the spinal cord. It would cause paralysis and rapid loss of blood. If it was not the skill of an expert – it was, how you say – *la suerte del diablo?*'

'The luck of the devil.'

It is DS Jones who translates the adage. Skelgill is scowling.

'The *work* of the devil, more like.'

They all nod in agreement.

'So he was stabbed where he lay?'

'*Si*, Inspector. Almost all of the blood is close to 'is body. Just a few smears spread around the sheets, probably made by *la esposa* – and stains on the lady's nightdress. It is there.' She points to a flimsy, bloodstained, beige garment that lies crumpled inside the small bathroom.

Skelgill appears to be warming to the Iberian medic's efficiency.

'When did it happen, Doc?'

'From 'is body temperature – and the room temperature – with just a top sheet on the bed – 'e died at very close to *las tres*.'

'Three a.m.' DS Jones again does the honours.

'No wonder his wife thought he was alive.'

Skelgill's tone is flat – as if to allow in his mind for the rejoinder, "Maybe he was".

He turns to face the woman. She is packing items into a small black Gladstone bag, and for a moment he seems to appraise her figure. She is of medium height, like his colleague, though slim to the point of being skinny, with a shock of raven hair and great dark eyes beneath curved brows.

'Thank you very much, Doctor. I may need to meet up with you when you've filed your report.'

She snaps shut her bag and stands upright. There is a conspiratorial glint in her eye as she glances at DS Jones. Then she reaches again to shake hands with Skelgill.

'*Encantada*, Inspector – you *old cuddy.*' And with a friendly nod to DS Jones she is gone.

Skelgill shakes his head ruefully.

'I'll swing for that Arthur one of these days. How am I supposed to know Herdwick's got a locum in?'

DS Jones has to suppress a grin; being a local lass she knows that a *cuddy* is a donkey. But Skelgill quickly gathers his wits.

'Any road – better have a quick shufti before SOCO kick us out.'

The room itself is smart but unremarkable. Only the half-glazed terrace door might strike one as unusual, though a pleasant facility, especially in this weather. All the curtains are still drawn, and they muffle the birdsong that drifts in through the open window noted by PC Dodd. More exceptional are the expensive toiletries that crowd the ledges in the bathroom, and rows of designer labels that grace the clothes rail.

'Not short of a bob or two.' Skelgill grips his gilet, rather in the manner of a dinner-jacketed announcer taking hold of his lapels. 'Must be alright, that advertising lark, driving round London in a flash motor, top restaurants, expense account.'

'Wouldn't you miss the fishing, Guv?'

'Thames is good for chub.' His reply comes as he absently pokes his finger into a half-eaten plate of what looks like cheesecake, left on top of the dresser. 'Not bad. And still fresh. Think he brought back his pudding to eat in bed?'

'Doesn't look like a sweet-eater.' DS Jones is regarding the athletic figure on the bed.

Skelgill glances at her for a second, a furtive question in his eyes. Then he turns his attention to the drawers, and begins to poke about amongst some underwear with the tip of his pen.

'What do you reckon, Jones?'

She peers at the neatly folded ladies' briefs.

'Expensive. You might say *sensible*.'

Skelgill nods and moves away. A small polished writing desk stands beneath the window. Upon it rests a briefcase and a scrolled flip chart. Skelgill avoids the briefcase – presumably for fear of smearing fingerprints – and instead he unrolls the chart.

'Looks like they've been doing pretty well.' He scans through the headlines. 'New clients – record turnover – won a load of awards –'

'Guv.'

They might be new to one another, but there is no mistaking the note of urgency in DS Jones's voice. He swings around to find that she has carefully peeled back the crumpled top-sheet. There, at the foot of the bed, lies a flimsy sheer black g-string.

'Extra small. Not his, Guv.'

'Nor hers, eh, lass?'

4. MRS GROTENEUS

Sunday 4.40 a.m.

After leaving Room 10 and ushering PC Dodd back to his post, DS Jones departs in search of the owner, Mrs Groteneus. Skelgill, meanwhile, has optimistically taken up residence in the empty dining room, harbouring the misguided hope that a plate of lavishly buttered bacon sandwiches will be forthcoming. However, it is barely four-forty a.m. and the hotel is still bereft of staff. He rises and pushes through a swing-door. It leads into the darkened kitchen, silent but for the gurgle of an industrial dishwasher and the hum of a bank of refrigerators. There are some continental breakfasts made up. Skelgill rips open a packet of muesli and pours its contents into his upturned mouth. Then he hears voices from the dining room. With limited success he tries to swallow the grainy mixture. Attempting to retrace his steps, he finds himself trapped by the unfamiliar system of one-way doors. An anxious-looking, tall angular woman releases him; she has a prominent nose, and is aged perhaps in her mid-fifties.

'Ah, Mrs Groteneus. Just wondered if we could get a cuppa?' He indicates over his shoulder with a thumb.

'Of course.' She nods and bustles past him. 'Please be seated and I shall bring it to you.'

DS Jones lowers her voice, as they wait for Mrs Groteneus to return. 'Seems a bit highly strung. She runs the place on her own – her husband left her ten years ago. She's Dutch.'

Skelgill scowls. 'What is this, Eurovision? It'll be a French maid next.'

'Polish most likely, Guv.'

Skelgill is about to retort, but the woman reappears; having

18

gathered assorted tea things on a tray. She takes a seat opposite the two detectives, and stares nervously as Skelgill loads a cup with extra sugar and then holds it out for her to pour the tea. He looks up, and appears surprised by her expression of concern.

'Mrs Groteneus, I realise this is not good for business, and must be very upsetting, but it's essential that I ask you some questions about last night.'

She twitches, perhaps by way of acknowledgement.

'I gather this was a company booking – they took all your rooms?'

She nods.

'Can you tell me about the sequence of events as they took place last night?'

'Oh, *ja* – of course.' She licks her thin lips and looks as if she could do with a drink herself. 'But first I should tell you there was one person who did not arrive – I have a list of guests and the room allocation at reception.'

'Excellent – very efficient. We'll take note of that.' He glances at DS Jones, who is already writing in her pocket book. He nods for the hotelier to continue.

'They met for cocktails in the bar at seven-thirty and came in here for dinner at eight-thirty. The meal was over by just after ten, and then they went either to the bar or to the Great Hall – they brought a music system which was set up so they could dance in there.'

'How long did you stay with them?'

'I served the wine during the meal, and I was at the bar before and after. I went to bed just after midnight as I was due to get up at six o'clock to prepare the breakfasts.'

'Do you have a night porter?'

She shakes her head. 'They could help themselves to drinks after I had gone. We usually have an honesty-bar, but with this company I agreed a price per head – it was a generous deal they made with me.'

'What about your staff – when did they leave?'

'Chef, about ten p.m. – I heard his motorcycle – he lives at Keswick. The three waitresses and two kitchen staff all left together at their usual time, just after eleven. They share a car – they live at Cockermouth or nearby.'

'We'll need their details. Do any of them have keys?'

'No. I am the only keyholder for external doors. My two chambermaids, they each have a master key for the bedrooms, but do not take them out of the hotel.'

'Was the place locked up last night?'

'Er – *ja en nee*. You see, Inspector, I set the latch on the main entrance when I left, and locked the door from the storeroom – it is through the kitchen. And also I locked the bar door, which leads to a small patio. But I am at the mercy of my guests. If they did not lock their bedroom doors that lead on to the West Terrace – or they could have gone out on to the terrace by the door from the Great Hall and left it unlocked.'

Skelgill looks pointedly at DS Jones as she diligently writes. When he gains her attention he signals with a toss of the head that she should go and check. While she is away, he makes small talk with Mrs Groteneus about the weather. When she returns, he abruptly switches back to business.

'Jones?'

'Store room and bar doors bolted from the inside. Terrace door from the Great Hall unlocked, as Mrs Groteneus suspected.'

The woman wrings her hands but does not speak.

'Don't fret, madam – there's no law that says you must imprison your guests.' He pushes back his chair. 'Perhaps we could get that list?'

Mrs Groteneus is quick to lead the way, evidently relieved to escape the interrogation. She disappears behind the counter in the lobby, leaving the detectives to peruse the artefacts on display. Meanwhile she bustles about, muttering in Dutch and shuffling papers. Then suddenly she exclaims.

'*Mevrouw Goldsmith... Ja* – here is the letter!'

She hurries around to where Skelgill stands facing a wall.

Insinuating herself between the two, she jabs at the list with a bony finger.

'This one – Mr Grendon Smith – he did not come.'

But Skelgill isn't looking. He inclines his head towards a curved knife held in an odd-shaped wire fixture.

'Mrs Groteneus.' His voice is calm and measured. 'This knife – it's a kukri, aye?'

She flaps the paper, apparently determined to get him to look at her list.

'*Ja*, my husband brought them back from Nepal, many years ago.'

'Mrs Groteneus.' Skelgill persists. 'You just said *them*?'

Mijn God! She jerks around to stare at the kukri. 'There should be a pair!'

5. BREAKFAST BY THE LAKE

Sunday 6.15 a.m.

'**O**kay.' Skelgill speaks through a mouthful of bacon-and-egg sandwich. 'What have we got so far?'

DS Jones gazes thoughtfully across the scene, her eyes involuntarily following the aerobatics of a swallow as it hawks for flies.

'It doesn't look like a bungled robbery. Wouldn't the average sneak thief have stolen the valuables without waking him – and done all the other rooms, too?'

'More often than not.'

'I suppose it could be something business-related – and yet his briefcase wasn't taken. It being locked, you would imagine that would be the first thing to go. Unless someone just wanted to eliminate him?'

Skelgill grunts and shifts position on the angular boulder beneath him.

'I can't see it being some kind of professional hit. You'd need too much inside information, right down to which room he was in. Why come to the Lakes and hang about on the off chance – when you can mow him down any day of the week in London?'

A small furrow bisects DS Jones's smooth tanned brow.

'The chap Smith who never turned up – he would have known about the location and maybe the timings.'

Skelgill glances at her quizzically – perhaps a little intrigued that she has already made this connection.

'He'd run a risk of being spotted. He'd stand out like a sore

22

thumb. He's probably at a funeral.' Skelgill reaches for the aluminium pan at his feet. 'Have another butty?'

This is a generous offer coming from Skelgill – the last of his fisherman's breakfast. But DS Jones shakes her head diplomatically.

'I feel quite full, thanks.'

Skelgill needs no further encouragement. He munches in silence, surveying the surface of the water for signs of rising fish. Taking a few minutes out to gather their thoughts, Skelgill has driven the pair to the outflow of the River Derwent, where it drains Bassenthwaite Lake. Encamped on the shingle bank, Skelgill has demonstrated his expertise with a battered vintage Trangia stove and a strange smoking contraption he claims is called a Kelly Kettle. Being self-sufficient in food and drink is a state of affairs he swears by.

'If it's an inside job –' His voice tails off as he tosses his last piece of crust at a shoal of tiny dace that shimmer in the shallows. He watches the bread bob as the voracious whitebait attack it from beneath. 'We'll have a heck of a time with the evidence.'

'Contamination, you mean, Guv?'

Skelgill picks his teeth pensively. The early indications are that virtually everybody in the hotel had flocked to the scene of the crime, and several of them touched the hysterical Mrs Tregilgis in her bloody nightie.

'Aye, that – and the fact that the place is like a rabbit-warren – anyone could have nipped along to the lobby, swiped the kukri and stabbed him – meanwhile the rest of them were probably so drunk they wouldn't have noticed a thing.'

'How long should we keep them, Guv? Mrs Groteneus says they're scheduled to check out after breakfast – the company's offices are in Edinburgh and London. They've got taxis booked and train tickets from Penrith.'

Skelgill shrugs.

'It depends what the search team turns up. We need that knife. Can't have someone slipping away with it in their luggage.'

'No, Guv.'

Skelgill stands and stretches his arms above his head. He has removed his gilet, and his shrunken t-shirt now rides up to reveal the effect of regular rowing upon a man's abdominals. DS Jones looks on innocently, though she averts her eyes when he glances in her direction. He stoops and begins to busy himself with tidying his equipment.

'Get a couple of your DCs over as soon as you can. Might as well take preliminary statements while we've got everyone under one roof. And events will be fresh in their minds. Pay particular attention to the period between two and three – when he went to bed – and when he was stabbed. Make sure the staff's whereabouts can be corroborated. And we need to speak to the chambermaids when they come in – find out when that bed was last stripped. Then we'll both talk to the wife – after I've seen this Lord Goldsmith character.'

6. DERMOTT GOLDSMITH

Sunday 8.15 a.m.

'So, Lord is a Christian name?'

There is a certain literal irony in Skelgill's question, although his tone of voice errs more towards the sceptical. He is interviewing the surviving partner of Tregilgis & Goldsmith in a small anteroom situated above the hotel lobby.

'Middle name, actually – initials DLG – *Delta Lima Golf* in your parlance.' Dermott Goldsmith is clearly pleased with himself for thinking of this and beams at Skelgill. 'Close friends call me Dermott, but I tend to use Lord in business circles – it has a certain cachet. Our mission is all about brands – creating distinctive identities that leave a striking impression in the mind of the customer. I try to do much the same.'

Rather short, prematurely balding and overfed, with dark arched brows that almost join above a nose and lips too large for his face, Dermott Goldsmith has sauntered into the room as if accustomed to being important. He wears deck-shoes without socks, designer jeans, an obscure French t-shirt and a gold Rolex Oyster. His cool-dude image appears not to impress Skelgill, who still smells faintly of last Saturday's eighteen-pound pike. Indeed, though he strives to be civil at all times, Skelgill is probably least endeared when being patronised, and the glad-handed-we're-good-friends-already manner of Dermott Goldsmith is not cutting a great deal of ice with the detective.

'I'll stick to Mr Goldsmith to avoid confusion.'

'As you wish, Inspector – I am your humble servant.'

'Mr Goldsmith, we'll be taking formal statements from everybody in due course. But I thought I should speak with you first to get a bit of a picture of Mr Tregilgis and your company. Perhaps you could tell me about your respective roles in the business.'

Dermott Goldsmith nods in a naturally condescending kind of way.

'Well, Ivan was our frontman – could sell sand to the Arabs – don't know how he did it – I couldn't be so brash. Whereas I basically run the company.' He pauses for dramatic effect. 'I am effectively Financial Director, Company Secretary, I look after Personnel, Technology, Administration – you could say I'm the brains behind the operation.'

'You must be a very busy man,'

Dermott Goldsmith smirks coyly, oblivious to any sarcasm in Skelgill's tone.

'I gather you're based in the Edinburgh office and that Mr Tregilgis worked from London?'

'Correct, Inspector. Edinburgh is where it all happens.'

'I would have thought London was more the hub of the advertising industry?'

Dermott Goldsmith's features are momentarily discomfited.

'Edinburgh is a vibrant international capital, Inspector. We have more restaurants per head than any city in Europe; a galaxy of *Michelin* stars. It is an internationally renowned financial centre; home of the world's greatest arts festival; extraordinary coastline, mountains – with sailing and skiing on our doorstep. Our neighbours are high-achievers, there are leading private schools – everything that London has, without the grime and the crime.'

Skelgill regards him evenly.

'I always find Edinburgh a bit on the cold side.'

Dermott Goldsmith frowns and shakes his head.

'We have the same level of rainfall as Paris and Rome. This time of year, it barely gets dark at night. We barbecue on our terrace most evenings.'

It is not often in Skelgill's experience as a detective that a close associate of a murder victim spends the opening minutes of an interview talking about himself. Under normal circumstances he would immediately suspect the person in question for trying to lead him astray – but Dermott Goldsmith appears to be an exception to this rule. His abiding preoccupation is with self-aggrandisement. However, Skelgill's time is precious, and he moves to regain the initiative.

'Have you had any recent disagreements with Mr Tregilgis?'

'What?'

'Conflict. It's normal between partners in a growing business, isn't it?'

Dermott Goldsmith is caught unawares, and a shadow darkens his features.

'We never argued.'

The reply lacks conviction, but Skelgill seems content to let it pass.

'Are you aware of anybody in the company, or connected with it, that might have wanted to harm him?'

'Nobody – of course not. What possible motive could they have?'

Skelgill shrugs indifferently, as though it is not for him to supply an answer – but then he does.

'How about – jealousy?'

'Naturally, Inspector, one can't get to our position without making people jealous.'

'Just what is your position?'

Dermott Goldsmith touches his collar bones, as a preening barrister might parade before a jury.

'Well, Inspector, between us and these four walls – as fifty-fifty shareholders – of course, we are multi-millionaires.'

Skelgill remains implacable.

'So, what happens now – to the ownership of the company?'

This question seems to blindside Dermott Goldsmith. The façade of self-importance momentarily cracks, and his reply when it comes is somewhat strangled.

'Well, Inspector – that is a very complicated matter. I shall need to consult with our chartered accountants back in Edinburgh.'

Coming from the brains behind the business, Skelgill is entitled to observe that this is a weak response. But he nods patiently.

'Perhaps you could let us know in due course. Otherwise, that'll be all for now, sir.'

Dermott Goldsmith looks suddenly indignant that he is being discharged. It is evident to Skelgill that the man is having to exercise substantial self-control.

'But, Inspector – you haven't asked me about the madman.' His voice is strained.

'Madman, sir?'

'The intruder – the burglar – about my thoughts on the crime.'

Skelgill returns a rather blank stare.

'When I've formed some of my own, sir – happen I'll take you up on that.'

Perhaps Dermott Goldsmith senses the opportunity to make a dignified exit. He stands and brushes at his clothing ostentatiously, like he might be removing some contamination from this unkempt country detective.

Watching on, as Dermott Goldsmith crosses in a stately manner to the exit, Skelgill would be excused for thinking that the assassin got the wrong man.

7. MIRIAM TREGILGIS

Sunday 9 a.m.

By nine a.m. the temperature is already pushing 70°F and Skelgill's thoughts drift to Bassenthwaite Lake, barely a mile distant as the crow flies. There has been much talk of medics this morning, but this hot spell is just what the doctor ordered – to warm up the water and rouse the fish from their late-spring torpor. Skelgill is absently practising fly-casting when DS Jones's voice reaches him in his secluded garden corner. Feeling claustrophobic inside the hotel, he has decamped to a cluster of garden chairs beneath an arbour of just-blooming climbing roses, a heavenly scented spot on the far side of the rear lawn. DS Jones, meanwhile, has succeeded in locating and returning with Miriam Tregilgis.

She looks a most unlikely widow. With a model's figure, shoulder-length blonde hair, perfect features and an immaculate white outfit – lightweight tracksuit bottoms and a close-fitting matching polo shirt – she could have walked straight off the page of a summer fashion catalogue.

'Pleased to meet you, Inspector.'

She smiles politely, flashing even white teeth, and sits down opposite him, calmly intertwining her ringless fingers upon her lap.

'Do you have a suspect?'

Skelgill allows himself a little grin. He glances at DS Jones, who is in the process of moving a chair so that she may rest her notebook on the small round cast-iron table that he has been using for his tea. Miriam Tregilgis's opening question is the one that blatantly eluded Dermott Goldsmith. He shrugs in a friendly manner, opening his palms in a gesture of uncertainty.

'You're Welsh.' Her brogue is soft, but distinct, and he says this as a statement.

'Barry – near Cardiff. You've probably heard of Barry Island?'

Skelgill nods.

'I've fished for conger off the Knap.'

'Oh, there's lovely, bach.'

Whether her response is borne out of concealed nervousness or simply just the liberation of speaking with someone, it is impossible to know – but in this phrase her accent blossoms.

'Now you sound really Welsh.'

She smiles again.

'I left home at eighteen to study PE in London – I met Ivan and never went back – now when I visit they tell me I sound like a Cockney.'

Skelgill shakes his head determinedly.

'Believe me, madam – I work with one, and you don't sound anything like it.'

She seems to relax, and settles back a little in the seat.

'I suppose it's all relative.'

Skelgill nods. He regards her thoughtfully for a moment or two.

'You seem very composed – if you don't mind me saying so.'

His tone makes this sound like a compliment rather than an accusation, but she seems to sense his dilemma.

'I know, Inspector. A couple of hours ago I was screaming the place down – here I am now as though nothing had happened.'

'It's probably just the effects of shock.'

'Actually, I think it's because I'm relieved.'

It takes a second or two for the gravity of this unexpected statement to sink in. Both Skelgill and DS Jones become still, and stare at the woman with unconcealed surprise in their eyes. But, for Skelgill, this is a little opening, and swiftly he moves through it.

'Are you trying to tell me something, Mrs Tregilgis?'

'Such as what, Inspector?'

'That you – had some involvement?'

'My word – no, Inspector.' It seems the faintest hint of a smile teases the corners of her mouth, as if she can't believe the turn the questioning has taken. 'But I should certainly like you to catch the person who did.'

Skelgill again watches for a moment, but her features remain serene.

'It's something I was going to have to ask sooner or later, madam.'

'That's okay, Inspector.' Now she smiles more transparently. 'It's often the wife, isn't it?'

Skelgill raises his eyebrows.

'More often the husband, madam.'

'But neither in this case.'

Skelgill gives a non-committal shrug.

'So, madam – when you say you're relieved?'

Miriam Tregilgis now leans forward apologetically.

'It was a poor choice of words, Inspector. It's hard to explain. If you'd told me yesterday that Ivan would be murdered in his sleep I'd have said it would be devastating. But now – well, I can only tell you how I feel. It's like a weight that I wasn't aware of has been lifted.'

'Were you happily married?'

She shakes her head slowly.

'I shouldn't say so, Inspector.'

Skelgill produces the kind of inquiring look that would befit a venerable physician, peering at his patient over a pair of spectacles. She opens her palms as a sign that she will elaborate.

'We've lived like flatmates for the past couple of years, nothing more.'

'So you didn't – er – *sleep* together?'

'Not – as they say – in the biblical sense, Inspector.'

'And – were you thinking of splitting up, divorce?'

She shakes her head.

'It might sound strange – but we never really discussed it. We just got on with our separate busy lives, doing our own thing.'

'Did you each have other partners?'

Skelgill puts the question tentatively, but she does not appear unsettled.

'Ivan spent his life falling in love with the most attractive and dangerous women he could find. He was a hopeless romantic. Though to his credit, only ever one at a time.'

Upon hearing this description, Skelgill's eyes narrow – although it is impossible to know which aspect so engages him. Perhaps he wonders if she considers herself to fall into the 'attractive and dangerous' category. Certainly she is attractive – but dangerous?

'And was there one at *this* time?'

'Undoubtedly.' Her singsong accent makes the word seem like it has extra syllables. 'But I can't tell you who, I'm afraid.'

'You mean you don't know – or you won't?'

She gives a little nervous laugh, as though she is amused by the idea of thwarting the police.

'The former, of course, Inspector.'

Skelgill smiles in a conciliatory manner. Then he asks quietly:

'And what about you, madam?'

'They say celibacy is good for the soul, Inspector.'

It is her first oblique answer, but she holds his gaze, unblinking, and he seems to find this a little disconcerting. He glances at DS Jones, as if he is checking that she has noted the reply – though she writes in shorthand, and there are only illegible squiggles to see on her page. He turns back to Miriam Tregilgis. It seems he decides to let the minor evasion pass.

'You're a PE teacher – you said you studied it.'

She shakes her head.

'These days I'm a Personal Trainer. I have clients at a number of gyms in the West End, and I lecture on anatomy and physiology for two half-days a week at my old college.'

Skelgill nods.

'What about Tregilgis & Goldsmith – how much are you

involved?'

'Really just occasional do's like this.' She shrugs languidly. 'I always feel a bit guilty, to be honest.'

'In what way?'

'Well, you see, Elspeth – Dermott's wife – she might as well work for the company – except Ivan didn't want that, you know – Directors' wives lording it over the staff? So she doesn't have an official position. But Dermott has her running round like she's his PA, organising this and that. She always knows what's going on in the business – the next big pitch, clients' names, latest projects, who's going to get the sack. I just turn up and drink the champagne.'

'Did you discuss the company with your husband?'

'Hardly ever. Ivan wasn't the sort to pass on his troubles. And that suited me.'

'How would you describe him?'

'He was the leader.' Her reply is immediate, and unequivocal. 'They'd follow him over a precipice. He was phlegmatic – but passionate under the surface. And I know it sounds daft coming from me – but he was one of the most loyal people you could meet. He'd die for those he loved. Maybe he did – I don't know.'

Skelgill nods slowly. This picture of Ivan Tregilgis is not that which Dermott Goldsmith paints. However, it appears to be one he can warm to.

'Presumably you now inherit your husband's shares in the company?'

'I've really no idea, Inspector. Ivan's hobby was climbing, and he always joked that if he fell down a mountain I'd be able to buy one of the Brecon Beacons in his memory.' She shakes her head, though rather casually. 'But I make a good living through my own job, so I've never really worried about the finances.'

Skelgill seems to consider this answer for a moment, and then determines to move on.

'I take it your belongings have been returned to you?'

'Your people kindly moved everything to the spare bedroom

once they'd finished, Inspector.'

'Was anything missing – jewellery, money, clothes?'

She shakes her head.

'As far as I can tell everything is still there – of mine, at least. I believe you have Ivan's briefcase? Someone asked if I knew the combination.'

Skelgill nods.

'We'd just like to check there's nothing of import.'

'I quite understand, Inspector – although you would think if there were, the intruder would have taken it.' She purses her lips and nods. 'Unless, of course, they knew the combination.'

Skelgill raises his palms in a hushing gesture, as if to reassure her that she need not do the police's job for them.

'Can you remember, madam, if the French door that leads from your bedroom was left unlocked at any time?'

'We had it open most of the afternoon. Just about everyone was out on the terrace – sunbathing, drinking, chatting.'

'What about in the evening?'

'I think Ivan locked it when we went up to dinner.'

'Are you certain of that?'

'Not absolutely.' She closes her eyes as if she is trying to picture the scene. 'But I don't remember any sense of leaving valuables unattended – you know that feeling you get when you stay abroad in something rather flimsy – a villa on stilts in the ocean, a mountain ski chalet.'

Skelgill looks like he doesn't, but he nods all the same. He gets to his feet in a chivalrous manner.

'Well, thank you – I think that's all for now, Mrs Tregilgis. If anything does come to mind please let us know. Where are you planning to stay?'

'Lenny Edwards, one of the boys from the London office, is going to drive me to my parents' in Wales this afternoon. Then my sister will come up to town with me for a few days.'

'Is that Central London?'

'We have a flat quite near to the office.' She raises her eyebrows

34

self-consciously. '*I've* got a flat. It's just off Endell Street.'

'Covent Garden.' DS Jones seems to know the area.

'That's right, Sergeant.'

Skelgill digs his hands into his pockets. He suddenly seems self-conscious of his unkempt appearance. In truth he looks more like a gardener than a police inspector.

'Subject to developments, we may need to look at Mr Tregilgis's documents, admin – that kind of thing. So I imagine we'll meet again soon.'

Miriam Tregilgis rises and shakes the hands of the two detectives. Then she takes her leave, depositing an arrow-straight line of dewy footprints in her elegant wake. Skelgill runs his fingers through his hair, and clasps his hands at the back of his head.

'Which was it, Jones – the truth and nothing but the truth – or is she looking for an Oscar?'

8. KUKRI & KEY

Sunday 10.15 a.m.

Skelgill spends the best part of the next hour making a nuisance of himself. He wanders about the hotel and its grounds, generally getting under the feet of the search team. He requisitions some hotel stationery, and draws a plan of the building, marking on all the possible exits. Then he fills in the names of the guests in their corresponding rooms. He notes that only the two company directors, Messrs Goldsmith and Tregilgis, had their partners with them, while all the rest were in single-occupancy. The more senior employees' rooms were on the ground floor, benefiting from access to the terrace.

DS Jones has been despatched to brief the DCs who are to conduct interviews. She is also checking upon a variety of technical points such as job titles and responsibilities in Tregilgis & Goldsmith. Sitting in on the first interview, with the aforementioned Lenny Edwards, she is rewarded with an immediate revelation. The reason for the absence of Grendon Smith is that he was dismissed last week by Krista Morocco, head of the London office. While this was apparently no great surprise, the bad grace in which he took the news rather was. "Started smashing up his desk," was the description provided by his erstwhile workmate. In due course, Ivan Tregilgis was fetched from a nearby wine bar, and was obliged to escort Smith off the premises and relieve him of his office keys and company credit card. No one witnessed what went on between the lift and the main door, but when Tregilgis returned it was with a look of having given Smith "a bit of a helping hand," according to Edwards. DS Jones is hurrying to convey this information to Skelgill when an animated PC Dodd scoops her with the tidings that the kukri has been found.

There is now a rendezvous at the ladies' toilet in the lobby. The knife had been hidden in the overhead cistern of the single-cubicle convenience. As Skelgill is quick to point out, it has been submerged for perhaps seven hours in a weak solution of bleach, and regularly flushed. This is not ideal for forensic purposes. He stares at the weapon, held aloft in a transparent evidence bag.

'What chance of prints?' The forensic officer produces a well-practised expectation-lowering glower. 'Okay – see what the boffins in the lab come up with.'

The man nods and shuffles away. DS Jones draws alongside Skelgill.

'Guv, could I have a word – it's about this Smith character?'

Skelgill glances at her – somewhat disinterestedly, it must be said – when a second scene-of-crime officer suddenly barges through the swing door from the bedroom block. Between finger and thumb of his gloved right hand he clutches a worn brass key.

'Sir – down the back of the radiator outside Room 5.'

Mrs Groteneus is summoned. To her credit – for she is plainly humiliated – she immediately identifies it as the master key belonging to the chambermaid responsible for the ground floor.

'But I do not understand.' She sounds most affronted. 'Why has Kasia not reported this to me? It is not correct procedure. I shall speak with her at once. She is in the staffroom with the others.'

'Leave it to us, madam.' Skelgill intervenes, in the process probably saving the poor girl from a roasting. 'We must do this formally.'

The hotelier reluctantly yields to his authority, and stalks rather bad temperedly from their presence. Skelgill turns to DS Jones, still eager to impart her news about Grendon Smith.

'You do this one, have a quick word now – she might be intimidated if I'm there – and I don't speak Polish.'

He grins mischievously, and disappears through the swing door.

*

Over yet another pot of tea (in Skelgill's case only), DS Jones insists on first recounting the story of Grendon Smith's ejection from the London office.

'What do you think, Guv?'

Skelgill scowls.

'I can't believe that someone's been hiding all day in the shrubbery waiting for a chance to have a pop at Tregilgis.'

'But he *could* have done it, Guv.'

'Jones – if getting the sack – which by all accounts he was expecting – is a reason for topping your employer, imagine what state the country would be in. When was he dismissed?'

'Wednesday.'

'Well, it's hardly heat of the moment.'

DS Jones compresses her lips.

'Say he was on the fiddle? Ivan Tregilgis might have threatened to turn him in.'

Skelgill shakes his head, and then gives a reluctant sigh.

'Look. I agree – he could theoretically have done it. How he crept in and took the knife without being seen – that beats me. But find out where he lives and get his whereabouts checked for Saturday night.'

DS Jones gives a satisfied nod. She is clearly surprised that Skelgill is perhaps not as pig-headed as his reputation might suggest. However, she tries not to make too much of her little triumph.

'The chambermaid, Guv?'

'Aye.'

'You were right – she is Polish.'

'I think you guessed that before me, Jones.'

'She speaks fluent English. But she's terrified of Mrs G.'

'Why does neither of those things surprise me?'

DS Jones grins.

'She misplaced the key yesterday; she thinks about one o'clock.

The party had arrived, but they hadn't checked into their rooms. She thought she must have left it in the door – she often does – but there was no trace of it. She was putting in clean towels and had reached Room 4. She borrowed the other girl's key to finish off, because she didn't dare own up. She was hoping it would appear when she went over the place this morning.'

'What about it being behind the radiator? That's outside Room 5.'

DS Jones nods.

'She agrees it's possible that she might have put it down, on the windowsill, or even on top of the radiator. But she doesn't understand why she would open Room 4 and then walk along the corridor to Room 5. She thinks someone must have moved it.'

Skelgill regards DS Jones pensively. While a master key would be a useful asset to a would-be murderer, last night the Tregilgis's door was unlocked. That said, the killer is unlikely to have been able to predict such a state of affairs. DS Jones waits for a few moments, but as Skelgill appears to have no further questions, she moves on to the second aspect of her interview with the girl, Kasia.

'The bed in the Tregilgis's room was completely stripped and changed yesterday morning. The underwear could only have got there some time later.'

Skelgill nods. This is as expected.

'Anything else?'

'Not from the chambermaid – but I did check the menu.'

'Enlighten me.'

'The sweet with dinner was sticky toffee pudding.'

'Hardly original.'

'I suppose they're all visitors – they wouldn't know we have it every day.'

Skelgill grins, amused by her sense of humour.

'Come on, Miss Marple – there's more, I know.'

'The plate of cheesecake that you noticed in the bedroom. There's a good three-quarters of a full-sized round in one of the fridges. Perhaps he got peckish and went and helped himself.'

Skelgill can no doubt identify with this behaviour, but he is suddenly overcome by an immense yawn, which immediately infects DS Jones in the mysterious way that yawns move.

'You must be bushed, Jones – you've been up all night. I had a lie-in until three.'

DS Jones shakes her head determinedly, though in her eyes there is a hint of strain.

'I suppose am a bit tired, Guv.'

Skelgill rubs a knuckle pensively against the stubble of his chin.

'Okay – here's the plan. Unless some devastating piece of evidence turns up, or someone confesses, let the advertising crowd leave once they've been interviewed. Politely remind your DCs that I want typed statements on my desk for seven a.m. sharp. Get a decent kip and we'll go through them first thing. And don't forget your toothbrush.'

9. POLICE HQ

Despite his best intentions to go home, get a hot bath, eat a late lunch and sleep for a very long time, Skelgill was unable to drive past his mooring at Peel Wyke without 'just checking the boat'. One thing led to another, and he spent Sunday afternoon afloat on his beloved Bass Lake. In turn, a late lunch became an even later Chinese takeaway and a few bottles of local Cockermouth ale, and a long hot bath became a hasty cold shower at six a.m. this morning. He arrives at his desk in Penrith an hour later to find a note from the forensic department stating that there are no fingerprints on the kukri. To add insult to injury, his in-tray is bereft of statements. He is just picking up the phone to berate the person unfortunate enough to answer his call, when DS Jones works her way backwards into his office.

'No ruddy statements –'

'Morning, Guv.'

Cheerfully, she turns and places before him a police-canteen tray bearing two mugs, three bacon rolls, and a stack of A4 papers.

'How come you've got them?'

'Sorry they're a few minutes late – I've been marking-up your set.'

She separates the bundle into two halves, and hands one to him.

Uninvited, he picks up the nearest mug of tea and takes a mouthful. He frowns suspiciously at the top sheet. The text is marked in places with fluorescent yellow highlights.

'What's all this?'

'I had to do the printouts this morning. I took photocopies of the handwritten statements before I left the hotel – then I went through them last night.'

'You've read them?'

'I thought it would give us a head start.'

Skelgill's features are still severe, though his voice softens.

'Jones, you're a star – but you need to get a boyfriend.'

She grins bashfully.

'I've got a boyfriend.'

'Aye – but one that lives nearer than – where is it – Chelsea?'

He glances away, as if he is thinking he should not have revealed that he knows this aspect of her private life.

'Clapham – but it's – kind of – near enough –' Her voice tails off, but then she rallies and grasps her share of the documents between both hands. 'I was wired last night – I would never have slept – I mean, the chance to work on a case like this.'

Skelgill appraises her more carefully.

'No wonder you've got bags under your eyes, lass.'

She regards him with a mischievous glint in her eye.

'So do you, Guv, if you don't mind me saying.'

'Aye, well – I was giving it some thought, myself.'

While there is something of a white lie here, it is accurate to say that, whilst afloat, he did inevitably ruminate over the events at Bewaldeth Hall. And if he has been left with any overriding sentiment, it concerns the chalk-and-cheese that were his brief meetings with Dermott Goldsmith and Miriam Tregilgis. For all their differences, what they held in common was a curious ignorance of the fate of the company. This is something he needs to know.

But now DS Jones lifts a handwritten list from the top of her pile.

'In chronological order, Guv – I think there's about a dozen significant points.

'Hit me.'

Unaccustomed to such luxury, Skelgill leans back and jams a bacon roll into his mouth. DS Jones takes a quick sip of her tea, and then begins.

'Everyone was due to meet in the bar at seven-thirty p.m. Ivan Tregilgis and Dermott Goldsmith were there already. The first employee to arrive overheard the end of a conversation. Apparently Goldsmith said, "Well, I need to see it," and Tregilgis replied, "Sure." Then they immediately changed the subject. Goldsmith was apparently looking quite exasperated.

'Make a note to ask Goldsmith what "it" was.'

Skelgill is proficient at talking whilst eating – he claims it is an essential quality for efficiency in police work. DS Jones turns her pad towards him to show the question already written down. He winks for her to continue.

'At midnight they opened champagne. It's the company's seventh anniversary. Ivan Tregilgis was seen to dance "intimately" with Krista Morocco, the girl who runs the London office. The pair of them may then have gone out on to the terrace to smoke. Apparently that door from the Great Hall was unlocked the whole time, and people were wandering in and out. Not long after, Ivan Tregilgis came back, and had a bit of an altercation with Julia Rubicon – she's head of their Edinburgh office. It's not known what was said – the music was pretty deafening – but she stormed off leaving him standing in the middle of the dance floor.'

'Who told us this?'

'It's from just one statement – a Melanie Stark, who works in the London office. And neither Krista Morocco nor Julia Rubicon mentioned these things.'

Skelgill taps on air with his half-eaten roll.

'Why would *you* notice something like that?'

DS Jones grins.

'She probably fancied him, Guv.'

Skelgill seems surprised by her directness.

'You mean the Stark lass fancied Tregilgis?'

DS Jones nods.

'Next thing – at about a quarter to one Dermott Goldsmith quite conspicuously signalled to his wife that he was leaving to inject himself – he's a diabetic. He omits this from his statement.'

'Do we know how long he was gone?'

'It couldn't have been many minutes – he was back by about one a.m. Someone came onto the dance floor with one of the voodoo masks from the lobby. In next to no time they were all hopping about with spears and drums and whatnot. One of the girls says Dermott Goldsmith asked her what his Zulu club reminded her of.'

Skelgill raises his eyebrows, but chooses not to comment. DS Jones continues.

'They eventually returned all the paraphernalia – Ivan Tregilgis made sure they did it properly. Then the next notable event was – as we know from his wife – that he went to bed at about two a.m. He didn't make a great fuss of going – most people said they hadn't noticed. Interestingly, Miriam Tregilgis says he was leaving early in the morning and would be away for two nights – but she didn't know where.'

'She claims not to know a lot.'

DS Jones waits to see if he has more to add, but he remains pensive, and she continues. 'After that, if I had to paraphrase the statements, I'd say it's all a bit of a blank. No one is admitting to going anywhere near the Tregilgis's bedroom – basically you just get a picture of twenty people milling around the public areas, getting increasingly drunk. Nothing happens until Miriam Tregilgis's screams are heard and they all descend on Room 10.'

Skelgill picks up the pile of statements from his desk and casually flicks through them. There are a good hundred pages, and he scowls at the sheer mass of information.

'Glad you couldn't sleep, lass.'

DS Jones shrugs modestly, and reaches for the plate with the single remaining bacon roll.

'It doesn't really help us in narrowing down the possibilities.'

Skelgill sighs wistfully, though it is equally probable that he has been hoping she would not be hungry.

'What was it Miriam Tregilgis said about him falling in love? Sounds like there's a few likely lasses in that mix.'

DS Jones nods.

'More than half the company is female – there are only five males, excluding Ivan Tregilgis.'

Skelgill affects consternation.

'Three to one ratio – shall I dare set foot in their offices?'

DS Jones grins reassuringly.

'Don't worry, Guv – I'll ride shotgun.'

10. MOFFAT AND BEYOND

Monday, 9.15 a.m.

A few wisps of morning mist still hang around the Devil's Beef Tub as Skelgill barrels his long estate car through the s-bends that cut into the green Borders hillside. DS Jones hangs on grimly to the scalding coffees collected from a busy Moffat café, now several minutes behind them. "Best bacon rolls south of The Horn", had been Skelgill's rather obscure comment. His knowledge of food-stops appears to be informed by their proximity to places he fishes.

'Source of the Tweed.' He gestures in an almost proprietorial manner towards an unprepossessing expanse of moorland to their right.

Before DS Jones can reply, their radio crackles into life.

'Got that appointment sorted for you, Ma'am.' It is one of her DCs. 'Ten-thirty and it's 77, Frederick Street. You're to ask for a Mr R Macdonald.'

'Aye – and a couple of Happy Meals?'

The constable chuckles, dutifully acknowledging Skelgill's quip.

'Straight up, Sir – and it's all cleared with Police Scotland.'

Prior to their departure, DS Jones had left instructions for her team to track down the Edinburgh-based accountancy firm that acts for Tregilgis & Goldsmith. She thanks her constable and terminates the call. She glances across at Skelgill.

'Will we do it for ten-thirty?'

At this same moment her head almost makes contact with the roof of the car.

'Cancel that question.'

Skelgill grins jubilantly.

'Okay – here's one for you.' He clears his throat, as if to buy a second or two in phrasing the question. 'Why would you leave your – *undies* – in someone's bed? I mean – surely you'd notice they were missing?'

DS Jones stares at the undulating road ahead, subconsciously adjusting the position of the paper cups as the car rises and falls, her arms acting as shock absorbers.

'I can think of circumstances when it wouldn't be a priority.'

'Such as?'

'Disturbed in the act. Panicked and ran for it.'

'What else?'

'Maybe she just couldn't find them in the dark.'

Skelgill tilts his head to one side and makes a clicking sound with his tongue.

'I'll give you that one. Many's the time I've arrived home to find I'm wearing women's knickers.'

DS Jones laughs.

'I could deduce that you went out wearing them in the first place.'

'You're too clever by half. They should have warned me.'

Now DS Jones smiles rather coyly.

'But, seriously – assuming they don't belong to Miriam – it's feasible that Ivan Tregilgis and his lover were disturbed, and the female went out through the French door.'

Skelgill nods pensively.

'I don't see Miriam Tregilgis throwing a sudden tantrum and knifing him. By her account, she's more likely to knock politely and give the mistress time to clear out. But, in any event – he wasn't prepared for the blow.'

'He could have been pretending he was asleep – thinking it was Miriam coming to bed.'

'Maybe.'

'I was wondering, Guv.'

'Aye?'

'Well – what if the underwear belongs to the killer?'

'Bit of a giveaway?'

DS Jones frowns.

'I know – but – if anyone could have contrived to take him unawares, at close range? Then she could unlock both doors and return to her own room via the terrace. It would be dark and probably deserted out there. In her own bathroom she could wash any traces and prints off the knife. Then just wait for the commotion and join on the back of it. And it would be easy to slip into the ladies' public toilet to conceal the weapon.'

Skelgill shrugs. It is not his habit to speculate beyond the facts – but perhaps the unfamiliar company he keeps today prompts him to break his little rule.

'Okay – here's a version for you. Miriam comes back to the room – disturbs the killer in the act – decides not to tell us about it.'

DS Jones's eyes widen.

'But that could put her at risk, Guv.'

'Not if she were in on it.'

11. MACDONALD & CAMPBELL

Monday, 10.30 a.m.

Within two hours of leaving Penrith the soot-blackened spires and steepling volcanic cliffs of the Scottish capital come into view. DS Jones's last visit was a school trip by coach to Edinburgh Zoo – and scenery was unlikely to have been much of a priority. Now she sits in something like awed silence as they weave their way through the Southside, heading progressively back in time towards the medieval heart of the city. Skelgill seems to know where he is going.

'Bit different from the Smoke, eh?'

DS Jones nods.

'Trams. Saunas. No kilts yet, though.'

But shortly their route bisects Princess Street, to the strains of busking pipers (kilted, of course). A minute more and they have crossed into the New Town, cresting the brae at George Street, and rumbling down the cobbles; glittering views of the Firth of Forth and the Kingdom of Fife open up before them. Skelgill slews left into Heriot Row. They exit the vehicle – he stretches extravagantly, while DS Jones reads a sign that details the parking regulations.

'Macdonald's here we come.'

Skelgill sets off at a pace, turning the corner and striding up the hill down which they have just driven. DS Jones has to scurry in pursuit, and she calls after him anxiously.

'But, Guv – we'll get a ticket – it says resident permit holders only.'

Skelgill waves away her protestations.

'Nay – that's just for at night – so the locals can get parked. Trust me.'

DS Jones does not look convinced. They pass a traffic warden who is at this moment affixing a ticket to the windscreen of a parked car. The man glances up – no doubt accustomed to keeping his wits about him – and his hungry eyes suggest he reads her plight. He smirks and stealthily resumes his task before an irate owner can return.

77, Frederick Street turns out to be an impressive Georgian tenement, five stories including the basement and loft levels. The former houses a clandestine nightclub, and the ground floor – much to Skelgill's liking – a brasserie. The floors above are all converted into offices, and entered by a communal stair, a place little changed since the building was erected two-and-a-half centuries ago. They climb broad stone steps, curving in a spiral, worn down at their centres, to the third floor. Here a smartly painted blue door bears a polished brass plaque with the words, "Macdonald & Campbell Partnership, Chartered Accountants."

The detectives announce themselves at the entry phone. Promptly there is an electronic buzz and they are transported into a modern world of pastel colours, brushed chrome and sparkling glass. A tight-skirted receptionist leads them into a meeting room, and Skelgill is noticeably polite as she takes their orders for refreshments. A couple of moments later, looking younger and less like an accountant than one might imagine, a well-groomed man of about forty bounces into the room. He wears suit trousers, and an open-necked striped shirt with the cuffs held by gold links.

'Inspector, Sergeant – Rory Macdonald – pleased to meet you – but such terrible news, *terrible* news.'

His refined accent is a product of the extraordinary influence that the independent school has upon the city's professional class, and reminds Skelgill of a rugby player interviewed after a game. His build is that of a stand-off, or full-back at a push.

'Such a young chap, too – what on earth happened, Inspector?'

They resume their seats, and Skelgill opens his palms

apologetically.

'I can't say a great deal, I'm afraid – we're still waiting for forensic information. However, I can tell you this is a murder investigation.'

Rory Macdonald blows out his cheeks and stands up, as though this is too much for him. He paces across to one of the great sash windows, shaking his head. The detectives wait patiently while he regains his composure.

'I only met him a few times – but he was the sort of fellow you immediately warmed to. Charismatic, but modest as hell. Can't imagine anyone wanting to – you know?'

Skelgill concurs, with a sympathetic nodding of his head.

'Unfortunately – in the absence of a definite suspect – we have to examine a number of lines of inquiry.'

Rory Macdonald folds his arms and leans forward on his elbows over the boardroom table.

'Shareholding.'

Skelgill is a little surprised by this seamless transition to business matters – he underestimates the silky skills of the accountancy profession.

'Has Mr Goldsmith spoken with you this morning, sir?'

'Actually, no – just that it's the obvious question, really. You know – who gets what?'

'And are you able to give me that information, sir?'

'Certainly.' He sits back and stretches out his legs, at the same time bringing his hands together. He twists the gold ring on his left index finger. 'Mrs Tregilgis automatically inherits her husband's shares, but then what's called a cross-option agreement kicks in. It triggers an insurance policy which pays out to Dermott Goldsmith – then, under the agreement he is obliged to buy the shares from Mrs Tregilgis – and she is obliged to sell.'

Skelgill's gaze drifts from Rory Macdonald to a landscape painting of a loch with a fisherman plying his craft on a distant bank. Whether this image distracts him, it is hard to say, but into the silence that ensues DS Jones poses a question.

'So, Dermott Goldsmith gets the company and Mrs Tregilgis gets a cash sum?'

'Correct, Sergeant.'

Skelgill is back with them.

'How much?'

'A million.'

Skelgill's eyes narrow.

'How much is the company worth?'

Now Rory Macdonald folds his arms and puckers his lips.

'Och, Inspector – if only you had asked me that yesterday I should have given you a different answer.'

'Why?'

'Ivan Tregilgis was alive.'

'And that makes a big difference?'

'I should say so, Inspector – these advertising agencies, they are not like ordinary companies – they have few fixed assets – merely their staff and their attendant skills.'

Skelgill is nodding.

'Take away the skills.'

'Precisely, Inspector. A million would have been a poor deal for Mrs Tregilgis yesterday – but today, who knows?'

Skelgill lifts an eyebrow.

'It's still not bad for a poor deal.'

Rory Macdonald nods several times, as if to say it's the sort of poor deal he too would be happy with.

Skelgill's grey-green eyes are alert, in the way that they gain light when he is fishing and senses a bite.

'Who would know about this?'

'Well, of course, I can't vouch for whom they might have told – but in theory it's quite possible that it never went beyond Dermott Goldsmith and Ivan Tregilgis.'

'Who thought up this scheme?'

'Er – I did, actually.' Rory Macdonald makes an endearing mea culpa face. 'It's not uncommon, Inspector. If I remember rightly Ivan was pretty keen on the idea. It protects you from suddenly finding that half of your company is henceforth controlled by your late-partner's spouse – who may or may not be a desirable business associate.'

He looks at Skelgill as though he would like to say more, but decides that a certain amount of diplomacy is called for. Skelgill eyes him suspiciously.

'There's no chance that Mr Goldsmith could just pocket the money and carry on as though nothing happened?'

Rory Macdonald shakes his head decisively.

'The administration process only allows the cash to be paid to the ultimate beneficiary.'

'And Mr Goldsmith would know that?'

'Yes, I'm certain. He was closely involved in all the paperwork. He's our main point of contact.'

At this moment there is a knock on the door and the receptionist enters.

'Penrith CID on the telephone for Sergeant Jones.'

She rolls her r's in the fashion of the Scots, although it might be a variant of this expression that comes to Skelgill's mind as his gaze is drawn to the pencil skirt that leads DS Jones from the room. As the door closes, he turns his attention back to the accountant.

'Mr Macdonald, I appreciate your being so open with us.'

The man regards him earnestly.

'We both need the facts to do our jobs, Inspector.'

Skelgill nods appreciatively.

'How would you describe Dermott Goldsmith?'

'Och – now you want some opinion.'

Skelgill opens his palms in a helpless gesture.

'I just get the feeling that his employees will be tight-lipped when I ask them the same question.'

Rory Macdonald grins sympathetically.

'Pretty harmless, I'd say, Inspector. Bark worse than his bite. He's successful – he likes to show it. Capable businessman. Bit of a know-all – always telling me how I should present their accounts.' He chuckles to himself and shakes his head. 'Positive, up-beat sort of character. Sometimes a bit brash – tries to haggle over our charges, not really the done thing. But we can't choose our clients – no more than you can yours.'

Skelgill grins ruefully.

'Reckon I'd go for damsels in distress, every day of the week.'

'I just get directors in distress, I'm afraid.'

'And where do Tregilgis & Goldsmith sit on that score?'

Rory Macdonald shakes his head.

'Och – they don't – at least not in financial terms. We're just starting their annual audit – looks like a seventh successive year of double-figure growth.'

'So, no pressing debts, angry creditors?'

'Not even an overdraft, Inspector.'

Skelgill frowns reflectively. Then with a flash of what might be insight, but what is certainly unaccustomed humility, he makes an unconventional request.

'What questions would *you* ask you?'

Rory Macdonald's smile is telling.

'It's a good question, Inspector. I think my answer would be, "Do I suspect any fraud?"'

'And do you?'

'No indication.' Rory Macdonald's expression becomes grave. 'But, given the circumstances, I shall wheel in our biggest magnifying glass.'

Skelgill nods gratefully.

'What sort of fraud could happen in a firm like theirs – that would be hard to detect?'

Rory Macdonald's eyes now narrow, and he perhaps for the first time looks a little uncomfortable. It is as if the grey areas of accountancy are gathering like clouds in his mind.

'I guess I'd be asking two main questions. Firstly, is anyone with access to the bank account spending money on themselves and disguising it as legitimate business expenditure?'

'And the second?'

'Are any employees living above their means?'

'How would that come about?'

Rory Macdonald puts his tongue into his cheek.

'Place an order with an external supplier – agree an inflated price and pocket the difference – a kickback, perhaps in the form of a continental holiday or a new car.'

'Could that happen in advertising?'

'Certainly – the firm spends hundreds of thousands with some suppliers.'

'And how do they normally prevent this kind of thing?'

Rory Macdonald frowns resignedly.

'It isn't always easy, Inspector. In a busy organisation, with delegated responsibility – they have to trust their employees. And for us, in an audit – when no two projects are alike it's not easy to establish whether a price paid for a service was competitive.'

Skelgill nods and, checking his watch, he indicates he must wrap things up.

'Mr Macdonald – I must thank you again – and perhaps you would let me know if anything irregular does crop up in the audit.'

As they move out into the lobby, Skelgill notices two office doors, both labelled with the name Macdonald.

'What became of Campbell, sir?'

'Och – I married her, Inspector – as we say in Scotland, I'm the *heid bummer* around here now.'

12. BRIEFCASE

Monday, 11 a.m.

Skelgill discovers DS Jones in the street below; a hand pressed over one ear and her mobile to the other. The traffic is not heavy, but the cobbles of Frederick Street amplify the sound of its passing. Skelgill indicates they should enter the brasserie. They take seats at a table a couple of yards back from the window, and he orders while she completes her call.

'He thinks Goldsmith's a bit of a donnat.'

DS Jones nods, but it is clear she has more pressing matters on her mind.

'That was Forensics. I called them back so I could come outside. It's about Ivan Tregilgis's briefcase.'

Skelgill eyes her inquisitively.

'The combination was his wife's date of birth.'

DS Jones looks surprised, though she grins widely.

'How did you guess?'

'Intuition.' Skelgill smirks in an exaggerated manner. 'And inside it was a piece of lead pipe and a passport belonging to Colonel Mustard.'

DS Jones chuckles, but quickly restrains her mirth – for he is not so far from the mark.

'Actually, there *was* a passport – Ivan Tregilgis's – plus a return ticket to New York, due to fly out this morning from Manchester.'

Skelgill tilts his head to one side.

'So that's where he was off to. Any indication why?'

'Not as yet – there are some papers – but nothing that's categorical – apparently there's a presentation about the agency – the sort of thing they might give to a potential new client.'

Skelgill nods.

'He is supposed to be the sales guy. Maybe that's it.'

'One interesting thing – there are no fingerprints whatsoever on the outside of the case.'

Skelgill stirs chocolate flakes into his cappuccino. In trying to suck the excess froth from the spoon, he gets it jammed in his palate, and for a comic moment he looks like a fish on a hook, his eyes bulging in surprise. With a jerk he frees the recalcitrant item of cutlery, and shakes his head in relief.

'Why would anyone do that?'

'Someone must have tampered with it, Guv – someone who doesn't want us to know.'

Now Skelgill purses his lips.

'What was it in the statements – when they were overheard at the bar?'

'Dermott Goldsmith said he needed to see something that Ivan Tregilgis had.'

Skelgill is silent for a moment.

'Makes you wonder if that had something to do with it.'

'Do you think Dermott Goldsmith would know the combination?'

Skelgill shrugs.

'Why don't we ask him? There he is.'

'What –?'

Dermott Goldsmith is just a few feet away, standing on the pavement outside the brasserie. Perhaps a combination of the bright day and the dark interior makes it difficult to see through the glass. Indeed, he surely cannot be aware of their presence, for he begins to use the window as a mirror, first checking his thinning hair, and then his clothing, including a look over his shoulder at his well-padded rear. Then he wheels away, and apparently disappears into the stair from which they recently emerged.

'He must be calling on the accountants.'

Skelgill nods.

'He won't be too chuffed that we beat him to it. And, when the cat's away –'

*

Having insisted they despatch their coffees in double-quick time, a striding Skelgill has his colleague skipping to keep up as they descend Queen Street Gardens West to the car. His cryptic reference to the cat being away signalled his intention to visit the Edinburgh office of Tregilgis & Goldsmith while its surviving principal is otherwise engaged. However, as they round the corner into Heriot Row, Skelgill lets out howl of dismay. There is a parking ticket on his windscreen. DS Jones pretends not to notice – she must figure that this is not a good time to remind him of her earlier warning. Skelgill clenches his fists at his sides, but fortunately for all concerned, there is no trace of the warden. A workman in a white boiler suit is loading tools into a plumber's van a few spaces along, and Skelgill approaches him.

'Hey up, marra – I just got a ticket along there.'

The man blinks several times, perhaps wondering if he is being blamed.

'Aye – ye cannae park there, ken?'

Then the man's mobile rings, and he takes the call without further reference to Skelgill, closing up his van and wandering over to a house opposite. Skelgill shrugs and returns to DS Jones.

'Looks like we've paid to park. May as well leave it here now. Come on, we'll leg it – it's only Charlotte Square.'

13. JULIA RUBICON

Monday, 12 noon

'Do you recognise these briefs?'

'They're not mine, if that's what you mean.'

'What type were you wearing on Saturday night?'

'Red, lacy.'

'What size do you normally buy?'

'Medium.'

'Can I see the label in the ones you're wearing?'

*

This was an impromptu examination that Skelgill had by necessity delegated to his female colleague, conducted in the privacy of Julia Rubicon's office. Now that he enters, a few minutes later, he sees the almost imperceptible shake of his sergeant's head – a pre-arranged signal that tells him this is unlikely to be their Cinderella. No classic beauty, Julia Rubicon has an allure in a bad-girl sort of way. The first impression is an aura of intense perfume and spectacular hair, full lips coloured scarlet, an excess of mascara, bare legs, and outrageous shoes. A bra appears to be an option not exercised today. If Skelgill were assessing her capability to find a weakness in Ivan Tregilgis's sensibilities, he would probably comment along the lines that she could drive a coach and horses through them.

DS Jones, on the other hand, appears inured to such gothic distractions, and continues unperturbed.

'You were seen arguing with Mr Tregilgis on Saturday night, just after midnight. What was that about?'

'I don't recall arguing with him.' Julia Rubicon's features are unmoving, but beneath there is the sense of anger suppressed.

'In her statement Mrs Stark says you strode off the dance floor leaving Mr Tregilgis standing alone.'

'She would.' Julia Rubicon's eyes narrow, catlike.

'So, you didn't have a disagreement of any kind?'

Julia Rubicon shakes her head, her features taut.

'It has been mentioned to us that Mr Tregilgis was having an affair. Would that be with you, Miss Rubicon?'

'No.'

Skelgill affects distraction – gazing out of the mullioned window at the trees of Charlotte Square Gardens – though he pays close attention. This is the first time he has witnessed DS Jones in action.

'We'll have access to all of Mr Tregilgis's credit card bills, telephone records, computers and so on. It will be a very easy thing for us to cross-check.'

There is no reply. Julia Rubicon sits obstinately, biting a cheek. Eventually she speaks.

'Then I think you'll find we worked together, Sergeant.'

'For work reasons, then – did you go into Mr Tregilgis's bedroom at any time prior to the discovery of his body at three-fifteen a.m.?'

'No.'

Julia Rubicon is determined, but DS Jones is tenacious. For Skelgill, there is a bizarre illusion of mud-wrestling.

'Miss Rubicon, did you have anything to do with the death of Ivan Tregilgis?'

'*No!*'

At last, there is a release of emotion. She bows her head away from them, covering her face with the veil of dark hair. She is not as tough as she tries to make out. For a few moments she sobs. DS Jones glances at Skelgill – as if she seeks permission to press home the advantage. But Skelgill shakes his head. And now he intervenes more softly. There is a peculiar glint in his eye – perhaps it is the novelty of playing good cop.

'Julia?' His use of her Christian name seems to have an immediate effect. She turns back to face the detectives, blinking, not wiping her eyes, allowing the mascara to run. 'How would you describe your working relationship with Ivan?'

She breathes heavily, and her reply is somewhat oblique.

'Mainly by telephone.'

'Could you elaborate?'

'Ivan was only involved in one of my accounts – Caledonian Bank. Their head office is here in Edinburgh. He came up for monthly creative review meetings. Other than that, I would speak with him most days, often several times, frequently late at night – there were production deadlines every four weeks.'

Skelgill nods broodingly.

'Wouldn't it have been more practical for Mr Goldsmith to attend these meetings?'

If Skelgill is angling at the suggestion of a convenient monthly liaison, Julia Rubicon scotches the notion.

'Their CEO insisted Ivan worked on the account.'

'What's wrong with Mr Goldsmith?'

'Ivan is an award-winning Creative Director.'

They must all note the redundant present tense, for there is a momentary hiatus.

'And what does Mr Goldsmith do?'

She sighs, and after a moment's consideration, pulls a face of dark disapproval.

'Tries to make us run with mediocre ideas we suspect his wife of dreaming up.'

Skelgill nods diplomatically.

'I take it you don't always see eye to eye?'

'You know what they say about the corporate ladder, Inspector.'

Skelgill permits himself a restricted grin. But he does not let this quip draw him off track.

'And you've been in charge of this office for about a year, I understand?'

'I was promoted last summer. I was in the London office for nearly four years.'

'And you worked with Mr Tregilgis then?'

'Some of the time. My line manager was Krista Morocco, but Ivan preferred to work directly with me on my accounts.'

'Why was that?'

Julia Rubicon looks at him as though this is a rather pointless question.

'Perhaps he thought we did a better job that way.'

'And more recently – Mr Tregilgis worked mostly with Ms Morocco?'

She shrugs indifferently.

'I imagine so.'

'And how did she get on with Mr Tregilgis?'

'She seems to get what she wants.'

'Why would that be?'

Again comes the shrug. 'I suggest you ask her.' Hostility is creeping back into her manner.

'Don't worry, Miss Rubicon. We shall.'

*

'You didn't pull your punches, Jones – given we've not got so much as a stray hair on Tregilgis's pillow.'

They are back inside Skelgill's illegally parked car, lunching on healthy vegetarian rolls procured by DS Jones, in Skelgill's case supplemented by potato crisps and a chocolate bar.

She makes a face – one apparently not intended for Skelgill's consumption – and which might be read as lacking in sympathy: that Julia Rubicon was evidently expecting to be interviewed by a male detective. She is more diplomatic in her reply.

'I think she's got a guilty conscience.'

Skelgill might indeed wonder if Julia Rubicon's exotic appearance had brought out the fighting spirit in his sergeant. Certainly, the pair are well matched, being of a similar age, and neither unaccustomed to turning heads. But, despite unleashing such forces, he was probably wise to let DS Jones lead the interview; he could not guarantee himself immunity from Julia Rubicon's unconventional charms.

'When you say *guilty*?'

DS Jones narrows her eyes reflectively.

'I remember when I was about thirteen; we'd played a game of consequences in class that turned a bit blue. The Deputy Head found the screwed-up notes in a waste-paper basket and interrogated us one at a time, trying to extract confessions. I hadn't even written anything bad. But that feeling of answering questions, knowing you were covering up – for yourself and your friends. You just don't act normally. You don't question the questions. That was how Julia Rubicon behaved.'

Skelgill nods – she has listened more closely than he.

'I mean, Guv – if you were completely innocent, how would you react if a detective asked you to drop your skirt?'

'You didn't do that?'

'No – I just checked the label at the back.' DS Jones grins, amused by his widening eyes. 'But why not tell me to get lost? Or at least ask what it's all about. And she wasn't affronted at being accused of having an affair. Nor did she want to know who told us. That's why I think she's hiding something.'

Skelgill is nodding slowly, but he means to test the hypothesis.

'Why would she lie about having an affair with Tregilgis?'

'Perhaps she thinks we can't prove it. If they were careful and didn't leave any incriminating messages – it's her word against ours.'

Skelgill gives a world-weary shrug.

'I reckon most folk would deny they were having an affair. It's human nature.'

'She didn't hold back when it came to Dermott and Elspeth Goldsmith.'

Now Skelgill scoffs.

'You heard what she said about the corporate ladder, Jones.'

'Look down and all you see is brains?'

Skelgill glances sideways at his subordinate – she has not completed the maxim – but instead is regarding him inquisitively.

'Aye, well – the rest of it doesn't apply in our case.'

Two-handed, he makes an assault on his sandwich.

14. ELSPETH GOLDSMITH

Monday, 2 p.m.

'Yes, we've just finished the kitchen. One's house is so much more of a home with an Aga, don't you think? My honey-and-tarragon roast chicken from the slow oven is simply divine.'

Skelgill stares vacantly across the stressed oak dining table; it is greedily expansive, like the deck of an aircraft carrier. But some relief arrives, a plate of jumbo scones glides in to complement a squadron of china, silverware, butter, clotted cream and preserves. He perks up.

'Not too early for a spot of afternoon tea, I hope, Inspector? Home-baked – absolutely to die for.'

The woman speaks with a clipped military delivery, and an officer-class accent.

'Very kind, Mrs Goldsmith – I hope we're not putting you out.'

'Must keep up one's strength, Inspector – especially after this awful business. Such a loss to the advertising industry. Dermott and I are simply devastated.'

Elspeth Goldsmith assumes a face of mourning, and it strikes Skelgill that she bears an uncanny resemblance to her spouse. Early indications suggest she is also on a par in the self-promotion stakes. But her proclaimed misery evidently does not extend to her appetite, for she immediately sets to – an act that corroborates another aspect of her appearance: Skelgill has already dismissed from his mind any requirement to ask her the embarrassing 'underwear question'.

Skelgill's strategy, as outlined to DS Jones en route from Edinburgh's West End, is based on the premise that Elspeth Goldsmith probably knows more about the company and its goings on than most. However, she is unlikely to be forthcoming if she senses the police consider Dermott Goldsmith a key suspect. To this end, he has decided to leave the latter to stew, while through gritted teeth he applies flattery to the man's wife.

'I'm told you're something of an advertising expert yourself, madam.'

'Oh no, these days merely a humble housewife.' Elspeth Goldsmith sends a great wave of false modesty crashing over them. 'I simply offer a little creative direction now and again. Before we set up Tregilgis & Goldsmith I used to work in one of the big London ad agencies – TW&TS, you've heard of them, of course – founded by the legendary Tim Wilson and Tom Smith? Hard to believe I met Dermott there when he was a lowly trainee Account Executive.'

'If you don't mind me saying so, Mrs Goldsmith, you come across as a pretty capable individual.' Skelgill raises his half-eaten scone, as if it bears testament to his claim. 'Mr Goldsmith no doubt relies on your judgement in a number of respects?'

Elspeth Goldsmith's small dark eyes glisten with pleasure. Perhaps she is unaccustomed to this kind of praise. Almost literally she preens, brushing crumbs from her ample bosom, and simpers affectedly.

'Well, behind the scenes, naturally, I effectively make a lot of the key decisions for the company. You could say I'm Dermott's sounding board.'

'Happen you could help us in much the same way.'

Skelgill's entreaty is plausibly earnest.

'I should be delighted to assist, Inspector. Another scone?'

'Don't mind if I do, madam.'

'Bother! We need more clotted cream.'

She heaves herself to her feet and pads across to a skyscraper of an American refrigerator.

'Mrs Goldsmith.' Skelgill opts to maintain momentum. 'The death of Mr Tregilgis has the hallmarks of a bungled robbery – but until we get a clear lead, protocol demands that we eliminate everybody who was on the inside, so to speak.'

Elspeth Goldsmith, leaning into the fridge and obscured by its great door, seems momentarily frozen. However, as she emerges, the apparent cause of her hesitation becomes clear: she licks what might be custard from her lips.

'I quite understand, Inspector – I am a crime fiction aficionado myself – so I am well versed in your procedures.'

Skelgill seems to cringe, but he succeeds in subduing whatever counterpoint troubles him.

'Then you'll appreciate, madam – more than most – that we must turn some stones that would be better left undisturbed.' He contrives an expression of contrition. 'Unfortunately, things tend to come out about innocent people's private lives that in the final analysis have little bearing on a case.'

The woman nods enthusiastically.

'Absolutely, Inspector – it just cannot be helped.'

Skelgill inhales portentously, and fixes her with a grave stare.

'Is it possible that Mr Tregilgis was having a relationship with one of the females in the company – Miss Rubicon, for instance?'

Elspeth Goldsmith raises a finger, as one would test the wind direction.

'It is odd you should say that, Inspector.' Her voice becomes a little hushed. 'Because I've had Dermott working on it for the last couple of months.'

'With any success?'

'Apparently whenever Ivan came up to Edinburgh, Julia always wore more – well, *tarty* clothes and make-up – if that were possible.' She adds the last phrase sniffily. 'And they spent a lot of time out of the office together.'

'What made you suspect in the first place?'

'Well, Inspector – Ivan would always have some excuse for booking into a hotel in town – that he would be out late with clients, that sort of thing.' She waves a regal hand upwards. 'We have six bedrooms here – seven if you include the maid's room – what possible reason other than if he were seeing Julia could he have for not staying with us?'

Skelgill shakes his head slowly, emphasising that he too cannot fathom such a state of affairs.

'I really can't imagine, madam – but could it be that Miss Rubicon just was wanting to impress him with her work?'

'But, Inspector – I believe she has no boyfriend – and she has been in Edinburgh for almost a year now.'

'Do you think they were having a relationship during the time she worked in London?'

Elspeth Goldsmith leans forward conspiratorially.

'Well, that's another thing, Inspector. I was catching up with Mel on Saturday night – that's Mel Stark, she's number two to Krista Morocco in the London office. She says there was all sorts of friction between Julia and Krista before Julia left – the girl was strutting about as though she owned the place. Mel thinks Julia got the promotion ahead of her – that Ivan pushed it through to get Julia out of their hair and calm Krista down.'

'What did Miriam Tregilgis think about all this? I take it you know her quite well?'

Elspeth Goldsmith taps the side of her nose.

'Still waters run deep, Inspector.'

Skelgill appears puzzled.

'Could you elaborate on that, Mrs Goldsmith?'

'Talk to her and you'd think she doesn't know what's going on under her very nose – Ivan – the money – but I don't believe it.'

'When you say *the money* –?'

'She likes her lobster thermidor at The Savoy. And what with the million from the cross-option agreement, and Ivan's life insurance – she's sitting pretty isn't she? Meanwhile we are left to keep the company afloat.'

Skelgill nods evenly, though it is a response that conceals his surprise. It seems that Elspeth Goldsmith is better informed –

ostensibly at least – than her Financial Director husband.

'And are you suggesting she's not exactly upset about losing Mr Tregilgis?'

'Always acted a bit aloof, I thought – and never slow to find fault.'

'Is it possible she has another man?'

'Well, not wishing to spread scandal, Inspector.' She folds her arms, rather indecently emphasising her cleavage. 'Mel was saying that Geri, one of the juniors in the London office, has spotted Miriam at the same gym she uses. You know – with one of her personal training clients? He's a well-known professional footballer. Apparently, the sessions sometimes get rather intimate.'

'When were they seen together?'

'It has been within the last couple of months.'

'It sounds like Mrs Stark is well informed.'

'Well, I am not inclined to gossip myself – but she acts as my eyes and ears in the London office.'

Skelgill glances at DS Jones, who raises her pen to indicate that has a question. She has been reading a message just delivered to her mobile. She clears her throat.

'Mrs Goldsmith, if I could just clarify a point in your statement – about your conversation with Mrs Stark?'

'Absolutely.'

DS Jones glances at her notes.

'You mentioned that when the alarm was raised at about three-fifteen a.m. on Sunday morning, the pair of you were together in the hotel bar?'

'That's right – that's when she was telling me about the toy-boy.'

'And you joined with the others to see why there was a commotion in the bedroom corridor?'

'Correct.'

'Can you recall if you took anything with you, from the bar?'

Elspeth Goldsmith strums her fleshy lower lip.

'You know – I don't think I was drinking – I was on mineral

water by then – but wait – yes! I believe I may have done. It had been a long time since dinner – we'd raided the refrigerator and found some delicious cheesecake – so I may have taken the dish with me – and of course I would have lost track of it while I was trying to calm Miriam.'

DS Jones nods and makes a note. She looks to Skelgill, that he should resume.

'How would you describe Mrs Tregilgis at that moment?'

'Positively deranged, Inspector.' Elspeth Goldsmith's small eyes widen. 'Screaming – trying to fight us off like she was having a night terror – and covered in blood. My dress was ruined.'

'What did you do?'

'A couple of the girls and I corralled her into the bathroom, splashed water in her face, got her to sit down on the seat of the loo. Then when she'd recovered a little we changed her into a hotel dressing-gown and took her to my bedroom.'

Skelgill nods. He exhales with an air of finality – Elspeth Goldsmith looks as though she might be disappointed – but he pre-empts any protest she may have.

'All this tea – and talk of loos, Mrs Goldsmith – if you don't mind, I'll just nip to yours before we leave you in peace?'

Elspeth Goldsmith, from her sitting position, manages to produce something that approaches a swagger.

'Be my guest, Inspector. There is a choice of six – the nearest is out in the hallway – but you must see our new en suite – first floor, last door on the left – we've just had the most marvellous heated marble tiles fitted.'

Skelgill takes some time to complete his expedition, though it is not the most marvellous heated marble tiles that detain him, but an extraordinary exhibition of photographic enlargements that lines the walls of the stair and landing. Dermott Goldsmith with a TV soap star; Dermott Goldsmith with a famous sportsman; both the Goldsmiths with well-known film director; and so on. Curiously, there is an impression that it is the gleeful Goldsmiths who are the subject of these pictures, while the bemused celebrities are muscled into the background.

'What did you think, Inspector?' Elspeth Goldsmith waits with DS Jones at the front door. 'Best part of a hundred pounds a shot. Not something you'll see every day, even in this neighbourhood.'

'It's certainly a pleasant area.'

'More than pleasant, Inspector.' She sweeps an arm across the driveway and front lawns. 'This is Ravelston.'

Skelgill nods politely, though perhaps unsatisfactorily.

'The home of Scotland's Great and Good, Inspector. I grew up in this very house.'

'I didn't realise you were Scots, madam – your accent sounds more English.'

'Inspector, I am a MacClarty – I simply went to the right school. So important, don't you think?'

Skelgill looks like he is grappling with the urge to run away. But it is just as well that he resists, for he would miss one final nugget of information that Elspeth Goldsmith wishes to dispense. She shadows them to their car and lowers her face close to the open driver's window.

'Did I mention Ivan and Krista Morocco?'

'Er, I don't believe so, Mrs Goldsmith – was there something?'

'Well, of course – it's just the old industry jungle drums – but word is they had a clandestine fling before Ivan married Miriam. In those days Krista was a client of Ivan's former firm, before she joined us. Naturally, client-agency liaisons are frowned upon – never mind by the fiancée, eh, Inspector?'

'We shall bear that in mind, Mrs Goldsmith.' Skelgill is fumbling for reverse gear. 'You've been very helpful, madam.'

As she waves them off, Skelgill notices through his rear-view mirror that she produces a mobile phone from somewhere on her person.

15. CALTON HILL

Monday, 3 p.m.

'S he obviously didn't want to part with her cheesecake, Guv.' Skelgill frowns pensively. This might be a sentiment with which he can identify.

'Aye – what was all that about?'

'I got a message from the office – there was just one set of fingerprints on the dish – so, presumably hers. She wasn't hiding it. And it seems the beer bottles had been left by a couple of the lads who'd gone in to help.'

Skelgill nods. He has decided to postpone further their interview with Dermott Goldsmith. The more they hear the more he feels unready for that meeting. Instead, he has suggested they take a time out, and has offered to show what he claims is "the best view in Edinburgh".

To this end, they have parked near St Andrew's House, home of Scotland's civil service, and climbed the stone steps to the summit of Calton Hill. One of Edinburgh's 'Seven Hills', and just two minutes from the east end of Princes Street, a short scramble rewards the breathless visitor with what is arguably the most dramatic urban panorama this side of the Atlantic.

Now DS Jones's mobile rings. Captivated by the vista, she continues to gaze out over the ancient town as she takes the call. Skelgill casually saunters away and unobtrusively joins the queue at a burger van stationed beside the old City Observatory. His philosophy is that, in their job, you never know when you might get your next meal. He returns to the viewpoint with various packets, and teas in disposable paper cups.

DS Jones has taken a seat on a bench in the shadow of the Nelson Monument. He settles beside her, and begins to tuck in.

As he listens to her directing her team, he reflects that he is actually enjoying working with her. She is far less exasperating than his regular partner, DS Leyton; she is smart and naturally hard working. And, while he does not exactly admit it to himself, she subtly panders to his ego. She completes her call, and turns to him.

'Guv, when did you become an expert on Edinburgh?'

'I lived here.'

'Were you a student?'

'It was more of a gap year.'

'What did you do?'

'I was in a band.'

'Really – what kind?'

'Punk – well, sort of folky rocky punk. We were called *Against The Grain*.'

'What instrument did you play?'

'I was lead singer.'

DS Jones suddenly seems to concentrate hard on the contents of her cup. She might be reflecting upon a couple of Skelgill's questionably melodic renderings on their recent journey from Penrith.

'Wow – that's – amazing.'

Skelgill looks a little sheepish.

'I had to get drunk – to get up on the stage – but it kind of went with our image.'

'I don't suppose you're on YouTube?'

'It wasn't invented.'

He sounds relieved. DS Jones grins. She raises her cup and indicates to their environs.

'Despite Dermott Goldsmith's hyperbole – it looks like a great place to live.'

Skelgill growls a little grudgingly.

'Aye – it was alright – decent ale. Fresh air. North Sea.' He casts about doubtfully. 'But I missed the fells.'

'I was a bit like that in London. It's a crazy city – absolutely brilliant in many ways.'

'Aye, well – you can be my tour guide tomorrow.'

DS Jones nods. They refer to their planned itinerary, which will take them this evening by air to the English capital, where tomorrow they will meet with the southern contingent of the advertising agency, Tregilgis & Goldsmith. For a few moments they eat in silence, perhaps each recalling their times in the respective metropolises. Then Skelgill screws up his empty bag, and casts about for a litter bin.

'What did you make of Lady Goldsmith's performance?'

'You make her sound like Lady Macbeth.' DS Jones tilts her head from side to side, as if she indeed might be reflecting that the comparison would be apposite. 'I think Miriam Tregilgis was right – that Elspeth Goldsmith is certainly in the know. And she didn't stand on ceremony when it came to stirring the pot.'

'Kicking up dust?'

'Maybe, Guv – she's not stupid – she must realise that we would have Dermott Goldsmith in our sights, given he gets control of the company. She didn't need much encouragement to suggest why some of the others might have been unhappy with Ivan Tregilgis.'

'Reckon she let slip that business of the cross-option agreement?'

DS Jones ponders this question.

'I don't know. I suppose at least it shows they haven't conspired not to tell us. Maybe Dermott Goldsmith was knocked off his stride yesterday – by the shock of the murder?'

Skelgill looks unconvinced.

'He was composed enough when it suited him.'

There is another pause, until DS Jones speaks.

'There were a couple of things in that call – forensic issues, and whatnot.'

'Aye?'

'There's no trace of anyone but Ivan Tregilgis having been in that bed – literally not a hair, like you said – no signs of sexual activity.' She allows a moment for reflection. 'No prints on that

master key – nor on the kukri, as we already knew. However –
remember the other kukri – the one that was in the holder on the
wall?'

'Aye?'

'It has a thumbprint on it that matches prints taken from Krista
Morocco's bathroom.'

DS Jones glances at her superior, for he does not respond, but
he seems to have nothing to add. Then he quips.

'Whatnot.'

'Sorry, Guv?'

'You said forensics and whatnot.'

'Oh, yes – it's about Grendon Smith – the sacked employee.
His alibi for Saturday night – it's not exactly conventional. He
claims he slept in his car – stayed out all night somewhere in
Norfolk – apparently he's a twitcher.'

Skelgill looks disappointed.

'You almost had me interested then, Jones – I thought you were
going to tell me he's a fisherman.'

16. FETTES AVENUE

Monday, 4 p.m.

'**D**an Dare. Long time awa'.'

These words are uttered by a stocky man of medium height with short grizzled hair, a stern expression and penetrating dark blue eyes that belie his fierce appearance with their warmth; to DS Jones's mind he must be aged probably in his late fifties.

'Can't keep a bad penny down, Cammy. So, how's it going, me old marra?'

'Ach, yer seein it, mon, yer seein it.'

'Still not speaking English, then, eh?'

'Tch. Are ye nae going to introduce me to this bonny lassie?'

'DS Emma Jones. I've warned her about you.'

'I bet he didnae tell ye fifteen years back he saved my skin?'

*

Skelgill's plan is to leave his car at Edinburgh airport, and fly to and from London, and collect it upon their return – when they can interview Dermott Goldsmith. To facilitate this, and deal with one or two other administrative issues, he has called upon his contacts in the Scottish police. As such, they are welcomed at the force's Edinburgh HQ, Fettes Avenue. (Skelgill's little joke is that this surely ought to be renamed *Letsby* Avenue.) Their chaperone, DS Cameron Findlay, now a deskbound administrator, is an auld acquaintance that Skelgill will never forget. A decade and a half

76

before, they worked together on a joint-forces operation to crack an organised poaching syndicate that parasitised the great border-country salmon rivers. A matter close to both their anglers' hearts – it was almost literally so in DS Findlay's case in the unwanted form of the contents of a 12-bore cartridge. Only a brave if somewhat reckless intervention by one rookie DC by the name of Daniel Skelgill saved the day. Henceforth, in these circles, he became affectionately known as Dan Dare. Skelgill's memory of the incident reflects the bizarre dry humour of his Scottish ally, who, whilst Skelgill was wrestling with a shotgun-wielding poacher, waist deep in the River Tweed, called out 'Yer spookin' the fish, Danny'.

Now he stands by awkwardly while DS Findlay recounts the tale of that stormy night. To his relief they are interrupted by a secretary who informs them that if they get their skates on they can make the six p.m. flight for Heathrow.

'Leave your wheels here.' DS Findlay is insistent. 'I'll drive you out to Turnhouse in a marked car so we can use the bus lanes – otherwise this time of night ye might as well walk.'

Ten minutes later they are forcing their way across the homebound commuter traffic choking the Queensferry Road. Edinburgh motorists are polite but stubborn – a trait that makes Skelgill think it would never be wise to invade. It takes a belligerent squawk of the squad car's siren to confirm its occupants are still on duty.

'That's the Goldsmith's place back there, isn't it?'

This observation comes from DS Jones, who suddenly seems to get her bearings as the giant spaceship of Murrayfield stadium heaves into view.

'Aye, that'd be it.' DS Findlay produces a rueful grin. 'How the other half live, eh?'

'You should see their new bathroom.'

Skelgill sounds in good spirits; perhaps he is secretly buoyed by DS Findlay's tribute.

'It wasn't funny, Guv.' DS Jones protests. 'While you were

absent I was subjected to the full-blown kitchen tour in every minute detail. Le Creuset, Sabatier, Dualit, Gaggia – you name it, they've got it.'

Skelgill shrugs.

'Small wonder Tregilgis avoided the place.'

DS Jones nods.

'What you said about her sounding English – I would have guessed Home Counties from her accent.'

'Ach, there's a thing.' This intervention comes from the taciturn DS Findlay. 'Ye see, we pretend tae hate the English – but in fact we know you're mostly just like us – and, after all, ye cannae help being English. But those Scots that *act* like they're English – that's what really gets our goat.'

Skelgill shakes his head in resignation; the Scots see subtleties in nationality of which their southern counterparts are blissfully unaware. But the conversation has prompted a thought.

'Cammy – any chance you could do a bit of digging on this lot up here?'

'Aye. Dare say I owe you one.'

'Just background stuff. You know – the Goldsmiths, anything on the company, employees, suppliers – that sort of thing.'

DS Findlay nods economically.

'I've got a pal over at The Scotsman. Works on the business desk. I'll see what a couple of pints of Eighty Bob will turn up.'

In due course, with a few deft manoeuvres and judicious use of the blues and twos, DS Findlay delivers his charges to the drop-off at Edinburgh airport with time to spare. A lively dash and some flashing of their warrant cards should see them make their flight.

'Much appreciated Cammy.' Skelgill reaches to shake hands across the roof of the car. 'See you in a day or two. No joyriding in my motor, now.'

DS Findlay grins.

'You mind to look both ways when you're crossing the road down there. I've heard they dinnae stop for anybody.'

'We'll be fine – this lass studied there for three years. She's an honorary Cockney.'

'Aye well, anything beats being a Geordie.'

'Very witty, Cam.'

17. EVENING FLIGHT

Monday, 5.30 p.m.

'What was that about being a Geordie?'

DS Jones sounds puzzled, as they ride the escalator up to the departures gate.

'He likes to wind me up – when I worked with them all the Scots assumed I came from Newcastle.'

'We sound nothing like Geordies.' DS Jones is indignant.

'Aye – but could you tell the difference between an Aberdonian and a Dundonian?'

'Hm – I guess not.'

'Same principle.'

*

The Edinburgh-Heathrow flight is barely half-full, so Skelgill turns his charms to the task of getting them moved to an empty row, where they can discuss police matters free of eavesdroppers.

'Are you sure you don't want the window seat, Jones?'

'Guv – it states on the instructions card – when a male and female are travelling together, the man must always have the window seat.

'What?'

'And the stewardesses must wear high heels and suspenders.'

Skelgill looks at his colleague to see she is smirking. A little colour breaks out upon his prominent cheekbones.

'Guv – *you* have it, really. I'll probably fall asleep, anyway. The view's wasted on me.'

Suitably chastised, he slides across to the window.

'You can have it on the way back, lass.'

Skelgill struggles until he gets comfortable with the seat belt. At five-eleven and three-quarters he is not overly tall, but there is something lanky about his rangy form, and it takes him a minute or two to settle in the cramped and unfamiliar environment. He takes a deep breath, and then clears his throat, though it is in hushed tones that he begins to speak.

'Talking of underwear, happen we're homing in on Krista Morocco.'

DS Jones nods.

'If the statements are accurate, it sounds like she and Ivan Tregilgis were getting along fine on Saturday night – and they did disappear, out onto the terrace. If his bedroom door was unlocked –'

But now Skelgill rows back a little; he harbours reservations about developing a scenario beyond the facts.

'We have to remember it was only midnight – whatever they did, it could be entirely unconnected to his death.'

'Maybe they went into *her* room, Guv?'

'What – and he kept her undies as a trophy?'

DS Jones chuckles.

'I believe there's a market for such things.'

Skelgill folds his arms and pushes back against his unyielding seat. He thinks of saying, "Surely you mean such *thongs?*" – but instead opts to change the subject.

'Remind me what was in Tregilgis's briefcase.'

DS Jones closes her eyes begins to recite from memory.

'A travel voucher for two nights at the Plaza – it's a hotel on Fifth Avenue. A couple of climbing magazines. Passport. Toothbrush. Radio. Condoms. And the printed showcase of their work.'

Skelgill seems dissatisfied.

'Something's not right. You wouldn't go on business to New

York without taking some reference to whatever meeting you were attending.'

'Maybe it was a new client visit – to receive a brief.'

'Run that by me.'

'Well, the first stage in advertising is normally that the client hands a brief to the ad agency. They conduct market research, develop a creative strategy, and then go back to make their pitch.'

'When did you become the oracle on advertising procedure?'

'Guy I dated for a while when I lived in London – he was a copywriter with an ad agency. Bit of a psycho. Hardly ever turned up for work. I dumped him when I found he'd been sleeping with my flatmate.'

'Sorry about that.'

'Don't be. My flatmate was also a guy. I think I was just by way of an introduction.'

*

Once airborne, Skelgill becomes silent, and distracted, as he watches Britain go by. The wind direction has dictated a westerly take-off, banking left above Glasgow – the sprawling city seems only a stone's throw from its neater east-coast rival. The pilot now tracks the motorway towards the English border, still climbing into a cloudless sky. Skelgill gazes transfixed as the Solway creeps nearer, a vast glistening bay drawing the eye across the Irish Sea, where the distant Isle of Man seems to float above the horizon. With a tingle of anticipation he begins to pick out the Cumbrian fells, first the blunt twin massifs of Blencathra and Skiddaw guarding the northern reaches, and soon the jagged cluster that makes up the Langdale and Scafell Pikes. The lakes themselves are harder to discern – blending as they do into the dusky landscape until fleetingly illuminated by the setting sun's direct line of reflection.

'Look at Bass Lake!'

Skelgill turns to his companion – but, good to her word, DS

Jones is fast asleep. Indeed, as he leans back into his seat her head lolls sideways and rests upon his shoulder.

'Jones.' His whisper is tentative. 'Jones.'

But these entreaties are to no avail. It seems the strains of the last two days have finally taken their toll. He cranes awkwardly to look at her, and slides into a more comfortable position. Then he sits very still, his hands folded on his lap. She sinks more heavily against him. Skelgill closes his eyes, and sighs.

When DS Jones wakes up, Skelgill is just finishing the last of her airline sandwich.

'Oh, Jones – didn't like to disturb you. I got you a coffee.'

'Thanks.' She frowns at the unappetising dark brown liquid.

'What do you want to do tonight – are you planning to see your fella?'

DS Jones does not answer for a moment. Then she shakes her head.

'No – he doesn't even know I'll be down. I didn't think I'd have any spare time. And he's away over in Clapham.'

'You're not obliged to be on duty round the clock. Feel free if you want to shoot off. I'll be fine.'

DS Jones could be excused for thinking she detects a plaintive note in Skelgill's tone, but it seems he has nothing to fear.

'If it's okay with you, Guv – I fancy a quiet Chinese, to be honest. I mean – we need to discuss tomorrow's interviews, don't we?'

Skelgill regards her reflectively.

'What time do you think we'll get to the hotel?'

It is plain that Skelgill has handed over the baton. She examines her wristwatch.

'If we land on schedule we should be on the tube by seven-thirty. Piccadilly Line all the way to Covent Garden – about an hour. Then it's only a couple of minutes' walk – the hotel's just off Drury Lane. We could be in Gerrard Street by nine – plenty of cheap places to eat.'

The aircraft, now well into its descent, banks heavily to the right; it makes disconcerting whirring and clunking noises. Skelgill is a far-from-frequent flyer, but he notices the stewardesses seem unconcerned, so he gazes down upon the London rooftops; they stretch as far as the eye can see. He makes the comparison that Europe's great metropolis appears to cover as big an area as the entire Lake District. There he knows every square inch, has trodden every path, climbed every pike, followed every rainbow. But, one rainbow he did not follow still niggles in the depths of his mind; the regret that he had eschewed a posting to the Metropolitan Police early in his career. Even his family had urged him to go, despite generations of accumulated suspicion of anything that smacked of 'offcomers', as Cumbrians call outsiders. "Spread thou wings, lad – do thysen justice." But Skelgill had succumbed to some perverse logic, that he would be a fish out of water, out of his depth – and other such oxymorons. Naturally, in the fast lane of London most provincial folk fear their own parochialism, but in Skelgill's case there was perhaps a more personal weakness that undermined his self-confidence, albeit one that hitherto even he has been unable to define.

'Something exciting, Guv?'

Skelgill is jerked from his reverie.

'What?' He is a little abashed, and waves a hand at the window. 'Just admiring the view. Tell me what's down there.'

DS Jones leans across him. She places a hand on his knee to brace her weight.

'Look – Westminster Bridge – you can see Parliament – then follow the road westwards – the first park is St James's – there's the Palace – then Green Park – Hyde Park Corner with all the traffic – see Park Lane running up from there – then Hyde Park to the left of it – the Serpentine – and there's Kensington Palace.'

Her commentary continues until they run out of obvious landmarks after Kew, although Skelgill stares for some time at a distant Wembley stadium – perhaps imagining its fabled twin towers and Bobby Moore, arm aloft, and wondering if England will ever again win the World Cup.

With hand luggage only, they are soon on a train. There is an air of despondency and fatigue, and it infects the two detectives, who sit quietly rapt. Skelgill picks up a discarded copy of the Evening Standard. He flicks absently through the pages, pausing at the classifieds, and becomes engrossed by the myriad of small ads seeking plasterers and plumbers, table dancers, meter-readers and mystery shoppers (whatever they are); and there are one-bedroom flats to rent at weekly rates you wouldn't even pay for a month back up north. Next he finds himself counting down the stops, his head nodding as he reads along the Piccadilly Line map displayed overhead. The journey is largely overground to Hammersmith, and they bisect rows of untidy houses with jumbled back-gardens and Heath-Robinson extensions, ramshackle sheds and lines of washing. Occasionally there are glimpses of families sitting out on white plastic garden furniture, seemingly oblivious to their dismal surroundings.

Station by station, the train fills up. Skelgill scrutinises the growing cross-section of humanity that begins to throng the carriage. Initially, new travellers are solitary, glum and mostly of foreign origin – maybe cleaners and night porters on their way to work? At Hammersmith there is an influx of smarter, office workers. South Kensington and Knightsbridge see them joined by well-heeled shoppers, jet-setty middle-eastern women wearing expensive western clothes. As the train dives deeper under the West End, there is an inrush of tourists and small groups of trendily dressed younger people, and many of these leave with Skelgill and DS Jones at Covent Garden, where they press as a body into a lift reminiscent of a scene from Quatermass.

Skelgill looks relieved to escape from the stale humidity of the underground. This is their first taste of fresh air since Edinburgh – if there can be such a thing in central London. However, there is a warm, almost continental ambience with the aromas of cooked spices and the clink of raised glasses. DS Jones leads the way assuredly up Long Acre, with its designer boutiques and disorderly beggars. They dodge between taxis and cross into Endell Street, where Bohemian sandwich-bars are mingled with outlandish clothing shops, open-fronted cafe-bars that spill onto the pavement, and a "lesbian sex club" that prompts a small debate as to where the missing hyphen should go, or whether it makes any difference.

They take their hotel by surprise, DS Jones suddenly ducking in ahead from the pavement. The rooms are threadbare but adequate, although not for the money. By agreement, they simply deposit their bags and retrace their steps – they have settled on DS Jones's proposal of a quick Chinese, and as early a night as possible.

'The Tregilgis's flat is down here.' DS Jones takes them on a minor detour to show Skelgill the location.

'Doesn't look that smart.'

'You should clock the price tags, Guv. And I bet it's pretty cool inside.'

'Sounds like Miriam Tregilgis.'

18. KRISTA MOROCCO

Tuesday, 9 a.m.

'Do you recognise these briefs?'

'I bought an identical pair last week.'

There is a silence. Skelgill, having thoroughly rehearsed a line of questioning vetted by DS Jones, has omitted to practise what to say if Krista Morocco replies in the affirmative. They sit in the latter's glass-walled office, set in a highly fashionable Soho condominium. Arriving on foot Skelgill had been surprised by the early-morning calm that pervades Covent Garden before the couriers, taxis and tourists get going. He stopped to watch great dripping-wet sacks of live mussels being unloaded into the back of a Belgian restaurant, and marvelled at the number of old ladies walking tiny dogs. There were even uniformed children on their way to school. Perhaps ordinary people did live here after all? This notion was soon quashed by the rows of shining cars parked in Soho Square: BMW, Jaguar, Range Rover, Porsche, Mercedes.

'Did you wear them on Saturday night?'

'I didn't wear any on Saturday night. My dress was sheer and clingy and partially see-through. Underwear simply wasn't an option.'

Krista Morocco's china-blue eyes are unblinking.

Skelgill's mouth appears to become somewhat dry. DS Jones steps into the breach.

'When did you last see this pair?'

Krista Morocco lifts up the plastic evidence bag.

'I guess when I packed on Friday night. I didn't wear these at all at the weekend.'

'You didn't mention in your statement that they were missing.'

DS Jones is quickly getting into her stride.

'If they're mine – I had no idea I'd lost them. I kept most of my belongings in my overnight case at the hotel, and I still haven't unpacked.'

'Can you explain the fact that they were found in Ivan Tregilgis's bed?'

'What?'

Skelgill, despite his momentary disorientation, is watching very carefully this reaction. DS Jones, however, presses for an answer.

'Ms Morocco?'

'Sorry.' She sounds genuinely apologetic. 'I can't explain it. Someone must have taken them from my case.'

'Did you leave your room unlocked at any time?'

'I don't think I locked it at all.' Krista Morocco regards them ingenuously. 'We usually take the whole place for these events, so there's never any need to lock your door.'

'How about the French door that led onto the terrace, was that unlocked too?'

'Yes – at least, from mid-afternoon onwards.'

'Can you recall anything happening that could explain how your underwear got into Room 10?'

Krista Morocco shakes her head.

'Just after midnight you went out onto the terrace with Mr Tregilgis. Why was that?'

She stares at DS Jones, and then, rather more pleadingly, at Skelgill. Her reply, slow to materialise, is couched in sad tones.

'I don't know.'

DS Jones persists.

'Surely something happened? Did you talk, smoke, maybe kiss one another – go to his room – or yours?'

Krista Morocco remains silent. Then her eyes flood with tears. She shakes her head again.

'I really don't know. I can't remember going outside with Ivan.'

The detectives regard her in silence. Skelgill is wondering if his colleague will relent, but she simply waits until Krista Morocco finally speaks.

'Look – we started drinking just after lunch – out on the terrace – then there was barely a break before we met for cocktails. You see, my memory – everything from somewhere in the middle of dinner is a blank – until the shock of, you know – the blood?'

She inhales sharply as if to suppress a sob.

'Do you normally drink that amount?'

'Me personally, hardly ever – but at the company do everyone lets their hair down – and partying, it's in the advertising industry's DNA.'

Now tears spill down over her sculpted cheekbones and she tugs a box of tissues from her desk drawer. Skelgill senses a wavering in his own resolve, and he recognises that his young female colleague has an advantage over him in this particular situation. Indeed, DS Jones presses on with what is perhaps the toughest question yet.

'Ms Morocco what we believe to be your fingerprints were found on an ornamental knife – a Nepalese kukri to be precise – it was identical to the weapon which may have been used to murder Ivan Tregilgis.'

Krista Morocco stares in disbelief.

'Can you explain that, Ms Morocco?'

There is no answer.

'And I suppose you wouldn't recollect if you stabbed Ivan Tregilgis?'

The woman twists the tissue between trembling fingers. Her nails are exquisitely manicured. She turns pointedly to Skelgill.

'Are you here to arrest me, Inspector?'

A note of panic permeates her voice.

Skelgill stares at her for what seems like an age. DS Jones seems poised ready to pounce should Krista Morocco make a break for freedom.

'Nay – it's not come to that, lass.'

The young woman bows her head, and wipes away more tears.

'I loved Ivan, Inspector.' She looks entreatingly at Skelgill, and there is fear in her eyes. 'I could never harm him – not in a million years. Is somebody trying to frame me?'

'Who would do that, Ms Morocco?'

She hesitates, as if sensing the gravity of the moment – of making an accusation – despite the opportunity it provides to shift the unwelcome burden of guilt from her own shoulders.

'I don't believe anyone in the company could commit a murder, Inspector.'

Skelgill sinks back into his chair, and DS Jones mirrors his movement, the tension draining from her athletic frame. He flashes a half smile, as if to show he recognises Krista Morocco's generous diplomacy.

'Put it another way. Who might take the opportunity to make things awkward for you?'

Krista Morocco shifts uncomfortably in her seat.

Skelgill offers a prompt.

'We understand there has been some tension with Miss Rubicon.'

Krista Morocco looks like she would prefer to disagree, but she nods reluctantly.

'I think she feels I've stood in her way.'

'With respect to Mr Tregilgis, or to her career?'

'Probably both.'

'Were you having an affair with him?'

Krista Morocco shakes her head. Her eyes glisten and the tears threaten to reappear.

'No. We had a short relationship about seven or eight years ago – before he was married. I lost out, I suppose. But we remained very close. The advertising business might seem glamorous, Inspector, but it's a constant battle – some clients – not the companies themselves, just certain maladjusted individuals who get into positions of power – they treat agencies very badly. It can feel like a battle for your very survival at times – and you form very

90

strong bonds with your colleagues.'

'Were Ivan Tregilgis and Julia Rubicon having an affair?'

'I think it's possible – at least until she went to Edinburgh. I don't know if it continued.'

'And how did you thwart her career?'

'Well – it was just in her mind.' Krista Morocco holds out her hands as an appeal for understanding. 'I actually helped to get her promoted ahead of other candidates – but apparently she thought she should leap-frog me and be put in charge of *both* offices.'

'How do you know?'

'Because Ivan told me.'

'Was she good at her job?'

'Yes, a competent operator, very efficient. But too self-absorbed to be a good senior manager.'

'What would you say to the suggestion that Miss Rubicon was transferred to get her out of your road?'

Krista Morocco seems unruffled by this.

'I don't deny there was conflict. But Julia only had to say the word to Ivan if she wanted to stay – I had no power to put her in the Edinburgh job, and I wasn't planning to remove her from my office.'

Skelgill nods, seemingly satisfied with her responses. He looks to DS Jones, and indicates she should address a prepared line of questioning. While a pressure valve has been released, she resumes in the same professional and decisive mode.

'Ms Morocco, I understand last week you did sack somebody. Mr Grendon Smith?'

'That's correct.'

'Why was he dismissed?'

'We think he defrauded us, though I doubt if I could prove it. I had to sack him on the grounds of incompetence. It was all a bit unpleasant.'

'What was the nature of the alleged fraud?'

'Kickbacks from a supplier. We cross-quote all of our out-work to make sure it's competitively priced, but there's still scope for dishonesty.'

'How did you find out?'

'We got a whisper from a chap who'd moved job from one of our suppliers to another.'

'How much is involved?'

'Around the five thousand mark. Perhaps more.'

DS Jones nods.

'And what was he like – Mr Smith?'

'He interviewed well – I made an error of judgement. At first he seemed very helpful and keen to learn, but as soon as things got tough he would start to blame everyone but himself – and that's not our culture. Underneath the charm he was a spiteful person – he had unpredictable mood swings – and he became unpopular with the rest of the team.'

'And on the day he was fired I understand he and Mr Tregilgis had a bit of an altercation?'

Krista Morocco nods.

'Grendon reacted badly. He was emptying his desk, slamming drawers and aggressively flinging items into the waste bin. Ivan was nearby with a client and I rang him. He came over and saw Grendon off the premises. I don't think it was too serious – but you wouldn't want to mess with Ivan.'

'Have you seen or heard anything of Mr Smith since?'

Krista Morocco shakes her head.

'Are you intending to report him to the police?'

'I never mentioned the kickbacks. As I say, I have no concrete proof. Though I expect he put two and two together – and Ivan may have said something to him as he left.'

'We may be able to find that out.' DS Jones taps her notebook with her pen. 'Perhaps before we leave you could give us contact details for the suppliers Mr Smith dealt with.'

'Certainly – but there is one firm in particular – they're called BDL – Ivan was about to take them to court.'

'Why was that?'

'I suppose you could say they did the dirty on us. They're a specialist media contractor and they came to us about a year ago and offered us a higher agency commission to place work with them instead of one of their competitors. It's standard industry practice – the client can only buy direct at a higher rate, so may as well go through an agency like us. We cover some of our costs that way. But then BDL went directly to one of our clients and offered them the agency discount. So they used us to build up the trading relationship, and then cut us out of the equation. We should never have trusted them – their MD has a reputation as an unscrupulous operator. Our lawyers have advised us that we can sue them for breach of contract, so we formally put them on notice last week.'

'And are you suggesting there could be a connection with Mr Tregilgis's death?'

Krista Morocco glances rather helplessly at the two detectives.

'I really don't know. It all seems unbelievable. I understood someone had broken in and killed him, and I've just been trying to think who might have had a reason.'

Skelgill clears his throat to speak.

'In that vein, Ms Morocco, are there any other unusual circumstances that affect Tregilgis & Goldsmith at the moment?'

Krista Morocco nods immediately.

'There is one thing. Although it seems far removed from a murder.'

'No harm in telling us.'

'About three weeks ago I took a phone call from an American – he said he was a recruitment consultant and could I talk? I was curious and said yes, but that I'd need to call him back via his company switchboard – just in case it was one of our clients' competitors trying to get confidential information. However, he gave me a number – in the United States – and I rang it and got through to him, no problem. He then said, sorry, he wasn't exactly a headhunter, but that his firm – I'd vaguely heard of them – was one of the leading New York ad agencies and they were opening an office in London, and were looking for someone to head it up.'

'And were you interested?'

'Well, flattered, I suppose. I wasn't thinking of leaving Tregilgis & Goldsmith, and to be honest I don't fancy working for a big shop again, what with all the bureaucracy and politicking.'

Skelgill raises an eyebrow – this small firm does not seem to be short of these qualities.

'Did it come to anything?'

'Well, it was a strange sort of interview. When I thought about it afterwards I realised he hadn't asked about my own achievements – it was more how I interacted with the principals – Ivan and Dermott – and the kind of systems and procedures that we use. He finished off by saying thanks and that he was coming over to London at the end of June, and would like to meet me then, and would be in touch.'

'So, what struck you as unusual?'

'Frankly, I felt he was more interested in the company than in me. And he asked me not to mention our conversation to Ivan or Dermott. Now if you're in the middle of getting a new job with a competitor, the last person you tell is your boss.'

Skelgill nods.

'So, are you saying this American crowd want to buy Tregilgis & Goldsmith?'

'It seems that way. We're known as one of the leading independents in the country. There's no Creative Director with more awards than Ivan.'

'And would the company be for sale?'

'I don't know – it's not something Ivan ever mentioned. But it is the normal thing in advertising – you start your own shop – build it up, sell it to a big company – and disappear into the sunset.'

Her eyes begin to well up again, as if she finds the image she conjures distressing.

'Ms Morocco, I take it you have this American chap's details?'

'Yes – sure – his number's saved on my phone.'

She reaches for her handset; it has been lying silenced on the table before them – and locates the contact. She turns the screen so Skelgill can see it.

'Ford Zendik? Sounds like one of my old cars. Mind if I borrow your office to give him a call?'

'Not at all, Inspector.' At last a faint smile hints at the captivating beauty that lies beneath what has been a mainly troubled façade. 'But right now in Manhattan it's four-thirty a.m.'

19. SEVEN DIALS

Tuesday, 11 a.m.

'Happen we can drop the underwear.'

DS Jones raises her eyebrows questioningly. She is not sure if he is fishing for a smile, the play on words. But he continues in a serious vein.

'Puts a different spin on it. How did they get into Tregilgis's bed – and, more to the point, why?'

'I suppose we should wait for Forensics to confirm they're unworn?'

But Skelgill seems more forgiving.

'She didn't try to talk her way out of anything she couldn't explain.'

DS Jones's eyes narrow slightly – there is the impression she thinks Skelgill has been unduly influenced by the woman's desolation.

'That was convenient amnesia – about events after midnight, Guv?'

He pulls a face, a curious expression that reveals his front teeth.

'Start drinking at lunchtime – I'd be struggling to remember what I had for tea.'

DS Jones looks ready to counter – but an alert from her mobile draws her attention.

'Ah – this is the lab, Guv.'

Skelgill begins to rise from his seat.

'Have a deek. I'll fetch another round.'

They are in a traditional West End sandwich-bar just a stone's throw from Seven Dials. Skelgill joins the assembly of waiting customers and contemplates the cryptically labelled fillings on display. Behind the eye-level counter bob an indeterminate number of small Italians; every so often a pair of hands pitches up a finished article for collection. Skelgill's mind drifts to the source of his intransigence as far as Krista Morocco is concerned. Behind her, on the wall of her office, were photographs of awards ceremonies, company nights out, outward-bound activity days. A cricketer himself, albeit largely lapsed due to a chronic back injury, his eye was taken by a shot labelled *"Client-Agency Test Match"*. It was a dated image – he had deduced from the time when Krista Morocco and Ivan Tregilgis worked for separate firms. The teams stand intermingled, and happily smiling Krista Morocco rests her head against Ivan Tregilgis's left shoulder, her right hand clearly visible clutching the other side of his waist.

'*Guv.*'

Skelgill turns sharply – there is a note of unfamiliar urgency in his colleague's voice. She beckons him across.

'Jones?'

She brandishes her handset. Now she speaks in hushed tones.

'Ivan Tregilgis wasn't killed with the kukri.'

'*What?*'

Skelgill sits down and rests his forearms almost belligerently upon the little table. DS Jones manipulates the details on her screen.

'It says the entry wound is consistent with a straight-edged blade at least five inches long and no thicker than an inch at its widest. It's nothing like the shape of a kukri.'

Skelgill stares out of the window and across the road. Through the glass of an eatery opposite he watches blankly as an eternal snake of sushi circles its victims. He curses. Some heads are turned. DS Jones makes a face of apology. Skelgill's jaw is set.

'Sucker punch.'

Clearly, he is kicking himself.

DS Jones makes an effort at mitigation.

'Guv – it was a scene of chaos – neither of us had had much sleep – there was Mrs Groteneus's shocked reaction. It was a natural conclusion to jump to – a stabbed victim and a knife stolen and then concealed nearby.'

Skelgill regards her reprovingly – perhaps that she seems to be taking an equal share of responsibility, when in fact the buck stops with him.

'Two teas!'

A call from behind the counter reminds him of his order. He rises again. He regards DS Jones somewhat contritely.

'Silver lining – for Krista Morocco.'

20. MELANIE STARK

Tuesday, 2 p.m.

While DS Jones had pointed out that the staff of Tregilgis & Goldsmith are predominantly females, had Skelgill been working with his regular 'oppo' DS Leyton it almost certainly would not have gone unremarked that they are disproportionately young, attractive females. Given his present company, Skelgill has felt obliged to keep this observation, and any speculation over there being a deliberate recruitment policy to himself. But now he wonders if the phenomenon has not in fact escaped DS Jones, for she regards their latest interviewee with an uncharacteristic degree of curiosity.

Melanie Stark, deputy to Krista Morocco, has an unfortunate lopsided, shrew-like face, and judged against the criterion of her peers would be considered plain. Her eyes are close together and her narrow mouth is pinched into a line. She sits, hunched across her desk, her gaze darting hungrily from one to the other of the detectives. DS Jones is conducting the interview.

'And when did you join the agency?'

'Just over six years ago.'

'So that makes you the second-longest-serving employee after Ms Morocco?'

Melanie Stark nods eagerly.

'And are these company do's a regular thing?'

'Oh yes, every year – sometimes twice if we've done particularly well.'

'And how did this year's compare to previous ones?'

'Pretty similar – high spirits, posh nosh, unlimited free booze.'

'You mentioned in your statement there was some friction surrounding Mr Tregilgis.'

Melanie Stark smirks primly.

'Julia and Krista fighting over Ivan. Miriam pretending not to notice. The usual form.'

'Could you elaborate?'

'Whenever Krista gets drunk, she gets the devil in her – and winds up Julia – by getting intimate with Ivan. He couldn't seem to resist her. So Julia would go crazy.'

DS Jones shifts momentarily in her seat, a movement that affords her a glance at Skelgill; briefly he raises an eyebrow.

'Was she drunk on Saturday night – Ms Morocco?'

'Who wasn't?'

'Do you recollect people dancing with various of the tribal artefacts taken from the lobby?'

'Yes, that was later on – a bit scary – all those masks and spears. I just had a set of tom-toms.'

'How about Ms Morocco?'

Melanie Stark thinks for a moment.

'It was a head-dress – with strings of Masai beads that covered her face. I remember she shouted to me something about Lowlife.'

'Lowlife?'

'It's a pet name for one of our most despicable clients. She was making stabbing motions with a dagger.'

Now DS Jones pauses to look more pointedly at her superior, but he watches their quarry implacably and she turns back.

'Did you see anyone else with a knife?'

Melanie Stark shakes her head.

'It was all a bit of a blur – and we had the lights down low.'

DS Jones nods and makes a note in her pocket book.

'What happened to all of the paraphernalia?'

'Ivan made sure we put it back. He always said in his opening speech about how we should behave – so we would be welcomed back at any hotel we hired. I don't mean he wasn't up for a caper himself – he abseiled down a stairwell at one place – but any gratuitous damage and he'd be really upset.'

'You said Mr Tregilgis had a weakness for Ms Morocco. What do you mean by that?'

'They go back a long way. Krista once said Ivan had her on his conscience – from when they went out together – but I suppose she told you about that?'

DS Jones responds with a question.

'There is talk that Mr Tregilgis and Ms Rubicon were having an affair. Is it possible he was involved with Ms Morocco at the same time?'

'No chance.'

The wary rodent-like eyes flash with indignation – or perhaps what might be anger.

'How can you be so certain?'

'Krista wouldn't put herself in the position where Julia could manipulate her. Not after all the hassle she gave us. Thankfully she deployed her charms on Ivan and had Julia shipped to Scotland.'

'You make it sound like a deportation.'

Melanie Stark's features crease into a Machiavellian smirk.

'Who would volunteer to have Dermott breathing down their neck – literally?'

The response takes them off at a tangent. Skelgill is interested to observe that his subordinate follows the lead.

'Mr Goldsmith is not so popular?'

'Adolescent – and jealous of Ivan. Not to mention obsessively anal. He tries to make us buy petrol in amounts divisible by the VAT rate, to keep our expenses in round numbers.'

'Mrs Stark, I gather that Mr Goldsmith is diabetic.'

Now Skelgill sees that there is some logic in DS Jones's willingness to take the diversion. Melanie Stark does not seem fazed by the question; thus far she has been a veritable cornucopia of information; she continues thus.

'Don't we all know it?'

She raises her eyebrows in a weary gesture.

'It was mentioned that at about a quarter to one he signalled that he was going to administer an insulin injection – did you happen to notice him leave?'

Melanie Stark shakes her head.

'I'd be surprised about that. Normally we get a public display – usually at the dinner table – never mind that half of us are nearly throwing up. And Elspeth revels in it, too, playing matron.'

DS Jones nods. Here is another small byway.

'We're told she has an important role in the company.'

Melanie Stark splutters.

'If by that you mean all the crap that Dermott doesn't want to do, then yes.'

She stares defiantly at DS Jones.

'Mrs Goldsmith told us that she was catching up with you on Saturday night – Sunday morning in fact.'

'Pumping me.'

She corrects DS Jones without embarrassment. The detectives would be excused for thinking she is grinding an axe that has been a good six years in the blunting.

'When exactly was this?'

'Just before the big commotion. We were leaning up against the bar eating some leftover pudding that she'd rustled up.'

'You didn't mention in your statement that you were with her just as Mr Tregilgis's death was discovered.'

Melanie Stark looks suddenly disconcerted.

'I must have got confused – I mean – when the policeman interviewed me, I hadn't slept and I'd got a terrible hangover. Seeing Ivan's body – and Miriam hysterical – it was such a shock – at the time it was hard to remember much before that.'

DS Jones remains silent. After a few moments Melanie Stark speaks again, her voice now strained – and, just as did Krista Morocco, she directs the question at a brooding Skelgill.

'Inspector – you don't think *I* had something to do with this, do you?'

Skelgill rouses himself from his torpor and stares at her menacingly. But then he relents and shrugs.

'You sound like you're telling the truth to me, madam.'

The woman visibly relaxes, and then she leans forward across the desk, as though she wants to share something with them. But she waits for the invitation.

'Madam?'

'About Dermott – going to inject himself?'

'Aye?'

'My husband's diabetic – he would never do it at that time of night – it could lower your blood sugars to a potentially fatal level.'

21. FORD ZENDIK

Tuesday, 4 p.m.

'Dead! You gotta be kidding, fella?'
'I'm afraid not, sir – he was killed by an intruder in his hotel bedroom.'
'You talkin' felony murder?'
'I reckon that would be about right, Mr Zendik. Would it help if I called you back in a short while?'

There is a pause followed by the sound of coughing and various muffled cusses, before the American voice returns.

'It's no problem, Officer – just a bit of a shock, that's all. Actually, I hardly knew the guy personally – met him just the once.'
'So, you don't mind if I ask you some questions?'
'Shoot.'

While DS Jones has been despatched to inspect any paperwork and electronic equipment kept at the Tregilgis property, and to catch up with developments filtering back to HQ, Skelgill has commandeered Krista Morocco's office in order to telephone the States. His patience in waiting is rewarded with the capture of Ford Zendik at his desk. A brief introduction has established both parties' credentials, enabling Skelgill to come quickly to the point with the straight-talking New Yorker.

'We believe Mr Tregilgis was due to fly yesterday to JFK – and thought he may have been intending to see you.'
'Dead right.' (The man coughs again, perhaps recognising his unfortunate choice of words.) 'In fact, Officer, he was due here in my office in less than an hour.'
'Where exactly are you?'
'Corner of third and fifty-second.'

'That's Manhattan?'

'Correct.'

'And can you tell me what the meeting was about?'

'Sure. We're buying his company. Tregilgis was coming over so we could put some flesh on the bones of the deal.'

'Do you mean the sale has already been agreed in principle?'

'What I'm saying is we'd agreed a ball-park figure.'

'Can I ask how much?'

'Sixteen million dollars.'

Skelgill pauses for a moment – he hopes the man does not hear him gulp.

'When did you hope to close the deal?'

'Today. Tregilgis was bringing the signed Heads of Terms.'

'That would be a printed document?'

'Sure. We *Fedexed* it last week – he called me on Friday to say he'd received it.'

'And do you know if he was in agreement with the main points?'

'He said it looked fine. Said he should be able to sell it to his partner, no problem.'

'Were they not entirely in accord?'

'They were in accord, alright – sixteen million bucks in accord. It was just a matter of swallowing the jobs we needed them to do for the next couple of years.'

'How does that work? I'm new to this advertising business.'

'When you buy an agency you keep the principals on for continuity – staff like it, clients like it – it's a people business.'

'Aye.'

'In this case we wanted Tregilgis to front the show, and Goldsmith to take a bit of a back seat – don't get me wrong, we'd keep him on – same package, impressive title with Vice President in it somewhere – but his skills are superfluous in an organisation the size of ours.'

'Whereas Ivan Tregilgis had more of a role to play?'

'Exactly. We'd made the usual discreet inquiries – talking

incognito to their staff, clients, industry contacts. Tregilgis was highly rated on all fronts – a top Creative with a string of international awards.'

'And not so, Dermott Goldsmith?'

'He's okay so far as it goes. But he doesn't really bring anything to the party – I've got bean-counters crawling all over me here, the last thing I need is another one – a puffed-up Limey, at that.'

When Skelgill's partisan sentiments might be roused, he finds himself in accord with the American's assessment.

'Was there some doubt that Mr Goldsmith would accept the position?'

'Like I said, Officer, sixteen million bucks buys a lot of humble pie.'

'Why were you dealing solely with Mr Tregilgis?'

'That's how they wanted it. It kept things simple – one point of contact.'

'Will Mr Tregilgis's death affect the deal?'

There is a moment's silence; Skelgill hears what he thinks is a slurping sound, and a muffled exclamation.

'Sorry, Officer. Let my drink get cold. Yeah, we'd still be interested, but it may alter the price.'

'Significantly?'

'Hey, buddy – are you their agent?'

'Sounds like it would pay well.'

'Sure would. But to answer your question, Officer, I'd need to think about it. Tregilgis had intrinsic value – some clients were loyal to him personally – and we'd need to hire a replacement head Creative – it's not easy to find top guns, even in London.'

'I understand. Who else would have known about the proposed takeover?'

'Couple of guys here – Tregilgis and Goldsmith over your side – I'd be surprised if they told anyone.'

'Why is that?'

'It could be unsettling if rumours got around – you don't want your clients or staff to start jumping ship. Best to present a fait accompli and show everyone that it's business as usual.'

'And there's no other agency in the mix? I mean – competing for your sixteen million?'

'Not in England, Officer.'

'Okay. Look – I appreciate your co-operation. Just one last question – what are your feelings about this?'

'We've lost one of the good guys.'

*

When DS Jones reappears forty minutes later, Skelgill is quick to note that she bears a deli-style sandwich bag.

'I thought this might fill a gap, Guv.'

Skelgill accepts the offering – she seems a little awkward about it – and there are several individually wrapped sandwiches. He extracts one and tries to hand back the bag.

'It's okay, Guv – I got them for you.'

Skelgill glowers reproachfully.

'Are you trying to tell me something, lass?' But he, too, finds the moment a little uncomfortable, and without waiting for a reply launches into another question. 'What of the Tregilgis place?'

DS Jones takes a seat opposite her boss.

"Not a trace of the agreement – but Miriam Tregilgis did take in a parcel from a courier on Friday.'

Skelgill, already biting into his ciabatta roll, nods pensively.

DS Jones continues.

'Miriam Tregilgis is pleading ignorance about the company sale.'

'How was she?'

'Phlegmatic, as before. And she denies having a relationship with any of her clients.'

'What did she say?'

'Initially just a straight "no" – then when I explained somebody had seen her, she said that it was after all 'personal' training and that sometimes a male client might get the wrong end of the stick.'

'Tell me about it.'

Skelgill's quip is somewhat forlorn, and DS Jones seems to eye him a little sympathetically. He takes refuge in his roll. She waits while he finishes the mouthful.

'How did you get on with Ford Zendik?'

Between bites he relates the details of his transatlantic conversation. When he reaches the part about sixteen million dollars, DS Jones sits up.

'Wow – that puts Miriam Tregilgis in the clear.'

'Explain.'

'Now she gets a paltry million pounds?'

Skelgill nods pensively. But he allows his colleague to continue.

'What did he say about the sale still going ahead?'

'That it would – but probably at a lower price.'

'But not half the price?'

'That's not the impression he gave.'

Skelgill can see where DS Jones is heading, and indeed she completes the algorithm.

'So, Dermott Goldsmith comes out ahead – he would own a hundred per cent of the company, and pocket whatever is the revised price.'

While Skelgill would not be in the least discomfited were they to find Dermott Goldsmith at the centre of the conspiracy, he feels obliged at this juncture to apply a modicum of devil's advocacy.

'Look, lass – we can't forget that Miriam Tregilgis is the only person that we've got concrete proof was at the scene of the crime – virtually at the time of death – and covered in Tregilgis's blood.'

DS Jones purses her lips – but she does not yet speak. Perhaps Skelgill is more inured to female charms than his manner at the time had suggested.

'And you might say paltry, but that's her mortgage paid off with change to spare, plus whatever his life insurance is worth – and she's got her own tidy little business.'

'But, Guv – say she had done it – what about the knife? She'd have to get rid of it in the couple of minutes before raising the alarm – in her nightie. Surely it would be nearby – and we'd have found it in the search?'

Skelgill grins.

'There's always the accomplice on the terrace, waiting to spirit it away. Maybe that's where your Smith character comes in. Disgruntled employee does the wife's dirty work.'

But DS Jones can tell he is now joking – in fact ribbing her for her reluctance to drop the Grendon Smith theory. She opts to backtrack, and find somewhat firmer ground.

'What about Dermott Goldsmith – I mean as far as the sale is concerned? The one thing that doesn't quite stack up is if he were being relegated to a backroom role – I can't see him buying into that – his ego just wouldn't tolerate it.'

'Happen that's what their barney was about – when they were overheard in the bar. I can see him being mithered by that – maybe Tregilgis was holding out on their new job descriptions – knowing it was the price of the deal.'

DS Jones nods.

'He hasn't told us any of this, Guv.'

'Aye. The questions mount for his lordship.'

22. WATERLOO BRIDGE

Tuesday, 9 p.m.

As Big Ben strikes nine times *post meridiem*, Skelgill can be found dining on Waterloo Bridge. He leans over the parapet and stares into the murky Thames as it streams below on the ebb tide. Experimentally, he drops a chip, and watches fascinated as it seems to tumble in slow motion, then suddenly to disappear beneath the oily surface, fodder for whatever foul and disfigured creatures inhabit these polluted reaches.

He studies a loose raft of flotsam drifting seawards: plastic bottles, rotting sticks, a tennis ball, clumps of weed, even a training shoe – an evolving aquatic pastiche, a diverse collection of parts that has coalesced for no apparent reason (although the tennis ball and training shoe are conceivably related). These individual clues to the raft's origins jostle for prominence in the eyes of the onlooker, while others perhaps are carried unseen by the undertow.

Skelgill rouses himself from his musings and stands upright. A heavily overcast sky heralds a premature nightfall, and the city is lighting up around him. Yielding to DS Jones's exhortations, he has taken up her suggestion to see "the best view in London" – in reciprocation of their visit to Edinburgh's Calton Hill; except he is alone. So he has ventured south along Drury Lane and Aldwych – via a couple of hostelries – and is surprised to find the river flowing so close by. Now, in the centre of Waterloo Bridge, he can only agree with his colleague's assessment. Views might be hard to come by in a city whose highest point is a building, but astride this great curve of the Thames many of the nation's most famous landmarks, ancient and modern, are visible in a single spectacular sweep of the eye.

The sandwiches, the remainder of which he ate as soon as they got back to their rooms, he now suspects were a kind of peace offering. For DS Jones has somewhat apologetically taken to public transport to rendezvous with her long-distance though long-standing boyfriend in Clapham.

Skelgill finishes his fish supper and crushes the greasy wrappings. Resisting any temptation to toss the ball into the river, he locates a waste bin. Then he returns northwards and swings left onto the Strand. He slows as he crosses Savoy Court. Beneath a gilded knight with spear and shield, a snake of taxis deposits bejewelled passengers outside the mouth of the eponymous hotel, where they are fed into a revolving door by a top-hatted commissionaire.

A man that looks like Prince Harry comes towards him from the direction of the hotel. Not wishing to stare, Skelgill moves away. A few paces further on a postcard lying on the pavement catches his eye and he picks it up. It features a surprisingly well-educated oriental lady offering her services. He realises it has fluttered from a nearby phone booth, which has much of its interior decorated with a catalogue of competing invitations. He peers through a vacant pane. The photographs leave little to the imagination.

'Scuse me, John – aw-right if I get in there?'

Skelgill spins round – it is Prince Harry – or, at least, his Cockney doppelganger.

'Aye – sorry.'

Skelgill rather staggers away, his expression sheepish. There is a gap in the traffic, so he allows his momentum to take him across the Strand. As he glances to his left he spies a distant Lord Nelson, proud above the rooftops, silhouetted against a sliver of orange horizon. When he reaches the opposite kerb he realises he is still holding the postcard, and as he strolls introspectively up Southampton Street he pulls out his mobile phone.

A few minutes later he presses the buzzer of an entry phone marked simply 'Flat 3'. He stands back so the spy-camera can see him clearly beneath the neon of a streetlight. A subtle click is his cue to enter. He pushes into a small, clean hallway that smells of new carpets. Then he hauls on a chrome bannister as he climbs swiftly to the penthouse landing. Panting now, he reaches out to tap on the heavy reinforced door. Like magic it swings slowly open. In front of him, pink-cheeked and a little breathless herself, stands Miriam Tregilgis.

'Good evening, Inspector.'

'Have you been drinking, Sergeant?'

'I can't be the only one?'

'Aye – but I've had more practise disguising it.'

'Did you make it to Waterloo Bridge?'

'I saw Miriam Tregilgis.'

'What – on the bridge?'

'Nay – I went to her flat.' Skelgill looks over his shoulder. 'Come on – the bar's still open – I'll tell you about it.'

They have arrived simultaneously to collect their room keys from the hotel's reception desk. Now they wend their way into the lounge bar, a large, over-bright room that is badly in need of refurbishment. Skelgill procures drinks and joins his colleague on a reasonably comfortable though beer-stained sofa.

'Cheers.'

'Aye, cheers.'

'So, what's the news of Miriam Tregilgis?'

Skelgill looks a little perplexed, as though in fact there is no news as such, and now he must manufacture something of merit. But he begins with a question.

'When you went round earlier – was her sister there?'

112

'I understood that she had to go back to Wales. There was an issue with one of her children.'

Skelgill nods pensively. In Miriam Tregilgis's apartment there had been a pleasant aromatic scent in the air. She had led him along a hallway, passing doors on either side. From behind one of these had come the sounds of a shower splashing, and a female voice accompanying a radio tuned to a music channel.

'When I arrived, there was someone there – a girl, a woman, I mean. I assumed it was her sister and that she'd introduce me later.'

'And did she?'

Skelgill shakes his head.

'The other one disappeared into thin air. She may have left completely – Miriam Tregilgis had a bottle of wine open in the lounge – we were in there.'

'Maybe she went to bed? Perhaps now that her sister's away she's got a friend staying to keep her company.' Then DS Jones regards Skelgill a little conspiratorially. 'It was a definitely a woman?'

She sows a seed of doubt in Skelgill's mind. He returns his colleague's gaze and it is likely that they share a similar thought pattern: the possibilities, and the implications.

But it is also likely that they have each drunk too much, and are too tired – still not fully recovered from the events of Sunday morning – to get drawn into a web of conjecture, such that is anathema to Skelgill at the best of times.

He downs his drink.

'Fresh start tomorrow, eh, lass?'

'Sure.' DS Jones reciprocates, and begins to rise.

They share the small cramped lift. DS Jones is on the fifth floor, Skelgill the eighth. Its progress is shaky and ponderous. Skelgill is not good at small talk.

'How was Clapham?'

'Fine.'

For a single word, her tone is revealing; it does not ring of fine.

But Skelgill lacks the guile that some might apply in these circumstances. However, DS Jones seems to appreciate his taciturnity. As the doors slide open for the fifth floor she suddenly clasps his sleeve and pecks him on the cheek.

'Night, Guv.'

'Night. Em –'

But she is gone.

23. GRENDON SMITH

Wednesday, 8 a.m.

Skelgill remarks that Pentonville Road is exactly what he had expected of a 'pale-blue' on the Monopoly board. No fan of the urban environment, he has confessed to DS Jones a certain admiration for the flowing harmony of the architecture in London's tightly knit West End. But now, as the two detectives stride uphill from King's Cross, all before them is disunity and strife. Buildings, entirely incongruous, in varying degrees of disrepair, jostle for space. Some are set forward, others set back. Some have cars crammed into improbably small courtyards; others are temporary construction sites. There are office buildings; headquarters of obscure institutes; and blocks of flats with grimy net-curtains and tiny balconies choked by washing and satellite dishes and neglected houseplants. There are few shops to speak of – just a cluster of narrow cafés, bookmakers and heavily shuttered sex emporia nearer to King's Cross. Not even the dazzling morning sunshine and brilliant azure sky can make it seem agreeable.

They are shortly to meet Grendon Smith – although he does not know it. And they are forearmed with information that DS Jones's team has unearthed concerning his past – chequered, as it turns out. There are several juvenile cautions and convictions: for taking pot shots at neighbours' pets with an air rifle, three counts of shoplifting, and possession of stolen goods (top-shelf magazines and videos); and one adult offence of fraud – the use of a deceased person's travel card.

Grendon Smith's address proves to be a ground-floor flat located in a small block down a side road about halfway to The Angel, Islington (another 'pale-blue', Skelgill notes).

Despite his relative youth, at twenty-three he seems aged and arthritic as he pokes his sharp, bony face around his door, blinking, and scowling like an angry fox roused from its lair.

'Yeah?'

Skelgill is standing to the fore.

'Cumbria CID – we'd like to talk to you.'

'Not again.'

'Just a few questions, Mr Smith. Then we should be able to leave you in peace.'

Grudgingly, the man turns and, leaving them to fasten the door, leads the officers into a sparsely furnished lounge that has a kitchenette on one side.

'I was just in the toilet – I'll be back in a minute.'

Without offering a seat, or waiting for a reply, he leaves the room.

'Mind if we make ourselves a cuppa?'

There is no reply to Skelgill's entreaty, just the click of a closing door. He looks hopefully at DS Jones, who sets about locating the necessary ingredients. Skelgill, turns to nose about the room.

Perhaps surprisingly, the tide of seediness that has stranded the district does not flow into the apartment, and the furnishings and carpets are new and clean, and the decor simple and actually quite stylish. Of greater salience, perhaps, in a single man's flat, is a corresponding lack of electrical goods – with only a small portable television opposite the sofa, set upon a unit capable of accommodating a much larger device. Skelgill is stooping to examine a loose comms cable when Grendon Smith re-enters the room.

He glances over his shoulder. 'Not had a burglary, have we sir?'

'Pressing debts, I'm afraid, Inspector. I was obliged to sell a few possessions.'

Skelgill stands up abruptly. While Grendon Smith has provided a plausible answer, it is his altered demeanour that elicits Skelgill's reaction. He wears a newly pressed collared shirt, neatly knotted tie, suit trousers and polished black shoes. His hair is trendily gelled, and he has shaved – there is even the waft of expensive cologne.

'You have drinks, officers? Sorry I left you to it – you caught me rather indisposed – is there anything else I can give you? And – please – do have a seat.'

This is evidently the Grendon Smith that, in Krista Morocco's words, "interviewed well."

'We're alright, thanks.' Skelgill gestures with an open palm to DS Jones. 'My colleague would like to ask you a few questions.'

'Whatever I can do to help, Inspector.'

DS Jones picks up her notebook.

'Mr Smith, presumably you know why we want to talk to you?'

'You're investigating Ivan Tregilgis's death.'

'That and other related matters.'

Perhaps now the man's eyes betray a hint of anxiety. However, he nods graciously.

'We'd like to confirm your whereabouts last Saturday night – between ten p.m. and eight a.m. the following morning.'

'Am I a suspect or something?' His tone is co-operative. 'I told all this to the policewoman who came on Monday.'

'We just need a few more details, Mr Smith. It's a routine elimination process.'

He nods.

'Well, as I said before, I was in Norfolk from about nine-thirty on Saturday night – and I got back here about midday on Sunday.'

'What were you doing in Norfolk?'

'I'm a birder, you know – birdwatcher? There was a collared pratincole at Holme bird observatory - it was a life tick for me.'

'How did you find out about this –'

'Pratincole.' Smith grins affably. 'I rang Birdline on Saturday afternoon – it tells you about any rarities that have been reported.'

'And you say you slept in your car?'

'I often do. It's the best way to be on the spot first thing in the morning. You never know how long a bird will stay. I bought fish and chips in Hunstanton on the way, and then parked down on the reserve at Holme. I'd got the tick before six a.m.'

'Can anyone vouch for your presence there?'

'Well – there were plenty of other birders – must have been close on a hundred by the time I left.'

'Any names you could give us?'

Grendon Smith pulls an apologetic face.

'Not off the top of my head – I mean, there were quite a few I recognised by sight – regular twitchers – maybe some of them will have made entries in the log book at the observatory?'

'Did you buy anything for which you have a receipt – fuel, for example?'

Grendon Smith shakes his head.

'I filled up before I left London, but I just paid cash.' He glances knowingly at Skelgill. 'Plastic's over the limit.'

'So, you can't actually prove you were in Norfolk?'

Grendon Smith gestures helplessly with open palms. To Skelgill's eye it is an almost-convincing act. The man must know it is not for him to prove his whereabouts, and there is little they can do.

'I can show you my life list? Collared pratincole is proudly added.'

Skelgill interjects. It is time for a change of tack.

'Mr Smith, you've mentioned a couple of times that you have some financial difficulties.'

Grendon Smith intertwines his bony fingers, and inhales in a worldly manner. His eyes are cast down, and he does not speak.

'Happen getting the sack doesn't help?'

The man starts.

'Oh, I wasn't sacked, Inspector – I left by mutual agreement.'

Skelgill remains patient.

'I got the distinct impression from Ms Morocco that you were dismissed.'

118

'Certainly not – it just wasn't working out for either party – nobody's fault – we each gave it a good shot – but these things happen, you know?'

Skelgill looks unconvinced.

'Mr Smith, by all accounts you had to be escorted from the premises by Mr Tregilgis on your last day.'

'They must have been mistaken, Inspector.' Grendon Smith's tone is soothing, if sickly to Skelgill's ear. 'Sure, I left with Ivan – but he wished me well – he offered to give me a reference when I need one for a new job.'

'And did he say anything else?'

Grendon Smith adjusts the knot of his tie, and shakes his head unhappily.

'Well – between these four walls – he was rather disparaging about Krista. He said she was prone to be emotional when she didn't get her own way, and that I was unlucky to have got the blame when actually the buck should have stopped with her.'

Skelgill folds his arms.

That Ivan Tregilgis might have had the good heart to offer Smith a reference is just feasible. But to have bad-mouthed a woman for whom he obviously had great affection – this is one lie too far. The slight stings Skelgill as sharply as it might have Ivan Tregilgis himself.

Skelgill does not reply, and now his colleague glances at him to see the colour has drained from his face, and there is a look of menace in eyes that have acquired a cold grey hue. Skelgill's reputation, though something of a mystery to her, revolves around the unconventional. She suspects that Grendon Smith can have no idea of the tightrope that at this moment he treads. But, for the sake of the investigation, she intervenes – she takes over with a stern warning of her own.

'Look here, Mr Smith – certain allegations have been made against you – and in view of your criminal record we may be obliged to investigate them – it would help if you were straight with us.'

Grendon Smith turns to her with a look of supplication.

'Sergeant – I always believe in honesty as the best policy.'

'Sir, it doesn't strike me as very honest to use your deceased father's travel card.'

'Ah – that was a very difficult situation for me.' He shakes his head despondently. 'You see – I needed to travel for job interviews – it was what he would have wanted. He had spent his last coppers striving to put me on my way.'

DS Jones, however, is unrelenting.

'You also have several juvenile convictions.'

Grendon Smith inhales heroically.

'I was a victim of chronic bullying as a teenager. The gangs in this area – I was forced to take the rap for quite a few things I didn't do – the alternative was to be ostracised – or far worse.'

Skelgill suddenly rises to his feet. For a split second DS Jones cringes.

But the expected does not happen. Skelgill's tone is perfectly controlled.

'We've more or less finished for the time being, Mr Smith. Sergeant Jones will take some details about your car. I shall just use your toilet and meet her downstairs. Let's hope your road tax is up to date.'

*

A few minutes later the detectives meet outside a corner store a short distance from the entrance to the flats. Its roof is guarded by a rusty array of horrible-looking curved spikes, which Skelgill seems to be admiring as he munches pensively. He offers a brown paper bag to his colleague as she approaches.

'Samosa?'

'Er – no thanks, Guv.'

'They're alright, these – the shopkeeper makes them herself – four for a quid.'

DS Jones gives her boss a wide-eyed look – as if to say he seems remarkably laid back considering what has just passed inside Grendon Smith's property. However, she misreads him slightly, for he succumbs to a succinct yet creative analysis couched in mainly unprintable Anglo-Saxon terms. More moderately, he continues.

'Lying little toad. I wanted to wring his scrawny neck.' He pauses reflectively. 'Let's hope our local crew nail him for those backhanders.'

'Don't you think he's a drug addict?'

Skelgill flashes his partner a sideways glance – there is a congratulatory gleam in his eyes, which have recovered much of their customary green tones.

'What makes you say that, lass?'

'The thefts – and probably others we don't know about. That he's sold off all of his electrical items. The mood swings that Krista Morocco talked about.'

'The mood swing this just now?'

'Yes – exactly.'

Skelgill is nodding. On top of his colleague's deductions, he also has the benefit of having surreptitiously pried around the remainder of Grendon Smith's flat, and seen the traces of white powder on his bedside table.

'Aye, I reckon you're about right.'

'But – Guv – what about Ivan Tregilgis?'

Skelgill shakes his head grimly.

'I'm not convinced.'

He does not elaborate, and DS Jones is momentarily crestfallen. She compresses her lips, and falls in silently as Skelgill turns towards Pentonville Road. But, as they begin to pick up pace, a look of determination slowly returns to her hazel eyes.

24. RON BUNCE

Wednesday, 10.30 a.m.

At King's Cross, the detectives take possession of a small rental car. The idea is to drive across London to interview Ron Bunce, Managing Director of BDL – the firm that Tregilgis & Goldsmith is about to sue – and then continue westwards to Heathrow airport, where the vehicle can be returned.

Their first stop, however, is at their hotel in Covent Garden, in order to collect their luggage. They set off rather tentatively, and at first Skelgill makes the same basic errors as any visiting motorist. But he soon gets the hang of red lights being only advisory, and showing courtesy to other drivers merely optional. In short order he is hooting and swearing with the best of them, much to DS Jones's dismay. Distracted by the contest, for the first time since their arrival in London he is really enjoying himself.

However, nearing their hotel, they become trapped in a one-way loop as they try in vain to get from the Kingsway to Drury Lane. Skelgill pulls over to give DS Jones more time to engage her mobile phone app. There comes a tap on the driver window. Skelgill glances up to see a fresh-faced constable standing beside the car.

'The cavalry arrives.'

But his friendly smile is not reciprocated.

'Is this your car, sir?'

Skelgill seems unable to answer.

The constable clears his throat.

'I'm sure you're aware, sir, that it's against the law to drive without wearing a seatbelt.' Then he indicates back the way they have come. 'I'd also estimate that you were travelling at well over forty miles per hour in a thirty zone, while you overtook as you came around that bend. You pulled across without indicating and the vehicle behind you had to take evasive action to avoid a collision.' He steps back and looks beneath the car. 'And now you are parked in a bus lane.'

Skelgill having clocked up in thirty seconds sufficient offences for a three-month ban, DS Jones watches in trepidation for her superior's reaction. Surely his only recourse will be to pull rank on the young PC by flashing his warrant card. But Skelgill has another surprise up his sleeve. He grimaces painfully, his face raised into the sunlight behind the officer.

'Aye – I'm reet sorry, marra – that wo' a ladgeful bit o' driving.'

Quite clearly the constable does not understand – other than perhaps to get the gist that this is some foreigner, who may be apologising. Skelgill, whose first urge had been simply to put his foot down and drive away (for once empathising with motorists he has pulled over in the past), now presses home his advantage. He moderates his Cumbrian brogue.

'It's like this, officer – we're visiting from up North – and to be honest – the speed everyone drives down here – every time I look in my mirror all I can see are the whites of the eyes of the bloke behind. And now we're lost and we'll be late picking up our daughter in Drury Lane. I'd appreciate if you could direct us.'

For a man unlikely ever to represent England at diplomacy, Skelgill does appear to have struck the right note. And perhaps the policeman is busy – and the traffic roars around them – and there is the time-consuming prospect of booking someone for such a confusing catalogue of minor offences. And perhaps he sympathises with the couple's plight – for he points out the exit from the one-way system and hurriedly waves them on their way, as though he has decided to pretend the incident did not occur. (Although as Skelgill lurches away with a screech of rubber, the poor lad can be seen stepping out into the road shouting "Seatbelt!")

'What?'

Skelgill glances at DS Jones, who has her arms folded and is shaking her head.

'Guv – our daughter?'

Skelgill grins mischievously.

'Daughter? I thought I said suitcases.'

'You said daughter!'

'Aye – well – she'd have just been a bairn, eh?'

DS Jones reluctantly succumbs to what might be an attempt at flattery, and sinks back into her seat. In due course, though not entirely uneventfully, they reach Hammersmith. They park in a dismal concrete multi-storey and eat an unsatisfactory lunch in a stuffy, overcrowded sandwich bar that is part of the tube station complex. Thence, on foot, it must seem a comparative relief to get back into the London air. The sun beats down from a still-clear sky as they thread their way through preoccupied pedestrians and hostile traffic. By sudden contrast, however, following the route recommended by DS Jones's mobile, they find themselves turning into the tranquil suburban oasis of Brook Green. Skelgill is drawn to walk down the long central strip of grass and trees that divides the two parallel strands of the street, like a sliver of pre-war greenbelt that has survived thanks to a planning error.

Now he muses reflectively.

'It's not so bad – London. They're no smarter than us, are they?'

DS Jones eyes her superior a little doubtfully. Uncertain of his train of thought, she is wary of saying the wrong thing. After a few moments Skelgill elaborates.

'You could do really well down here, Jones.'

'The streets paved with gold.'

Her tone is ironic.

'You should think about it.

Now she looks at him more pointedly.

'What – apply for a transfer?'

'Aye, well – look for a promotion, at least.' He grins ruefully. 'Then, one day – Inspector Jones of The Yard.'

'Are you trying to get rid of me, already?'

124

Skelgill looks suddenly alarmed – as if the conversation has slipped out of his control. Then he realises she is grinning at him.

'Nay, lass – what I meant – well – you know?'

Now DS Jones nods, her expression more earnest.

'I realise it would probably advance my career – but I don't think I could leave the North for good. I loved London while I was at college, and being here now reminds me of the things I miss – the shops, the weather, the nightlife –'

'The fella?'

DS Jones seems to pull a face at this suggestion, but she turns away to gaze at the properties lined up along her side of the road. She might be reflecting on domesticity in such a suburb.

'Most of my school friends are still in Cumbria. And Dad's not so good lately – I like to be around for Mum.' There is a sombre note in her voice, and she seems to realise this and to make a deliberate effort to brighten. 'Anyway – right now, where would I be without you to teach me how to do everything by the book?'

Skelgill seems buoyed by this backhanded compliment.

'Well, keep it in mind. Don't make my mistake and leave it too late.'

She glances at him sharply.

'You're still plenty young enough, yet, Guv.'

Skelgill feels his cheeks colouring and like she did a moment earlier now he peruses the properties on his side of the green. They continue in silence, and within a minute or so they reach the premises of Bunce Display Limited. The company is housed in a dilapidated former cinema encased in billboards of all sizes.

To their surprise, the run-down exterior belies a relatively tasteful lobby, equipped with comfortable modern furniture and a reception desk manned by a pneumatic blonde.

'Mr Bunce is ready to see you now. Through the double-doors, first on the right after the statue.'

The "statue" proves to be a hand-painted polystyrene bust of Lord Nelson, with his one good eye melted out where somebody has stubbed a cigarette. Signs of subversion continue at the door of Ron Bunce's office where, beneath a small plaque of HMS Victory, the words 'Captain Ron' have been scrawled in biro and only half-heartedly scrubbed away. However, any expectation the two detectives harbour of encountering a Nelson-like figure within is quickly dispelled. In fact known euphemistically by his associates as 'Big Ron' – the bigness a function of girth rather than height – Ron Bunce is cast more in the Churchillian mould. From behind an ornate mahogany desk decked with model barques and imitation seafaring instruments, he rises slowly to greet them. Overweight without being flabby, his turgid suntanned skin seems oiled by an evenly distributed layer of fat beneath, ready to ooze from his prominent pores at the slightest squeeze. Skelgill makes the introductions.

'Mr Bunce, I assume you know why we're here?'

'No idea, Inspector. Please enlighten me.'

His accent is more sophisticated than Skelgill would have anticipated; he was expecting something more akin to the Cockney twang of his regular partner, DS Leyton.

Ron Bunce leans forward and places his hands on the desk; there is gold aplenty in the form of a chain, cufflinks, sovereign rings and a wristwatch. His manner, neither guarded nor friendly, betrays no sign of discomfort.

'What does the name Tregilgis & Goldsmith mean to you, sir?'

'They're an advertising agency.'

'I understand they're about to sue your company.'

Without taking his eyes off Skelgill, Bunce gives an indifferent shrug.

'I doubt it.'

Among her notes, DS Jones has a copy of the solicitor's letter to which Krista Morocco referred. Skelgill gestures to the page.

'It doesn't look that way to me, sir.'

Ron Bunce is impassive.

'With the greatest of respect, Inspector, all a solicitor's letter ever tells me is that the sender has no intention to sue. Otherwise, why not just slap a writ on me?'

Skelgill is aware of skating on thin ice. Ron Bunce probably knows as much about corporate litigation as he does about pike fishing.

'What about the adverse publicity?'

Ron Bunce's upper lip twists into the semblance of a snarl.

'If they bad-mouth me I'll sue them for slander. If they issue a writ and the press get hold of it I'll counterclaim for defamation.'

Skelgill persists, albeit he senses his words lack conviction.

'Mr Bunce, there seems to be a large sum at stake here – I can't see Dermott Goldsmith letting go of that.'

'I deal with Ivan Tregilgis. I'm sure he'll be far more reasonable.'

'I don't think so, Mr Bunce. Ivan Tregilgis is dead.'

Ron Bunce's porcine eyes narrow to mere slits. But it is without emotion that he speaks.

'I'm sorry to hear that. What happened?'

'He was murdered, Mr Bunce. I'm surprised you haven't heard.'

'I've been away for a week.' Ron Bunce seems unperturbed by the news. He reaches forward and turns a framed photograph. It shows him standing on a Mediterranean quayside, a blonde on his arm and the prow of a boat above his shoulder. Just legible is the name, *Victory*. 'I've got a yacht at Puerto Banus. Flew back last night from Gib.'

'Can anyone confirm that?'

For the first time Ron Bunce permits himself a smile. He gestures towards the photograph.

'Ask Sam – you just met her at reception.'

There are battles to contest and those to avoid – or, at least, to postpone – and Skelgill has determined this is one of the latter. To fight another day, more ammunition is needed, probably a thorough consultation with the Met Police. He signals to DS Jones and begins to rise.

'Thank you for your time, sir – that was all we needed to know.'

Ron Bunce shadows them from his office to the double-doors, and through one of the porthole windows watches them sign out at the desk. He notes that the Detective Inspector's exchange with the receptionist appears to be of a flirtatious rather than interrogative nature.

When he strolls back towards his office, he pauses to stand to attention and salute the bust of Lord Nelson. Then he notices the loss of his hero's good eye, and his expression becomes one of intense anger. He storms back to the double-doors and wrenches them open.

'Sam. Here. Now.'

*

'I shouldn't like to work for him, Guv. I doubt we'd have to try hard to find a disgruntled employee in there.'

Skelgill nods broodingly.

'Aye, but we'd have to try a sight harder getting them to talk. He's a hard case.'

'I think we should check with the Met to see whether they've got anything on him, Guv?'

She makes the point speculatively, her intonation questioning.

Skelgill grins.

'And what makes you say that?'

Now she takes a couple of quick paces to get ahead of him, and turns, walking backwards.

'Ron Bunce has a boat moored in the Med. He could be moving drugs from North Africa. He could be connected with Grendon Smith. Smith might be some sort of local courier. That would explain the kickbacks – a means of disguising payments to him. What if Ivan Tregilgis stumbled across something that made the connection?'

Skelgill is shaking his head – but his smile is broadening. She has rapidly joined the dots – far too swiftly for his comfort – but, despite his inner misgivings, and his customary recalcitrance, he senses he should not quash her enthusiasm.

Accordingly, and lacking a suitable counter argument, Skelgill suddenly darts past her, and sets off at a jog.

'Race you to the car.'

25. HILLEND

Wednesday, 7.30 p.m.

'Jones, time's getting on – I reckon we'll get a taxi to Letsby Avenue. I don't trust anyone to drive my motor out here – it's temperamental.'

DS Jones grins, he might be describing its owner – but then something in the crowd beyond the arrivals door catches her eye.

'Guv – look – no need – here's DS Findlay.'

Skelgill strides ahead.

'Cameron – am I glad to see you – how did you know when we'd be back?'

'Och – I'm not as green as I'm cabbage looking.' He winks conspiratorially. 'You'll have had yer tea?'

'Aye – on the plane – in-flight rations.'

'Aye – well not tae worry – I'm under orders to take you home fae a proper meal.' He reaches for DS Jones's overnight bag. 'When he worked up here, we called him Two Dinners.'

DS Jones has seen enough in the past couple of days not to be surprised. Her superior must have some extreme metabolism, for he is lean to the point that he invites feeding, which must suit him very well.

'Where's your hotel, Emma?'

'It's in an area called – Corstorphine?'

DS Findlay grins. He leads them out of the terminal building. 'Try Kus-*tor*-fen.'

'Ah – thanks for putting me right.'

'Nae bother – it's over there.' He indicates to the east, towards the city. 'See that big wooded lump? That's Corstorphine Hill.'

They round a corner of the multi-storey to be greeted by the sight of a large marked motorway patrol car sitting in a restricted zone. Skelgill's eyes light up.

'Nice one, Cam.'

'It was all they had spare. I need tae get it back in a hurry.'

'Then I'm your man.'

DS Findlay shakes his head resignedly – but nonetheless he tosses the keys to Skelgill. The homecoming evening flights have clogged the airport with traffic, so their initial progress is slow. DS Findlay begins to recount his findings to date.

'Seems these Goldsmiths like to keep a high profile – be seen about town with the right people. They appear in every edition of the local society magazine.'

Skelgill's eyes flick between the road ahead and his various mirrors.

'Who's driving that? Goldsmith, or the wife?'

'Apparently Goldsmith's got some financial interest in it. My pal at The Scotsman spoke tae the editor, but he was a bit cagey. Knows which side his bread's buttered.'

Skelgill nods grimly. DS Findlay continues.

'Goldsmith being from down south – it's harder to get information on him. But I discovered more about her – another pal of mine's a retired Sheriff and there's a legal connection.'

'Go on.'

'Aye – your Elspeth Goldsmith, she was adopted. The MacClartys were both lawyers, well heeled – old Edinburgh firm. They were childless into their forties – then after they'd taken in Elspeth an unexpected younger sister came along. But the wee lassie drowned in the Water of Leith. She was aged five and Elspeth about nine or ten. They used to play unsupervised by the river – it runs right through the city, but ye cannae see it most of the time – it's down in a wooded gorge, their property backs onto it. It looks like a daft wee burn in places – but when there's been a couple of days rain on the hills –' He tails off to indicate the Pentlands, the range that shields Edinburgh's southern reaches and supplies its water. 'It can turn into a raging torrent before your eyes.'

'What about the parents?'

'The old man was killed about ten years ago in a car accident – up north on a fishing trip – had been on the bottle. The wife died in a nursing home a couple of years later – by all accounts she'd never been right since the wee one drowned.'

There is a period of silence as they each mull over these facts. They are held by lights at the main intersection of the city bypass. Then Skelgill suddenly exclaims.

'Hey up – what's this?'

A sporty hatchback jumps the lights from the city direction and swerves between vehicles taking their turn of the roundabout. A few of seconds later a small police squad car, its blue light flashing, follows in hapless pursuit.

'It's the Keystone cops!' Skelgill's eyes narrow. 'They'll never catch it in that rattletrap.'

DS Findlay leans forward and switches on the warning systems. They join the chase. As motorists swerve for cover, the hot hatch rapidly pulls away from the first police car. Skelgill almost literally barges his way past, leaving DS Findlay to make apologetic hand signals to his astonished local colleagues.

He establishes by radio that the fugitives have robbed at knifepoint the service station at Drumbrae. Now, at the wheel of a vastly superior machine, Skelgill is soon on their tail – but getting past them is another matter. The bypass is thick with traffic, and all he can do is to tailgate the hatchback. There are two occupants, and the passenger, a leering gap-toothed youth, leans out and gives them a one-fingered salute.

'They're taking the A702 exit – heading south.'

DS Findlay provides commentary over the airwaves. The two cars slew across the carriageway to gain the off-slip, and ignore approaching vehicles at the exit roundabout.

'They've turned up for the ski slope. It's a dead end.'

Skelgill is forced to wait for a line of oncoming traffic – until an alert bus driver grinds to a halt. The access lane is steep and winding, and at intervals there are unforgiving speedbumps. DS Jones leans forward from the rear seat.

'What is this place?'

DS Findlay replies with a characteristically dry turn of phrase.

'Longest artificial ski run in Britain.'

Indeed, the slopes are coming into view, and skiers like lines of ants zigzag down the hillside – an incongruous sight on a pleasant early summer's evening. DS Findlay perhaps reads his colleagues' thoughts.

'Ye dinnae want tae ski in Scotland in winter – plenty of snow, but ye cannae see fae the blizzards.'

It is a curious irony – but their minds are jolted back to the imminent emergency as they swing into the car park. It is the end of the road.

Immediately they spy the robbers' car – and remarkably they see that one of the offenders is being held over the bonnet by a couple of men in ski outfits. DS Findlay identifies them as off-duty police officers.

'These are our boys – they must have picked up the all-cars call.'

The three new arrivals trot across towards the scene of the action. The men recognise DS Findlay and one calls out.

'Cameron – the big yin's away.'

He gestures towards the chair lifts, where a tracksuit-clad figure, some two hundred yards off, is running at speed up the artificial slope. Skelgill mutters under his breath.

'Big yin – big mistake.'

And he sets off at a steady trot.

'Danny – yer wasting yer time!'

But DS Findlay's entreaty is in vain. Skelgill raises a hand in acknowledgement, but carries on regardless. And did the youth only know it; he *has* made a big mistake. The policeman pursuing him might be twenty years his senior, but in his day was a record-breaking fell runner. So, when the cocky lout has the temerity to pause and shout an obscene taunt, believing it is just a matter of time before the chase is given up, Skelgill has the luxury of feeling a small pang of sympathy for him. But it is short lived. And slowly but surely Skelgill with his long, loping stride makes ground. When the gap is down to about twenty yards, he can hear his quarry panting, the breaths starting to come in desperate gasps. And when the villain realises he is going to be overhauled, and spins around, brandishing a carpet knife and screaming unintelligible threats – his final exclamation reflects the moment Skelgill's size tens thud into his chest and take him down.

In the stramash that follows Skelgill quickly gains the upper hand. He wrestles to free his belt one-handed, intent upon using this to secure his captive.

'Danny – I can see the pub frae here!'

Skelgill glances up. Almost directly overhead, borne in a double chair of the ski lift, DS Findlay and DS Jones swing past. The chair behind brings the two constables from the squad car. They are deposited just a short distance further up the slope, and DS Jones clatters pell-mell with panic in her eyes.

'Guv, Guv – are you okay?' She falls on her knees beside Skelgill and frantically pats his back and chest. 'They said he'd got a knife!'

Skelgill, grimacing as he subdues the protesting yob, indicates with a toss of his head. The carpet knife lies safely out of range.

'That's not a knife.'

He grins at her and gives way to the two uniformed officers. They relieve him of his charge. He rises, DS Jones still looking alarmed and a little disbelieving. DS Findlay picks his way over the last few yards of the fibrous matting. At the foot of the slopes a swarm of blue lights is gathering, as nearby units respond to the emergency call. The handcuffed felon is led away, leaving the three detectives to their own devices. DS Findlay has a twinkle in his eye.

'Nothing like making an unobtrusive arrival in Edinburgh.'

Skelgill grins rather uneasily.

'Cam – will your good lady's dinner keep for half an hour?'

'Aye – it's haggis 'n' neeps 'n' tatties.'

Skelgill nods with satisfaction.

'I believe you mentioned you could see the pub from here.'

26. DERMOTT GOLDSMITH

Thursday, 9.30 a.m.

'What's he doing?'

Skelgill's voice is hushed. DS Jones squints through a peephole in the interview room door.

'Fiddling with some sort of gadget – like a pocket calculator. He keeps looking this way.'

'Howay, lass – let's go in.' Skelgill flips four paracetamol tablets into his mouth and swills them down with the last of his machine tea. He drops the plastic cup into a bin and rubs his temples with the tips of his fingers. 'No hangover my backside.'

He refers to the events of last night. His post-chase thirst for a swift half proved to be more of a drought, and it was fortunate that the traditional Scottish dish of haggis, potatoes and swede keeps well in a low oven. At DS Jones's behest, as a peace offering for Mrs Findlay they had collected some flowers (and some claret), and the ensuing bonhomie was capped with the breaking out of a precious bottle of twenty-five-year-old Glenmorangie. DS Findlay had set about schooling them in the correct modes of both pronunciation ("I tell ye, it rhymes with *orangey*") and tasting, insisting he had never yet suffered any morning-after complaints from 'the water of life'. But, then, he is a Scotsman.

Accordingly, it is an under-the-weather Skelgill that approaches the interview room. This state of affairs is not improved by the news that a second search of the grounds of Bewaldeth Hall has drawn a blank. Now, as they enter, Dermott Goldsmith, with impeccable timing, pricks his finger and squeezes out a droplet of blood. Slowly, he looks up, as though it is a less pressing matter that interrupts him.

'I shan't shake hands – I am just testing my blood sugars.' He gives a condescending smile. 'One of life's little burdens.'

If he had hoped for sympathy – or even a response – none is forthcoming. The two detectives take their seats opposite him. His eyes still on his task, he tries a different tack.

'How is the murder hunt going – any nearer to catching the madman?'

'No thanks to you, Mr Goldsmith.'

Skelgill's abrupt retort causes Dermott Goldsmith to glance up sharply.

'I'm sorry?'

'I'm minded to charge you for obstructing the investigation.'

Dermott Goldsmith's face falls.

'What on earth do you mean, Inspector?'

Skelgill watches with distaste as Dermott Goldsmith pushes aside his equipment and winds a tissue around his bleeding finger.

'You didn't bring a solicitor?'

'Why should I? I have nothing to hide? I'm here voluntarily – as a witness.'

Skelgill regards him impassively.

'In that case perhaps you can tell me why you tried to conceal the sale of your company?'

'I d-don't know what you mean.'

Skelgill continues to glare.

'Are you saying you *weren't* about to sell the company, Mr Goldsmith?'

The man is plainly tongue-tied – no doubt an unfamiliar experience.

'Well – it's, er – we, er – we receive lots of approaches – this goes on all the time – in the corporate pond big fish eat little fish.'

'Really, sir?'

Dermott Goldsmith seems unwilling to elaborate. He produces what might be an abbreviated shake of the head.

Skelgill folds his arms and tilts back his head imperiously.

'Mr – Ford – Zendik.' He iterates the words individually. 'Now, he tells me he was expecting to seal a sixteen-million-dollar deal with you this week.'

Dermott Goldsmith's prominent features are swathed in dark unease; he looks ugly, angry, cornered. But still he does not speak.

'You do know Mr Zendik?'

'Yes, but –'

'But what, Mr Goldsmith?'

Dermott Goldsmith's voice comes out as something of a squeak.

'Nothing is agreed.'

'So you are selling the company?'

'Certainly they were interested – but so are other firms – like I say.'

'Mr Goldsmith.' Skelgill intones wearily. 'On Monday Mr Tregilgis was due to fly out to New York to conclude the Heads of Terms.'

Dermott Goldsmith stares blankly.

'Then that's news to me, Inspector.'

Skelgill takes hold of the edge of the desk with both hands. He leans forward.

'Come off it, Mr Goldsmith – how could you possibly not know?'

Dermott Goldsmith begins to offer some tremulous resistance.

'Well – I'm afraid you'll have to take my word for it. I have signed nothing as far as Ford Zendik is concerned.'

Skelgill intertwines his fingers and leans back and cracks his knuckles. He folds his arms once more and casts a pained look at DS Jones. She is to take over.

'Mr Goldsmith, on Saturday night at about seven-thirty you were in the hotel bar with Mr Tregilgis?'

Dermott Goldsmith regards her suspiciously, but he seems to nod.

DS Jones refers to her notes.

'You were overheard to say, "Well I need to see it", to which Mr Tregilgis replied, "Sure". What was it that you needed to see?'

And now, instead of feeling like a rabbit in the headlights, Dermott Goldsmith perhaps senses a small light at the end of the dark tunnel in which he finds himself. A sly look enters his eyes.

'It was the presentation to the staff – the company update. We always do it over cocktails before dinner.' He wipes moisture from his fleshy upper lip with the tissue. 'I asked Ivan about the charts.'

DS Jones is not yet knocked off her stride.

'I thought you were the Financial Director, Mr Goldsmith?'

'That's correct.'

'Surely it would be for you to produce performance charts?'

Dermott Goldsmith's confidence is growing.

'Ah – but Ivan liked to take centre stage – I agreed to let him do it this year.'

DS Jones does not react to his response.

'If I may take you forward a few hours, sir. At a quarter to one you indicated that you were leaving to give yourself an insulin injection. Where did you go?'

'I went to our bedroom. All my equipment was in there.'

He gestures to the monitoring device and toiletries case on the table.

'Is that not an unusual time to take insulin – perhaps risky, even?'

Dermott Goldsmith swallows a gulp of water from the cup provided.

'Well – I, er – just went to do a test – I felt my blood sugars were getting low and that I might need to eat something.'

'I thought you just agreed you went to give yourself an injection?'

'I, er – I didn't realise you were drawing the precise distinction.'

'Which way did you go to your room?'

'Straight along the corridor from the lobby.'

'And you were in Room 9, beside Mr and Mrs Tregilgis?'

Dermott Goldsmith nods.

'Did you go into their room?'

'Just later on – after it had happened.'

Skelgill interjects.

'Mr Goldsmith, I don't think you went to your room to inject yourself – I think you went snooping in Room 10 – for a peek at the contract that Ford Zendik had sent to Mr Tregilgis.'

Dermott Goldsmith shakes his head in desperation.

'No!'

'It wouldn't look very good for you if we found your fingerprints on Mr Tregilgis's briefcase.'

Dermott Goldsmith's features twist despairingly.

'But, I – I might have accidentally touched his case when we were all in the room – I can't remember – I was the one who ushered everyone out and locked the door until your constables arrived.'

'Where was the room key?'

'It was lying on top of the dresser.'

'But you didn't lock the terrace door?'

Dermott Goldsmith regards Skelgill with bewilderment.

'It didn't occur to me that it might be open – but, anyway – Ivan's briefcase was probably locked.'

'Why should that be?'

'I just know he usually locked it – I've been at plenty of meetings with him over the years.'

'So you know the combination?'

'No.'

Skelgill takes a moment. He considers Dermott Goldsmith rather disparagingly.

'Why didn't you mention in your statement that you went to your room?'

'I'm not sure – I, er – I think the officer who took it just wanted to know where I was after two a.m.'

'Why didn't you explain about the cross-option agreement when I spoke with you on Sunday?'

'Well – I, er – it's a very complicated document – I didn't know if it was relevant.' Again he rubs a hand over his upper lip. 'The, er – the insurance policy – it may not have been valid in the event of murder – in which case it would have been irrelevant.'

'And is it valid?'

'I'm still waiting for confirmation – from our accountants – they arrange that sort of thing.'

Skelgill shrugs resignedly.

'But why didn't you just say, yes – there's this instrument called a cross-option agreement and you needed to check its validity? We're bound to think you were trying to hide that information from us, Mr Goldsmith.'

Dermott Goldsmith's features collapse into a wounded grimace.

'Look here –' His voice is strained, almost whining. 'I haven't done anything – I never had anything to do with Ivan's death.'

Skelgill stares implacably.

'I don't recall mentioning that you did, sir.'

Dermott Goldsmith appears speechless.

Skelgill leans back in his chair.

'Mr Goldsmith, on Sunday you described yourself as the brains behind the business. Financial Director, Company Secretary – various other titles. While Mr Tregilgis was just the sales guy. You remember?'

Dermott Goldsmith gives a single reluctant nod.

'So, you can probably appreciate that I find it more than a little implausible when you claim not to know what's been going on.'

Skelgill indicates with a nod to DS Jones that she should gather up her papers, and then he rises.

'Mr Goldsmith, I suggest you have a think for a few minutes, and when we come back, let us know if there's anything that might help.'

Dermott Goldsmith sits unmoving. From the door, Skelgill turns back.

'By the way – why didn't you close your offices on Monday – as a mark of respect to Mr Tregilgis?'

There is a glint of avarice in Dermott Goldsmith's dark eyes.

'Ivan wouldn't have wanted that – there were deadlines to meet – we could have lost a lot of business.'

Skelgill does not deign to reply. He holds the door for DS Jones and follows her from the room. Then he stalks across to a desk where a duty constable presides.

'Do us a favour, marra – the guy in there. Let him stew for an hour then tell him he can go – say we got called away and we'll be in touch.'

27. HAYSTACKS

Friday, 6 a.m.

It is not unknown for ideas to come to Skelgill while he is fishing. This is convenient, for he needs little encouragement to paddle his trusty craft beyond reach on Bassenthwaite Lake. But angling can be an unreliable medium in this regard. Though he might set out with the best intentions to unravel a particular tangled conundrum, the plain fact is that he can become so engrossed in outwitting some imaginary monster pike that he will forget about the riddle altogether.

More dependable – and he knows it – is a good session out on the fells. Not running, mind, but a steady pull (albeit at a pace that will leave most casual walkers floundering in his wake). In this state of autopilot, requiring just sufficient concentration – navigation of the rocky terrain – the subconscious is left to its own devices. With a fair wind, it will make the connections that defy logical thought. If serendipity really strikes, Skelgill will recognise the signs.

This early Friday morning finds him chaining his Triumph motorbike to the gate of his mother's terraced cottage in Buttermere; it is still a tad early for her to be up and about. He sets off purposefully across the valley floor, and gains the summit of Red Pike within the hour. Thence he strikes off in an easterly direction along the roller-coaster ridge that comprises High Stile, High Crag, Seat and, finally, the smaller and imperfectly formed Haystacks – resting place and favourite peak of the legendary Lakeland biographer, Alfred Wainwright.

He unpacks a hot flask and cold bacon sandwiches, perched on a ledge just below the summit, from where he can survey the dale and the lakes below. It can be no coincidence that Wainwright wrote of this place, *"For the man trying to get a persistent worry out of his mind, the top of Haystacks is a wonderful cure."* Skelgill thumbs through his precious copy of The Western Fells, warmed by the cantankerous humour that sustained the writer throughout his monumental journey. He must one day find the perched boulder of which Wainwright had observed, *"Note the profile in shadow. Some women have faces like that."*

He returns the volume carefully to a pocket of his rucksack and leans back against the rocks. So much for the best views in London and Edinburgh. Small white cumulus clouds drift eastwards on a light breeze. Parachuting from above, a Meadow Pipit proclaims in urgent tones its territorial rights. Across the dale, from somewhere on the razor edge of Fleetwith Pike resonates the abrupt bark of a Raven. Beneath him, a little to his left, Buttermere and the more distant Crummock Water lie mirror-like, reflecting the sapphire sky and emerald fells, a bejewelled composition that might be the box of a jigsaw puzzle.

Indeed, this notion recalls the nature of his present conundrum – and a distant parallel to which he sometimes refers. As a small boy he endured a wearisome wet week in a holiday caravan near Fort William, with an uncle and aunt who had taken pity on his own family's poverty, and had tucked the youngest of four Skelgill brothers under their wing. But they might have well as set sail across Loch Linnhe and out into the Atlantic Ocean, for all that the weather threw at them. The caravan rocked and swayed as if it were on the move, and rain drummed relentlessly on the tin roof.

Stranded below decks, so to speak, Skelgill had discovered a plywood box containing a couple of thousand scrambled jigsaw pieces. There were no cover pictures. It took him a day to realise there was more than one puzzle, and another to determine how many. More by trial and error than by systematic logic he found himself with three frames and a series of floating fragments – a kilted piper, a wildcat, a ruined castle, a highland cow, Nessie. But where did they go? Which fragments fitted inside which frame?

Such is the paradox of the murder at Bewaldeth Hall. Like

every investigation, it has thrown up fragments of interest – intrigue, even. But which of these belong to the case, and which are purely incidental? Take the sexy undies, for instance. Had they, as Krista Morocco suggests, been stolen from her luggage – and then planted in Ivan's bed? If so, by whom? Was it a practical joke by one of the lads who'd had a few too many beers? Or is it the work of an agent provocateur? If so, do their motives concern the crime, or does it have more to do with matters of the heart? Could it have been Krista herself?

Another perplexing fragment is Ivan Tregilgis's briefcase. Thoroughly wiped of fingerprints, such a meticulous act surely has some connection to the murder. And the circumstantial evidence points to Dermott Goldsmith – at least as far as being the most likely candidate to have rifled its contents. However, if others got wind of the sale – and Krista Morocco certainly had an inkling – then Goldsmith is not the only person with an interest. A sale of the company would mean job changes, promotion opportunities, and redundancies perhaps.

Then there is the decidedly crooked Grendon Smith. If, as DS Jones would have it, he lurked in the rhododendrons with his binoculars, perhaps anything of potential value would catch his magpie's eye. What if he had been burgling Room 10 when he noticed a slumbering Ivan Tregilgis? But was his sacking sufficient a motive to merit such drastic revenge, or – giving credence to DS Jones's more advanced theory, that Ron Bunce, and narcotics had their claws into Smith – was there a more sinister explanation?

Particularly galling to Skelgill is his inability to eliminate names from the list of suspects. They have no murder weapon, the forensic evidence is compromised, and more than a dozen people had the opportunity to commit the crime. Almost as many have a motive, however tenuous.

But, as Skelgill mulls over these competing and intertwining lines of enquiry, he is troubled from deeper within. His subconscious is discomfited, albeit not ready to reveal the source of its disquiet. But what Skelgill does know – has recognised all along

– is that on that first morning at Bewaldeth Hall something of significance passed him by. That is to say, it passed by his conscious wits. And there have since been other such clues, related to this. But they are locked in. And the hike to Haystacks has not succeeded in turning the key.

With a sudden start Skelgill realises he has just heard the sound of a boot dislodging a rock. He stands up and peers around from his ledge. A rather unlikely couple – perhaps in their mid-forties – approach the summit, thirty or so feet beyond. The man is small and wiry and totes a large tripod with a tiny camera perched on top. Despite the warm weather he wears a blue-and-white bobble hat and a red cagoule, and has round spectacles with thick lenses and a sticking plaster on one of the hinges. The woman, about the same height as her partner, though younger looking, seems more sensibly attired, in stretch jeans and a close-fitting t-shirt that highlights her femininity. A pair of rather overweight chocolate Labradors, sensibly kept on a leash, stretch her arms out in front of her. The dogs have detected Skelgill, and no doubt the scent of bacon.

'It's Haystacks, I tell yer, doll.'

'T'int much to look at.'

They have a rather obscure accent, East Midlands, Skelgill guesses.

'It's what yer do wi' it, though, int it, doll?'

They both cackle; this is obviously some private joke.

Then the woman notices Skelgill. She beams and calls down to him.

'Yoright, me duck?'

Skelgill returns the smile and raises a hand.

Now the man stares at him fiercely. He points with the folded legs of his tripod to the ground at his feet.

'It's Haystacks, int it?'

Now Skelgill replies.

'Aye, it certainly is.'

The man turns triumphantly to his wife.

'There y'are. Told yer.'

He looks again at Skelgill.

'Wainwright's ashes are up here, you know.'

Skelgill is about to reply when his mobile rings. It can be a drawback of fell walking, that there is usually a good signal on the pikes, whereas the dales provide the excuse of blissful ignorance. He returns to his ledge to take the call; behind him the man wrestles to set up his camera, while the woman wrestles with the hungry dogs.

'Jones.'

'Guv – where are you?'

'Haystacks.'

'The mountain?'

'Aye – what is it?'

DS Jones sounds a little breathless. He might hope for news of some breakthrough, but is disappointed.

'The Chief wants to see you – to recap on the case.'

'It's my morning off, Jones – I've had no leave for weeks.'

'That's just what she's threatening, Guv – if we don't get a move on. She wants to know why we've made no arrests.'

28. TWITCHING

Saturday, 5.20 a.m.

The sly fox that is Grendon Smith emerges hesitantly from the communal door of his apartment block and stops to sniff the early morning air. He carries in one hand a smart black leather holdall, and on his back a small and rather worn green army-surplus rucksack, matching his fatigues. Satisfied there are no lurking threats, and manipulating a bunch of keys, he hurries across towards a row of dew-covered vehicles on the opposite side of the cul-de-sac. There is a strident squawk, and the flash of the hazards of a new-looking crimson roadster. He drops his luggage into the passenger footwell, rounds the bonnet and slides into the low-slung driver's seat. The engine fires into life, wipers flick a film of condensation from the windscreen, and tyres protest as the car snakes out onto Pentonville Road.

Were Grendon Smith a courteous driver, an observant driver, rather than a selfish, lazy driver, he might have checked his mirrors and noticed the long brown shooting brake with a wire coat hanger for an aerial in the shape of a fish that has pulled out behind him.

Skelgill, for his part, is having two thoughts. The first is that the vehicle in his sights is not the car of a destitute, unemployed young man – the insurance alone must be in four figures. The second is that, flash and appealing though the car might be, it is not the sort in which one could get a comfortable night's sleep on an obscure bird reserve.

They are heading due east. The sun slants over the rooftops and makes everything look either black or orange. Squinting, Skelgill lowers his visor and reaches for his sunglasses. There is some respite at Angel as they turn north, but soon they begin to veer eastwards again, bringing the sun back into play. At this time of day there are few cars on the road, and keeping a low profile is difficult in light traffic. Skelgill's dilemma is compounded by Smith's penchant for overtaking anything that gets in his way, forcing him to complete the same unpopular manoeuvres. At one point Smith gets himself into a race with a gang of youths in an old BMW – and for a while Skelgill knows his quarry's attention is occupied – but the gang spins off into a housing estate and Smith is freed of the distraction.

Soon after, he takes the slip for the M11, and Skelgill might now reasonably speculate that his destination is Norfolk once again. Indeed, their course proves almost arrow-straight (the exception a small dog-leg at Cambridge), and in due course the Fens flatten out before them. Above these agricultural levels Ely cathedral towers like a great gothic spaceship that has landed from another time, and Skelgill wonders how folk live in this land of lonesome horizons, with not even a hillock for company. Joining the A10 they skirt Downham Market, and reaching King's Lynn Smith holds his northwards course as he crashes through amber lights at a large island. The route is now signposted for Hunstanton – a name that Skelgill recalls mention of in Grendon Smith's statement.

A couple of miles shy of this cliff-top resort, 115 miles into their journey, the red roadster takes an abrupt left, towards the adjoining holiday village of Heacham. Skelgill has difficulty maintaining contact along the winding lanes, and only a fortuitous glance to his right gives him a glimpse of Smith's car – it has all but disappeared into one of the area's many sprawling caravan sites. He draws to a halt and turns his vehicle. A prefabricated shop guards the entrance to the site, with stalls displaying faded flip-flops and sets of cheap plastic beach-toys. He pulls onto the hard standing meant for customers, and switches off his engine.

It is seven a.m. and Skelgill's only sustenance has been a packet of chocolate digestives and a bar of Kendal mint cake. There is a smell of baking in the air, and he yearns for something savoury. But for the time being he watches the comings and goings. The shop is doing a brisk trade, and not just from occupants of the mobile homes. A steady trickle of cars brings mainly elderly folk, who collect newspapers, loaves, milk and paper bags that he suspects bear hot pies and sausage rolls. Skelgill is increasingly torn. But he has already nearly lost Smith once – if he ventures inside, he will never know whether he has slipped past in those few vital seconds. Then a movement in his wing mirror catches his eye. A newspaper delivery boy is leaning his bike against a railing. Skelgill winds down the window.

'Hey up, marra – do us a favour, will you?'

He waves a ten-pound note.

The boy's brow creases with distrust.

'It's alright, lad – I'm a plain-clothes detective – I can't leave my car. Nip into the shop and get us a couple of pies and a can of Coke – and whatever you want.'

The boy wavers. But the incentive seems to do the trick. The boy approaches – though only to within arm's length – and snatches the money and steps back. Now Skelgill displays his warrant card.

'Quick as you can, son.'

The boy gives a barely perceptible nod. Then he retrieves his bike and, taking a wide berth around the car, wheels it over to the shop doorway, where he lays it on the ground, casts another doubtful look at Skelgill, and disappears inside.

Maybe one minute later there is the roar of an engine – decelerating, in fact – and the crunch of gravel as tyres skid on the caravan site track. Smith is leaving, in a hurry.

Skelgill curses.

The paperboy is just emerging from the shop, the requisite goods cradled in his arms. Gaping, he watches Skelgill shoot past him.

'Keep the change.'

*

Skelgill manages to locate Grendon Smith ahead of him on the coast road. Weekend motorists are beginning to appear in good numbers, and the narrow Norfolk lanes make overtaking almost impossible, even for a reckless driver like Smith. They pass through Old Hunstanton, Holme-next-the-sea (puzzlingly landlocked) and Thornham, where an ancient smugglers' inn is advertised. Shortly after the village, Smith turns off, down a track signposted for Titchwell bird reserve. An oncoming van is signalling to turn in, and Skelgill gives way to put a screen between himself and Smith.

The track curves into an extensive parking area, divided into bays by thick stands of hawthorn. Despite the early hour there is a bustle about the place. Birders are busily jamming boots onto feet and hauling telescopes onto tripods. From a covert position Skelgill is able to watch Grendon Smith do likewise, and depart on foot.

Skelgill climbs out of his shooting brake and throws up the tailgate. Already clad in suitable outdoor gear – fishing and birding share a colour scheme – he complements his outfit with his worn Tilley hat and a pair of inherited field glasses. He completes the ensemble with his sunglasses, and sets off in search of Smith.

To enter the reserve it is necessary to pass through a small visitor centre. There is a gift shop and – much to his relief – a serving hatch where refreshments may be purchased. Safe in the knowledge that Smith cannot leave without returning this way, he procures a sausage roll and a tea. Presenting his change, the smiling, rosy-cheeked woman at the till addresses him in a singsong Norfolk accent.

'Beener see the hoopoe?'

'Come again?'

'The hoopoe – that's why everyone's heyer – boss made us all come in for seven.'

'Lucky for me – I'm starving.'

'And I had you down as a twitcher.'

Skelgill grins a little sheepishly.

'First things first, love.'

But it seems his improvised get-up has him marked out as one of the birding fraternity. While he eats at a picnic table a group of four men arrives at the counter. In their mid-forties they are evidently a group of friends, joshing with one another and breaking wind in turn, largely ignoring one another's efforts to impress, until one particularly tuneful rendering elicits the rather cryptic observation, "'That's yer rabbit for yer."

There being only one bench, Skelgill makes short work of his roll and tea, before the blazing saddles have him surrounded. As he heads for the salt marsh he hears them arguing over who was supposed to be looking after the communal kitty last night.

The path takes him through a shrubbery and onto a raised embankment, a kind of an inland seawall. Ahead he spies a crowd of fifty or so birders, all-male as far as he can tell, like a ragtag army in baggy green and khaki lined up to defend their position, telescopes and long-lensed cameras in lieu of proper artillery.

Suddenly a cry of instruction goes up – evidently the bird has popped its head above whatever grassy knoll was hiding it – and to a man the twitchers put their good eyes to their optics. After a couple of minutes, another exclamation proclaims that the rare hoopoe is on the wing, and mass observation switches to binoculars. It appears that the creature is departing the area, for one by one the watchers drop their hands, and the gathering loses its unity. People begin to mill about, exchanging congratulations for their new tick. Skelgill notices the blazing saddles – too late – hobbling and trumpeting from the direction of the visitor centre, hurriedly eating on the move.

Of Smith there has been no sign, but suddenly Skelgill realises he is approaching – he must have been concealed in the midst of the main body of birders, and now is only five or six yards away. He threads his way through the dispersing group, an expensive-looking telescope slung over his shoulder. Skelgill has but a second to react – he has to fight the urge to turn tail – but he braves it out, and keeps walking towards the gaunt figure. As they close to

152

within a few feet he receives a glare of barely concealed distaste – but he realises that it is not his inadequate disguise, but his patently outmoded binoculars that attract this treatment.

Skelgill continues for another twenty yards or so, and then turns around – pretending, initially that a bird passing overhead has caused him to look back. Smith is now some way off, still heading for the visitor centre. Casually, Skelgill begins to follow, subtly increasing his pace. When Smith reaches the little cluster of buildings, Skelgill is sufficiently close to see him enter the toilets. By the time Smith returns to his roadster, Skelgill is in position, slumped low behind the wheel of his own car.

The car park is otherwise deserted, and now Grendon Smith casually saunters across to a new 4X4 that stands opposite. With a cat burglar's salute he shades the reflection as he inspects the rear seat. Something wins his interest, for now he casts about upon the ground. Skelgill unfastens his seatbelt – this is not something he can stand by and ignore – but just at this moment a new arrival, a pick-up truck, swings into the area, and Smith is forced to abandon his scheme.

*

Given the bird-related theme of his day, and the erratic driving of Grendon Smith, the words 'chase', 'wild' and particularly 'goose' occur to Skelgill more than once during the next few hours. A merry dance along the Norfolk coast takes in such local attractions as Holkham Hall (for Hawfinch – heard but not seen), Holkham Meals (for a visiting Serin – neither heard nor seen), Cley Marshes (Garganey and Spoonbill – both present and correct), Salthouse Heath (singing Nightingale – not a peep), Weyborne Hope (Ortolan Bunting – already flown), and a futile dash back to Titchwell (where a report of a Marsh Warbler turned out to be nothing more than its uninteresting cousin the Reed Warbler).

Skelgill is able to keep abreast of these attempted sightings by reference to the Birdline telephone service, and thus understand exactly what his quarry is up to. The jaunt concludes at around six p.m. on Hunstanton cliffs, where Smith spends a few minutes eating a bag of chips, before hurling the wrapper angrily at a passing Fulmar. Evidently, a bird not worth ticking.

It seems that Grendon Smith is a bona fide twitcher.

Now his way leads back to the caravan park. Skelgill tails him and once more waits near the shop. After half an hour there has been no movement. He decides to take a chance. Cautiously he drives into the site. An ochre track of compacted local carrstone makes an undulating one-way circuit. Some ninety or a hundred static caravans, mostly aged and stained by the elements, are arranged in a rudimentary grid pattern. The grass in between is in need of mowing. Here and there stands a car, but on the whole there are few signs of life. There is a brick-built toilet-block with cracked windows that looks like something from an abandoned army camp. There is an atmosphere of post-war austerity, and Skelgill pictures demobbed men in string vests marching each morning to perform their ablutions.

In the far corner of the site Skelgill finds Smith's convertible concealed between the last caravan and hedgerow. The car is empty and the curtains of the mobile home are drawn. Skelgill notes the number – 88 – and continues driving. He returns to the shop and goes inside. In the absence of customers, a sullen youth seated at the counter is engrossed in a game on his mobile phone.

'I'm interested in buying one of the caravans. Number eighty-eight. I believe it's for sale.'

The youth stares blankly.

'You'd have to speak to the owner.'

'And how would I get in touch with him?'

For a moment the youth's expression suggests this is too demanding a question. Then he turns away and with a grunt brings down a ring binder from the shelf behind him. He hands it to Skelgill.

'It's all in there.'

The file contains a series of handwritten pages detailing the

154

particulars of the various proprietors. Skelgill takes a photograph. He closes the binder.

'Reet.'

The youth does not look up.

Skelgill slams the folder on the counter. The youth almost falls off his stool. Now he looks up. Skelgill is grinning at him, rather manically.

'How often does he use it?'

Fearful of what might come next, it takes the youth a moment to answer.

'Hardly ever. But his son stays sometimes. He drives a flashy sports car.'

Skelgill nods.

'Good answer.'

*

Skelgill's next port of call is the fish and chip shop patronised an hour or so earlier by Grendon Smith. Having availed himself of a fish supper – and a pie for good measure – he wipes his hands on the wrapper and drives the short distance to Hunstanton police station. Here he makes the acquaintance of the provincial constable with whom DS Jones has been liaising, for the purpose of investigating Grendon Smith's alibi for last Saturday night. They settle over a welcome pot of tea in the staffroom.

Skelgill begins by requesting that no mention be made of his visit. The constable seems sufficiently worldly wise merely to raise an eyebrow, though he must be wondering what a detective inspector is doing in his own time, two-hundred-odd miles from his home patch.

Skelgill must be wondering this, too – but he has felt an obligation to convey what he has gleaned about Grendon Smith. First, he is sure there must be a local problem of unsolved thefts of optical equipment from vehicles – and he is proved right. Second, he is able to suggest a culprit, and that the young man in question is quite probably masquerading as the son of a Mr Victor Collinson from West Bromwich, and appears to have obtained a key to his caravan.

At this, the constable's ears prick up. Two crimes potentially solved for the price of one, so to speak. But there is more. He proceeds to relate to Skelgill that there is another felony that is troubling the local force, that of drug trafficking. County lines gangs are moving narcotics up from London, and using for their temporary bases unoccupied holiday caravans.

It is food for thought: certainly it is news that would whet the appetite of his colleague DS Jones.

Skelgill thanks the constable and makes his excuses – and decides to take one last look at Grendon Smith – or, at least, to see if he is still at the caravan, and whether he can stealthily approach and observe him. But just as he reaches the turn off for Heacham, the red roadster tears out of the junction onto the London road.

It is still a couple of hours to dusk, and the crisp evening air affords good visibility. The stretch of coast road that runs parallel to the Wash is straight and true, and Skelgill has no need to get too close. Smith's route takes him onto the Snettisham bypass, and through the oak woods of Sandringham estate, thence down to the main junctions at King's Lynn. On this latter section Skelgill finds himself closing on Smith and, indeed, when they eventually reach the island where Smith will take the A10 south and Skelgill the A47 west, he approaches to within thirty yards.

Entering the roundabout first, Smith veers off as expected. Just as Skelgill crosses behind, an arm snakes out of the driver's window of Smith's roadster and gives a sporting farewell. Or is it a V-sign?

156

29. THE LETTERS

Monday, 1.15 p.m.

'Guv – some news.'

'Aye?'

Skelgill's reply is downbeat.

'Something to cheer you up.'

'I am cheered up.'

'You don't look it, to be honest.'

'You should have seen me in the pub last night.'

DS Jones smiles charitably. She has located her superior in the canteen.

'The Met have just been on – when Grendon Smith claims he was driving to Norfolk on the evening before the murder, his car was caught by a speed camera heading west out of London – roughly the opposite direction, I'd say.'

Skelgill lifts his melancholy gaze from his empty plate. His eyes are bloodshot and he looks tired.

'Was he inside or outside the M25?'

DS Jones ponders for a moment.

'It would have been inside, why?'

'Happen he were just going out of town that way. Pick up the M25, swing round.'

'Not from Pentonville – surely he would have headed north?'

'Do we know where he started from? What if he was already over that side of London?'

But DS Jones sees an opportunity here.

'Well – that's true – he might have been in Hammersmith. He could have called on Ron Bunce. And then headed for the Lakes. The Norfolk police still have no trace of him being there at the time he claims.'

Skelgill is tempted to relate his knowledge of Smith's genuine interest in ornithology, despite other more nefarious pastimes. But he bites his tongue. His situation is not helped by the cloud that has hung over him since Friday's meeting with the Chief – and the dressing down which prompted his somewhat desperate stalking of Smith on Saturday, in spite of his reservations.

A brutal killing on their doorstep and the culprit still at large. No prime suspect. No arrests. No murder weapon. Two costly searches. And Skelgill swanning about between Edinburgh and London clocking up expenses. To rub salt in the wounds he gets himself in The Scotsman for apprehending one of the Scottish capital's local villains.

DS Jones interrupts his unwelcome reverie.

'Think we should pull someone in? Even if we get the wrong person, it might cause the real killer to drop their guard. And it would take the heat off with the Chief.'

Skelgill glowers broodingly. Not patient by nature, fishing has taught him an important lesson. If you strike too soon you risk spoiling your chances for good. Spook the fish, reveal your presence, and there may be no second bite.

'We need a break, Guv.'

DS Jones's voice sounds beseeching. Then, perhaps a break occurs.

'Hey up, Skelly, lad!' The balding pate of George Appleby, Desk Sergeant, protrudes around the door of the canteen. 'You've got a visitor – Interview Room 3. Bewaldeth case.'

*

When Skelgill and DS Jones enter a few minutes later they find Elspeth Goldsmith brushing crumbs from her lap; she crumples a paper bag and pushes it into the mouth of her handbag.

'Mrs Goldsmith.' Skelgill forces a smile as he and his colleague settle opposite her. 'To what do we owe the pleasure?'

It seems the pleasure is Elspeth Goldsmith's, and she composes herself with ostentatious self-satisfaction.

'Well, as it happens I would have been passing anyway, Inspector. You see, there's a whole heap of our material still at the hotel – the music system, outdoor games – that sort of thing.'

'And you were coming down to collect it?'

'It's only a couple of hours from Ravelston, Inspector.'

Skelgill nods, and waits; but it seems she must be invited.

'So – er, what exactly did you want to see us about?'

Now she rubs her hands together and dips again into her bag.

'This morning, Inspector,' (she pauses for dramatic effect) 'I received this.'

And with a flourish she produces a clear polythene wallet that holds a single sheet of white office paper.

'The envelope is behind the letter.'

Skelgill takes the wallet and places it on the table between himself and DS Jones. In the centre of the page are printed the words, "£10K OR THE COPS FIND OUT. ONE WEEK TO GET THE CASH IN. AWAIT INSTRUCTIONS. TELL NOBODY." Skelgill turns the wallet over to see the envelope. It is printed in the same typeface, "PRIVATE & CONFIDENTIAL – MRS E GOLDSMITH." There is no address, stamp or postmark.

'Where was this delivered?'

'It was in Dermott's pigeon-hole at the Edinburgh office – post for me gets put in there, too. I take care of Dermott's admin.'

'This morning, you say?'

Elspeth Goldsmith nods.

'I made a flying visit at about nine-thirty to collect our mail.'

'Had it been opened?'

'No, Inspector.'

'And there wasn't one of these for your husband?'

'No. I opened all of his mail – just routine correspondence.'

'Who else has seen it?'

'Nobody.'

'How about Mr Goldsmith?'

'He's in London today – caught the red-eye.'

'Have you phoned him?'

She shakes her head.

'It's a big client powwow – strictly phones off.'

'So nobody else knows about this?'

Again she shakes her head.

'I thought I should tell you ASAP – and since I was driving literally right past –'

Skelgill taps the envelope, still inside its clear wallet, with the chewed end of his biro.

'This has no address on it, Mrs Goldsmith. Any idea how it got there?'

'Julia Rubicon arrived first and she took the post upstairs, and then one of the juniors sorted it out when she got in at nine. She thinks she remembers a 'Private & Confidential' envelope – but she can't recall whether it was just lying loose with the rest of the items delivered by the Royal Mail, or if it came in the zip-pouch from the London office. Apparently Julia had already opened it to extract her own letters, and she'd tipped all of the contents out onto the post table – so the two lots were more or less mixed up. I asked Julia, but she says she didn't notice it at all.'

Skelgill nods.

'Very thorough, Mrs Goldsmith.'

Elspeth Goldsmith looks pleased with herself.

Now DS Jones raises a question.

'When was Mr Goldsmith's pigeon-hole last emptied?'

'Dermott brought back all the mail on Friday evening.'

'And was anyone in the office over the weekend?'

'Not according to Julia.'

'So, this envelope was either posted by hand through the front door in Edinburgh – after the office closed on Friday evening – or it came in the internal mail pouch sent from the London office on Friday?'

'That seems to be about it, Sergeant. I put it in the plastic wallet

– in case there are fingerprints?'

She waits eagerly for more praise, and turns her attention back to Skelgill. He crunches his pen between his teeth.

'Who do you think sent it to you?'

Elspeth Goldsmith's eyes widen in surprise.

'Good heavens, I have no idea, Inspector.'

'Surely you must have your suspicions?'

Elspeth Goldsmith folds her arms, rather belligerently.

'Really, Inspector – I don't have a clue.'

Skelgill is contemplating reminding her that she only recently bragged about her sleuthing abilities. But he takes a softer line.

'Surely madam – you've just had a couple of hours in the car to think about it – who's the most likely person?'

She considers for a moment.

'Well, to be honest, Inspector, under normal circumstances I would have said Ivan.'

Skelgill raises a questioning eyebrow.

'Inspector, it would be typical of his practical jokes. Recently he left a toilet roll in the ladies' loo in the Edinburgh office. He'd put a printed sticker on the cardboard tube and wound the paper back on. It said, *"Call now, you've won a car!"* – and the person who used the last of the tissue was taken in by the hoax – it turned out to be a Mercedes showroom in London – but of course they knew nothing about it.'

Skelgill thinks he has a good idea of the identity of the person taken for a ride, so to speak.

'And do you think this is a practical joke?'

'Well – my immediate reaction was that it must be.'

'And now?'

'Well – it's not funny, is it?'

Slowly and deliberately, Skelgill shakes his head.

'What does it mean?'

'*Mean*, Inspector?'

'Aye.'

'Well – they're demanding money – ten thousand pounds.'

'Aye, I see that – but what will the cops find out?'

Elspeth Goldsmith, putting her malleable features through their paces, makes a face of extreme bewilderment.

'Your guess is as good as mine, Inspector. I certainly haven't done anything wrong. Being successful isn't a crime, is it?'

Skelgill smiles patiently.

'Of course not, Mrs Goldsmith. But, are we not supposed to think this has got something to do with the death of Ivan Tregilgis?'

'But – Inspector!' She sounds indignant, not so much at Skelgill, who has couched his question with some guile, but that this might be the intent of the mystery correspondent. 'Then why on earth send it to me?'

Skelgill nods reflectively.

'I know, madam. Then what if it's a coincidence – what if it concerns the sale of the company?'

Elspeth Goldsmith shakes her head, her expression blank.

Skelgill continues.

'You see madam, we have it on good authority that Tregilgis & Goldsmith was due to be sold last week – surely your husband would have mentioned that to you?'

There comes another shake of the head. Perhaps now, however, there is the faintest narrowing of her small brown eyes.

'I'm completely in the dark on that one, I'm afraid.'

'Not even an inkling? If I recall, you described yourself as your husband's sounding board.'

Elspeth Goldsmith does not do a good line in humility, but she clears her throat and shifts uncomfortably in her seat. But still she retains a good degree of incredulity in her expression.

'Inspector – if there *were* something as significant as selling the company – which I doubt – Ivan could be quite touchy about confidentiality.'

Skelgill must appear unconvinced, and his silence prompts her to elaborate.

'So, you see, Inspector – there is absolutely no point in

someone sending this to me. But, of course –'

It seems Skelgill must ask.

'Madam?'

'Well – you mentioned Ivan's tragic death.' She gestures to the letter. 'Surely this is the murderer trying to throw you off the scent – by making an accusation at, well – at me!'

Skelgill leans forward to place his elbows on the table; he intertwines his fingers, and rests his chin upon his knuckles.

'That would be one dense murderer, wouldn't you say, madam?'

For a second Elspeth Goldsmith looks alarmed – she reminds him of her husband, the way his face dropped when he threatened to charge him with obstruction, and of course the pair look alike – but then she seems to get the gist of Skelgill's meaning, and she laughs, a little hysterically.

'Exactly, Inspector – what are they thinking of? How ridiculous! Of course – by all means, send one to Miriam – I thought myself she must finally have run out of patience and snapped – but, well – you would have arrested her by now, wouldn't you?'

Skelgill has to suppress a grin; and other emotions, too, not all of which he understands. He settles for a somewhat oblique rejoinder.

'Mrs Goldsmith – you did the right thing in coming to us.'

She nods uncertainly. But she is not finished.

'This letter, then – does it fit with anything you have found out?'

'I really can't say, madam.'

Elspeth Goldsmith looks a little crestfallen. Perhaps she realises she cannot probe further – his phrase is ambiguous.

'What should I do, Inspector?'

Skelgill raises his shredded biro. As is customary, he has not written any notes.

'I'd like you to work closely with us on this one, Mrs Goldsmith. I suggest we try not to put whoever sent it on their guard. So I would prefer if you didn't mention it to anyone –

including your husband. And then we just wait. The minute you hear anything, get in touch. And on no account act alone – you could place yourself in danger.'

*

'What do you reckon then, bonny lass?'

Skelgill and DS Jones have returned to the canteen. DS Jones is studying the blackmail demand, still inside its protective wallet.

'The English isn't too good. That might tell us something.'

'What's wrong with it?'

'I was taught you should never end a sentence with a preposition.'

Skelgill takes the wallet and glares at the page.

DS Jones watches his expression; she comes to his rescue.

'It would read better if it said, "One week in which to get the cash".'

Skelgill continues to scowl.

After a moment he raps with a knuckle on the table.

'This sounds more threatening.'

DS Jones shrugs; he has a point.

'Still, Guv – it might help us to narrow down the identity of the blackmailer – either way, disguised or natural.'

Skelgill nods, but with some reluctance. Then he recognises in his colleague's demeanour that she has a suggestion.

'Aye?'

'Well – surely, this would be right out of Grendon Smith's copybook? We know he's on the hunt for money – and what's the betting he's still got access to the London office? He could easily have slipped the envelope into the internal mail system – say on Thursday night.'

Skelgill is forced to laugh – he holds up his hands in defeat – but DS Jones is aware of his antipathy to the 'Smith Theory', and now she offers some mitigation.

'Guv – I'm not saying this is to do with the murder – not by

164

Smith, anyway – obviously. But with his track record this is exactly the type of scam he would try to pull.'

'But why target Elspeth Goldsmith?'

DS Jones already has an answer.

'When you think about it, it could be quite clever. What if she thought her husband had killed Ivan Tregilgis – and someone has evidence to prove it? Her world comes crashing down if Dermott Goldsmith is jailed for murder.'

Skelgill ponders the scenario.

'Aye, well – happen so long as we don't arrest or charge anyone, they can all suspect one another.'

DS Jones raises the plastic wallet.

'I wonder if we can get any conclusive forensics from this.'

'Don't hold your breath. It looks like bog standard office stationery. Any of them might have touched the paper or the envelope. Not to mention any of them could have done it.'

DS Jones frowns. Skelgill is right, to slip an ordinary-looking envelope into the internal mail would be the simplest and most unobtrusive act. It could have gone in at either office. Come to that, even Elspeth Goldsmith could have done it.

She glances up at Skelgill to see he is grinning. Perhaps he is reading her thoughts – or, at least, having the same one. He rises and picks up the file.

'I'll drop this down at the lab – there's a couple of things I want to check with them.' He flaps the wallet and the envelope falls out. A little sheepishly, he carefully picks it up and replaces it. 'Catch up with you later – say, four?'

'Sure. I'm leading a self-defence class – but it can keep for ten minutes.'

Skelgill departs the canteen. His route takes him through reception, where he holds open a door for an attractive young civilian staffer. Her high heels produce an unusually penetrating clicking sound, and his gaze is drawn to its source. From off to one side, a voice barks a reprimand. It is George, the desk sergeant.

'Behave yourself, Skelly.'

Skelgill raises his hands to appeal his innocence, but realises he is wasting his time. And now George beckons him over. He speaks conspiratorially.

'Skelly, lad – I'm gannin' fishing on the Upper Eden, Wednesday night – got two free rods on a prime beat – if you fancy coming with?'

Skelgill taps the side of his nose, rather cryptically, it must be said. Then he turns to move away.

'George.'

'Aye, lad?'

'Never end a sentence with a preposition.'

*

DS Jones arrives punctually at Skelgill's office for their four o'clock review to find him listening intently on the telephone. He signals for her to enter and take a seat. She has changed into gym gear, black trainers piped in duck-egg green and matching figure-hugging Lycra that does not leave a great deal to the imagination, and tanned abdominals on display. Perhaps she was running late, for now she slips on a loose-fitting hooded top. Skelgill ends his call, and gazes at her interrogatively.

'We have a coincidence.'

'Guv, that's just what I was thinking.'

'Aye?'

'As I came past reception – George called me over –'

'Why am I surprised?'

DS Jones glances away diffidently.

'No – what I mean – he wanted to know something.' Her expression is solemn. 'He asked me, what is a preposition?'

It takes Skelgill a second to realise she is ribbing him – she is quick to catch on. He waves a hand to acknowledge her wit.

'But mine is more serious. Krista Morocco just walked into Charing Cross police station with a blackmail note just like Lady

Goldsmith's. They're scanning it now. Same wording except they asked for five thousand instead of ten.'

DS Jones looks keenly at Skelgill.

'Then, it suggests opportunism, after all. Surely they can't both know something?'

Skelgill does not demur.

'And why stop at two? Who else has had one and not told us?'

DS Jones nods.

'It's like someone's doing our job for us – trying to flush out the guilty party. But they put themselves at risk, don't you think?'

Skelgill looks momentarily alarmed. Then he notices his female colleague glance up at the clock.

'What's your class?'

'Oh – it's boxercise combined with a series of self-defence techniques. Something I've put together myself.'

Skelgill makes a casual appraisal of her outfit.

'I didn't realise you were an instructor. I'll remember not to argue with you.'

She chuckles.

'I've heard you don't need any help in that regard.'

'What – being argumentative?'

Again DS Jones laughs; he is uncharacteristically self-effacing.

'I had better go, if that's okay?'

'Aye.'

DS Jones rises. Skelgill's gaze follows her to the door.

'Jones?'

'Guv?'

'If you want my advice – the best form of defence is attack.'

She regards him, a glint in her eye.

'I thought you might say that.'

30. WNKR ADVERTISING

Penrith might seem an out-of-the-way place. But hop on a train in this small Cumbrian town and, three-and-a-half hours later, the traveller may alight in central London, untroubled by the delays and monotony of the motorway, and benefitting from the continuous availability of refreshments, albeit of a questionable pedigree.

Travelling first class on the grounds that a certain degree of privacy is required to enable them to discuss the case, Skelgill and DS Jones have not made any significant inroads in this regard. Between regular visits from the passing trolley, Skelgill has seemed preoccupied by the countryside that flashes by, or irritated by fellow passengers, businessmen wrestling ostentatiously with large newspapers and barking loudly into their mobiles.

Although the blackmail letters have introduced a thought-provoking new dimension, there has been no further enlightenment. And in the continued absence of a murder weapon and an obvious suspect for circumstantial reasons, the jigsaw is still far from complete. When motive becomes the crux of an investigation, as Londoner DS Leyton is prone to put it, "All bets are off, Guvnor."

There can be no denying a bloodstained knife, or fingerprints, or traces of DNA, or CCTV footage, or an eyewitness account – but anyone can deny a motive, and the police can flounder unavailingly, "until the cows come home", as Skelgill is more wont to remark.

Accordingly – and not least under growing pressure to achieve a breakthrough – Skelgill has little option but to drive the investigation forward along speculative lines. But there is some method in the madness. If motive will shine a light upon the dark melodrama acted out at Bewaldeth Hall, then its roots may be found in histories of its players. As the two detectives disembark at the Euston terminus, their onward destination is an advertising agency headquartered in Baker Street.

Skelgill has once more delegated the job of navigation to DS Jones, and now as they alight upon the platform he sniffs the air with some trepidation, but the aroma of fresh doughnuts dominates. They pass the great locomotive, its reptilian headlamp-eyes glowing a brooding red, and cross the main concourse where a silent multitude stares perplexed at the departures board, as a skilfully muffled announcer contributes additional disinformation.

'Where are we going?'

'Euston Square, Guv – it's a different tube station – further up the road – confusing isn't it?'

'Why don't they call it something else?'

'That's the sort of common-sense thing only the Americans would do.'

They pass out of the station into a seventies-style open-air precinct surrounded by office buildings, where a scattering of modern-art pieces and solitary people on mobiles frozen in various listening poses form a surprisingly congruous exhibition. Reaching the broad pavement on the north side of Euston Road, Skelgill is struck by the sheer volume of traffic jamming what is in places an eight-lane urban highway, a clogged artery relentlessly exchanging precious oxygen for unseen poisons. He marvels at the plane trees, which seem to thrive in this polluted environment. An ambulance, its plaintive siren appealing for cooperation, is hopelessly stuck somewhere among the vehicles that have nowhere to go.

Just ahead of them a stream of pedestrians pours down a flight of steps beneath a red underground sign. As he and DS Jones join the press, Skelgill becomes conscious that the predominantly

169

Manchester accents of the train journey have been replaced by the more bellicose London brogue. *"I ain't got no manny,"* complains a harsh female voice just behind him.

Two stops on a waiting train, standing and swaying, find them clip-clopping through the echoing Victorian labyrinth that is Baker Street station. Skelgill gazes around hopefully; perhaps these august surroundings will bring him inspiration – if only he could decipher the unease that rumbles within; it ought to be elementary.

Baker Street itself is alternately deafeningly busy and uncannily silent, as pulses of its one-way traffic are released by successive sets of lights. It is during one of the noisier intervals that they come upon a large and rotund male parking warden mid-confrontation with a small, slim, fair-skinned young woman attached to a great mass of frizzy flame-coloured hair that would surely threaten to lift her in a moderate breeze. Though their voices are drowned out by the roar of traffic, hostilities are evidently quite well advanced, and the girl appears to be winding up for a frontal assault upon the man mountain. The detectives make a precautionary detour towards the ill-matched pair – but to their relief the girl settles for tearing the ticket in half in front of the dumbfounded warden's face, hurling the pieces to the ground, and stamping upon them. She marches away, defiantly.

The detectives watch as she crosses the wide pavement and bangs through a pair of smoked-glass doors. Skelgill pats the perspiring warden on the shoulder and stoops to collect the scuffed remnants of the ticket. Then he and DS Jones follow in the girl's tracks – for she has entered the magnificent premises of WNKR Advertising.

'What is it with all these initials?'

Skelgill hisses his question as they cross the airy and minimally furnished reception hall.

'As I understand the convention, the advertising types like to have their names over the door. I suppose when there's a bunch of them, initials are the only practical solution.'

Behind the long reception counter the full names of the

founders are displayed in three-dimensional stainless steel, Wayne Nomark Kerr Rank. Skelgill scowls rather disparagingly.

They are signed in and directed to a broad cream sofa designed for appearance over comfort. A bank of TV monitors continuously screen commercials, presumably created by the agency. Skelgill thinks of a mug of tea – surely the purpose of the commercial break?

His attention becomes drawn by a group emerging from a lift. They begin an elaborate ritual of shaking hands and air-kissing. The agency staff are exclusively female: young, slim, blonde, tanned, black-clad in close-fitting skirts and tops, with impeccable finishing school accents. The client, male and older, wears a creased off-the-peg business suit and scuffed shoes, and carries a dog-eared briefcase. The girls hang on his every word, and greet his comments with choruses of "Super" and "Absolutely".

Skelgill leans across to DS Jones.

'Look at that, Jones – they're picking his pockets.'

DS Jones grins.

'Notice the smart ones are all women, Guv.'

'Not all of us, I'm glad to say.'

This rather theatrical voice takes them by surprise. From close behind, its owner has emerged from a small service lift. He leans forward, hand outstretched.

'Gary Railston-Fukes. Client Services Director.'

In the confined space of the lift, Skelgill breathes through his nose; their chaperone smells of stale cigarettes. His clothes are casual but clearly expensive, his haircut likewise; his build average, plump around the face and midriff; his eyes, behind long lashes, somewhat furtive; his nails are bitten and his fingertips nicotine-stained.

There is a contradiction in his still-boyish appearance that is prematurely going to seed. Identified by DS Jones's team, at thirty-four Gary Railston-Fukes is a survivor from the days when Ivan Tregilgis had learned his craft at this agency, including the period during which Krista Morocco numbered among his clients.

'Fly down?' Railston-Fukes makes desultory conversation.

'Train.'

'Shambles, aren't they?' Railston-Fukes does not wait for a reply. 'Privatise some sense into them, I always used to say – but they've botched that and left a worse mess. You should try commuting by rail down here. National disgrace.'

His accent is somewhere between Park Lane and the Old Kent Road, though it is difficult to tell which side is affected. His resting facial expression conflates a self-satisfied sneer with a cynical grimace.

'Last door on the right.'

He steps aside from the lift and ushers them along a broad, thickly carpeted corridor between floor-to-ceiling windows of darkened glass. Inside his office they realise the glass partitions enable the occupant to see out, but not the other way around. They must have been observed with some curiosity.

'Have a seat.'

Railston-Fukes slumps into his own swivel chair and rests his feet on an open drawer of his desk, stretching out languidly and folding his hands across his lap.

'You wanted to speak with me about Ivan Tregilgis?'

Skelgill nods and indicates with an open palm that DS Jones will begin the questions.

'You heard of course that Ivan Tregilgis was murdered?'

'The marketing press were wetting themselves all last week.' Railston-Fukes grins wryly. 'Just like Ivan to go out with a bang.'

DS Jones pauses just long enough to convey that she will not be drawn by his provocative manner.

'When did you last have contact with him?'

Railston-Fukes looks like he would revel in the idea of being a suspect.

'How does eight years ago sound?'

'Not since he left here, then?'

Railston-Fukes nods.

'Naturally I've seen him at the odd industry bash – we generally exchanged slurred insults and best wishes.'

'When was the most recent occasion?'

'Just before Christmas. His crew picked up a top creative award.'

'Can you think of any reason why someone might want to kill Ivan Tregilgis?'

Railston-Fukes shrugs.

'Jealousy?'

DS Jones detects a faint stiffening in her colleague's demeanour.

'Could you elaborate?'

'Good looking. Talented. Successful. Rich.' He squints, as though he is accustomed to speaking through invasive tobacco smoke. 'And still had a woman on each arm at that last awards ceremony.'

'Did you recognise them?'

'Krista Jonsson, yeah. *Morocco*, as she is now.'

'And the other?'

'Never seen her before. Looked like a tart on hire for the night.'

His gaze comes to rest casually upon the lowest unfastened button of DS Jones's blouse; she has to fight the urge to move a hand towards it. But she responds with a certain alacrity.

'Were you jealous, Mr Railston-Fukes?'

'Yeah.' Perhaps to their surprise, Railston-Fukes replies without hesitation or inhibition. 'Jealous – why not? But I'm not bitter.'

DS Jones nods. He is not a pleasant character, but he is candid, at least.

'Either way, it is hardly grounds for murder, is it, sir?'

Railston-Fukes shakes his head slowly.

'Not in my book, no. But maybe somebody closer.'

'Such as?'

'Wife. Girlfriend. Wife's lover. Girlfriend's husband? It would be something like that, knowing Ivan.' He grins at his own humour. 'Unless it was that dork he set up with?'

'Are you referring to Dermott Goldsmith?'

Gary Railston-Fukes nods slowly.

'Look – it was no surprise when Ivan told me he was starting his own shop – but when he mentioned Goldsmith I thought I was hearing voices.'

DS Jones, without conveying any sense of urgency, homes in on this latter point.

'What makes you say that, sir?'

'Goldsmith? I've never met anyone who could stand him. Not the best qualification for this business.'

Along such lines, DS Jones might justifiably question Gary Railston-Fukes's own rise to seniority.

'How do you know about Dermott Goldsmith?'

'He worked here before they broke away.'

'For how long?'

'Under a year, thankfully. He joined from TW&TS.'

'Ivan Tregilgis presumably got on well with him?'

Gary Railston-Fukes sighs.

'He must have seen something no one else could.'

'How well did you know Ivan Tregilgis?'

'I wouldn't say we were best mates – didn't socialise outside work – but we shared a few nights out with the same crowd. We joined WNKR on the same intake – took the same induction course.'

'And did you subsequently work together?'

'Not really. I was in a different account group – fags and booze clients.'

Here he produces his boyish smirk, as if he realises there is no need to point out that this was manifestly right up his street.

'You mentioned Krista Morocco – she was a client at the time?'

'Of Ivan's group, yeah.'

'And was there a relationship outside of work?'

'Your guess is as good as mine.'

'Not really, Mr Railston-Fukes – *you* were there at the time.'

Gary Railston-Fukes swings his feet down from his part-supine position and absently taps the trackpad of the laptop on his desk. He seems suddenly bored with the interview. He looks back at DS

174

Jones, his eyes narrowed.

'I only ever saw her at client-agency shindigs. We have annual cricket matches, tennis, that sort of thing – pain in the backside, if you ask me. Krista was quite an attraction. They obviously got on well – but that was standard form with Ivan – charm the knickers off a nun. Undying love, though?' He shrugs indifferently.

'When Tregilgis & Goldsmith was formed, did they take any of WNKR's clients with them?'

'Nope.' Railston-Fukes affects admiration. 'A breakaway with zero business. Hardly qualified as a breakaway.'

'Not even Krista Morocco's account?'

He grins sardonically.

'No enemies here, if that's what you're driving at.'

'They must have been confident of their abilities?'

'Dammed stupid, I thought – but what do I know? Look at me. Look at Ivan.' Then he seems to realise what he has said, and perhaps for the first time he exhibits a moment of self-censorship. 'Cancel that.'

DS Jones nods forbearingly.

'Just one last question, sir – is there anyone else still here who might have worked with Ivan Tregilgis?'

Gary Railston-Fukes begins to shake his head, but then he raises a finger and reaches for his phone. He dials an internal number, and inhales as it is answered.

'Mooro – did you join before Tregilgis left to set up with Goldsmith?' There is a brief hiatus before he continues. 'Got a couple of people like to hear from you.'

31. THE IRISH GIRL

Tuesday, 2 p.m.

'*ooro*' – Marie O'Moore, Planning Director, according to the plate on her door – is revealed as none other than the combative redhead, scourge of traffic wardens, whose fiery nature they had witnessed earlier. Of this, she shows no sign, nor any inkling that she recognises her erstwhile audience; perhaps they were shrouded in red mist. Skelgill finds himself approving greatly, and takes the lead with enthusiasm.

'Ms O'Moore –'

'Please –' She holds up a hand in protest. 'You must call me Marie.'

Skelgill obliges with a nod.

'Marie. We understand you worked with Ivan Tregilgis?'

Now she brings her palms together, fingertips uppermost.

'I did indeed – and what a terrible tragedy. I only pray you catch the devil behind it all.'

Skelgill nods again, more determinedly, but before he can respond the girl jumps to her feet, arms akimbo.

'I don't suppose that ignoramus Fukes offered you so much as a cup of tea?'

'Er, well –'

'And what about food? You'll have a bite? Don't worry – I deal in the art of the possible.'

Without consulting then further, she reaches for her telephone. She taps out a number; her nails are long and painted green.

Somebody now answers and the girl beams into the handset.

'Hi, Charlie – it's Marie. How's it going now? Grand. Look – thanks for that mountain of bacon rolls this morning – the client crowd were in seventh heaven. They'd been on the batter, by all accounts. That's right. I know. Now – I've got a couple of starving visitors in my office. Is there any chance you could rustle me up a plate of sandwiches and a pot of tea?' She listens for a moment and then laughs heartily. 'I already *do* owe you, Charlie. I shall – I promise – just remind me on the night. Thanks a million, Charlie – oh, and be sure to code it up to one of Fukesey's accounts, now.'

She ends the call and smiles graciously at her guests for their patience. Then she fixes her emerald eyes upon Skelgill. They seem to have a light of their own, that flickers and sparkles.

'I grew up in a village near Galway – have you been, by the way?' (Skelgill shakes his head apologetically.) 'You must – we've a beautiful cathedral. I studied media at Trinity in Dublin and like a lot of my contemporaries I headed across the water. That would be about eight years ago. I started here on the graduate trainee scheme – they move you around – and that's when Ivan was my boss for a few months. Great fella. Of course, he was a Celt, you know – Cornish, as if you couldn't guess, a name like that.'

Skelgill's own name and heritage are together somewhat more nuanced, but he shares a degree of provenance, and feels a common bond.

'How long after you joined did Ivan Tregilgis leave?'

'It was actually while I was working for him. You know, Inspector – he asked me more than once to join him.'

'You didn't.'

Skelgill states the obvious – but it seems to prompt some deeper thought on the girl's behalf. She purses her lips reflectively and lowers her gaze, and the Irish eyes begin to glisten. Suddenly she taps herself on the thigh.

'Come away with yourself, Marie – you'll never plough a field by turning it over in your head.'

She looks from one detective to the other, and grins apologetically.

'To answer your question, Inspector – I wasn't ready for it. For your first job, a big agency like this is ideal – get a couple of years under your belt. We have training schemes and courses, and you get to work in various departments, so you can find a discipline that suits you. I was most interested in planning, while Ivan's start-up was more of a creative hothouse.'

Skelgill nods comprehendingly.

'And where did Dermott Goldsmith fit in?'

The girl frowns.

'That's a good question – which I really can't answer. I didn't have too much to do with him, but he certainly wasn't the most popular one about the agency.'

'That seems to be the unanimous view.'

'Well, now – he was harmless really – once you got to understand him – the maturity of a teenager in the body of a man. I'm sure he was talented an' all – but he didn't take kindly to not getting his own way. And there was that business about calling himself Lord.'

'Did you work directly with him?'

She shakes her head, and has to part red locks that fall across her face.

'He was never my line manager – but we were alongside one another in a project team for a short while.'

'Did you by any chance have a client called Krista Jonsson?'

Marie O'Moore is about to answer when there comes a knock and she springs from her seat to get the door. A woman in a catering uniform bears a tray laden with refreshments. Now it is Skelgill's eyes that light up.

'Come in, Gina – that's grand, now. You're a star – and give Charlie a hug for me.'

Skelgill shifts his chair so the woman can more easily deposit her burden. There is a small triplicate pad on the tray, and Marie O'Moore leans over, pen poised. As Skelgill watches, she makes a squiggle that might read "Railston-Fukes", and winks as she catches his eye.

Now she insists they tuck in. She oversees the dispensing of plates, sandwiches and teas, and settles back with just a drink for herself.

Skelgill rotates a ciabatta two-handed until he finds the most propitious angle of attack. While they eat, he seems to feel he ought to postpone the subject that is left hanging, and instead make small talk.

'So, what is it you do here, Marie?'

She prefaces her reply with a self-effacing grin.

'Not a lot, some would say. But in a nutshell planning is not as dull as the ditchwater it sounds like. It's all about identifying insights that will help our ads engage the right people.' She indicates to the window, where a pile of art boards is propped against the wall. The foremost displays a sketch of several men in business suits, walking apelike, with legs bowed; they all appear to be wearing underpants inflated by air. 'That's what we do to our toddlers when we put them in diapers. The trick is making the blindingly obvious connection – that to which most folk are blind.'

Skelgill continues to stare with interest. Something about the concept strikes a chord. He murmurs approvingly.

'Happen we have something in common.'

Now the girl regards him reproachfully.

'I can't help feeling your job's rather more worthy than mine, Inspector.'

'I wish we had your resources.' Skelgill makes a sweeping movement with his sandwich to indicate her hi-tec, high-spec environment. 'Have you ever seen inside a police station?'

'Only when the guards invited us into their Christmas parties – under drinking age we were, an' all!'

Skelgill grins amenably – but now he opts to restore the connection to the purpose of their visit. Good company she may be, but the garrulous Marie is prone to digress.

'You were going to tell us about Krista Morocco – Krista Jonsson, as was.'

The girl leans back in her chair and runs slender fingers through the great fan of hair.

'Things were all going pretty smoothly, as I recall. We were in the run-up to making a new commercial, so there were a lot of meetings – pre-production, casting, location checks and suchlike.'

'And how would you describe the personal interactions?'

'It was obvious Krista had a soft spot for Ivan, which helped. But anyway she was a generous client – and that's a rare thing. A kind word never broke anyone's mouth.'

Skelgill glances at DS Jones to see she is grinning at him.

'Were you aware of a personal relationship between them?'

The girl rocks her head from side to side, and her keen eyes lose their sharp focus.

'It was basically professional as far as I could see. I'm not sure how long they'd known each other before I joined. Sure – they got on swimmingly – but I never saw them do anything improper, so to speak.'

Skelgill smiles briefly, but his tone becomes graver.

'Marie, we believe something from that time may have a bearing upon recent events. Can you remember anything that struck you as out of the ordinary – thinking of the people we have mentioned?'

Now she slides her fingers over her scalp, drawing her hair into a reluctant ponytail. A frown creases her brow, and she seems to wince as some memory pricks her conscience.

'I recall one time Ivan had asked me to come up to his office. He never closed his door – he said he detested the barriers of rank, you know? Well, he must have taken a phone call in the time it took me to get there – because I could hear his voice as I came along the corridor. Then just as I was putting my head round the door he exclaimed, "What do you mean, *baby*?"'

She pauses, and stares expectantly at Skelgill.

'Go on.'

'Well, that's it really. As soon as he saw me he ended the call.'

'Who was he talking to?'

She shakes her head, her great tresses spreading once again.

'I don't know – but the way he said it – it didn't sound like he was calling a girlfriend *baby*.'

180

'He didn't comment to you about it?'

'Not a word – but he seemed unsettled. I'd only just started working here – and I didn't know him so well then – but I never saw him like it again.'

Skelgill takes a drink of his tea, as if to punctuate the subject matter.

'What about Dermott Goldsmith – concerning his personal behaviour?'

'I do remember once – when we were on a night out – a bit of a celebration, after we'd got the ad in the can – I witnessed something of an awkward moment between him and Krista?'

Her inflexion invites his approval. He indicates with a palm that she should continue.

'We were in a crowded bar – there was a lot of noise. I don't quite know what had passed between them, but as I approached I heard Krista say something like, "I must be going deaf – I shan't embarrass you by repeating what I thought I just heard you say." She did it with a smile, but I could see Dermott's face had fallen, like a naughty schoolboy caught cheating in an exam. He made himself scarce – and Krista leaned over to me and said, "Boys will be boys." I think she thought I'd heard more than I had.'

Skelgill nods pensively.

'And was there ever anything beyond that, between the two of them – that you were aware of?'

The girl grins widely.

'Inspector, there was more chance of Dermott catching hold of a leprechaun than of Krista – she was way out of his league.'

Skelgill glances again at DS Jones. She seems to be amused by reading between the lines of his conflicted reactions. He reverts to Marie O'Moore.

'But he did end up marrying a woman he met in advertising – I believe at the agency he had worked for previously?'

'That's right. TW&TS – they used to be over in Berkeley Square.'

'Did you ever meet the woman?'

She shakes her head.

'No – I can't say I did – though now you mention it I do remember Dermott having a bit of a tirade about her – we were driving up the M40 to a client meeting in Birmingham.'

Skelgill leans forward encouragingly.

'I think he was having second thoughts about getting engaged. I remember thinking afterwards it was strange. You know – you might worry about infidelity or infertility or – well – any number of things? But he just kept saying if they got married how could he trust her not to get fat? And he'd got a fair old belly on himself!'

Skelgill is wondering how to respond – but there comes another knock on the door, and a fresh-faced young man hampered by an armful of art boards backs into the office. He looks alarmed when he realises he has interrupted – but Marie O'Moore puts him at his ease and explains to the detectives that she has an imminent meeting, but will happily delay it. Skelgill, however, is content that this is a good moment to bring matters to a close. As they are making their farewells, he remembers something and digs into his jacket pocket. He holds out the crumpled halves of the parking ticket.

'Marie – I think this belongs to you.'

She has a twinkle in her eye.

'Oops-a-daisy – how on earth did I mislay that, now?'

*

The detectives retrieve their overnight bags from reception. Exiting the monogrammed swing doors of WNKR Skelgill gasps – whether at their escape from the quixotic frying pan of the advertising agency or their emergence into the fire of a London heatwave, it is hard for his colleague to know. But he slips off his jacket and tugs at his shirt at the small of his back. The midsummer sun has burned off the cloud that had blanketed the capital on their arrival in the capital, and now just a hint of smoggy haze blurs its bright outline. DS Jones makes a unilateral decision, and diverts to the kerb to hail a cab.

'Good thinking, Jones – this is evil.'

An old-style black taxi lurches dangerously close. Skelgill makes to wrench open the nearside front door.

'No, Guv – we get in here.' DS Jones turns her head to hide her grin.

'I was just going to give him directions.'

Skelgill sounds unconvincing. He clambers awkwardly into the back seat. DS Jones smiles reassuringly at cabbie, lest he think this is some bungled hijack.

'Drury Lane, please – Holburn end.'

The man nods warily and slides shut the interconnecting window.

Skelgill wipes a bead of perspiration from his brow and casts about the dark interior.

'Do these things have AC?'

'Not even DC, Guv.'

Skelgill grimaces and settles back in the seat.

'It doesn't get this hot up north, Jones.'

DS Jones nods, rather wistfully it seems to Skelgill.

'We used to sunbathe on the roof of our flat. It was really quite private.'

Skelgill gazes out of the window, his eyes raised to the undulating line of parapets; he might almost be speculating whether they are passing this very minute beneath a secret colony of nudists. If so, then perhaps it is what triggers his next remark.

'Miriam Tregilgis has no kids. Krista Morocco has no kids.'

DS Jones nods.

'It could have been anybody, Guv – it could have been one of his pals telling him he and his wife were expecting.'

Skelgill sticks out his chin and rubs the underside with the tips of his fingers.

'The way she told it – it had the ring of a skeleton in the closet.'

They both become silent at this, for it is an unfortunate choice as a figure of speech. Skelgill is thinking back to something that

Krista Morocco said, about losing out.

DS Jones inhales – but she compresses her lips. If she has something to add, for the time being she holds her peace.

Skelgill changes the subject.

'What did you reckon to Railston-Fukes?'

'Another one that never reached maturity.'

Skelgill makes a scoffing sound.

'That's just blokes in general, isn't it?'

'I wouldn't say that, Guv.'

'No?'

'No, Guv.'

Skelgill raises his eyebrows – if this is intended as a compliment, he banks it and moves on.

'But he's a straight talker.'

DS Jones makes a murmur of agreement.

'He seemed to confirm what we know about Ivan Tregilgis and his ongoing romantic liaisons.'

Skelgill does not respond immediately; he stares broodingly at the passing sights, the pavements crowded with pedestrians, moving more languorously now, it seems to him.

'Aye – what he said – about jealousy – not easy for us to judge that, from the outside. Greed, power, revenge – they're more obvious. Jealousy's hidden away, like a little parasitic worm.'

DS Jones looks at her superior with no little alarm – but perhaps it is the simile rather than the notion that troubles her.

'It's a big step to kill someone, Guv – for reasons of jealousy. It seems to me that, in a case of unrequited love, it would be cutting off your nose to spite your face.'

Now it is Skelgill's turn to look bewildered.

'Are you quoting Shakespeare? It's way over my head, lass.'

DS Jones grins.

She is about to answer when Skelgill interjects.

'I could murder a cuppa.'

'Actually, Guv – I was going to make a suggestion?'

'Aye?'

184

'Well – we could go for tea around Covent Garden – and the sales are on – you could get a real bargain on a nice polo shirt – it's what you need for this weather. Trendy, too.'

32. LONDON BY NIGHT

Wednesday, 3.30 a.m.

Skelgill, leaning once more over the parapet of Waterloo Bridge, reflects that he should have listened more forensically to his colleague. When she slipped the word 'trendy' into her proposal, he might have divined that it was not without significance. Now he watches as the lightening eastern sky, threatening dawn, reflects off the sebaceous Thames and illuminates the pallid limestone dome of St Paul's. A steady, cool breeze drifts up river, bringing with it the iodine scent of the marshes. At his side, DS Jones shivers, and he – short-sleeved – does too.

'We ought to get some sleep, lass.'

DS Jones nods, and they turn, and link arms. In similar fashion they have promenaded for an hour or more, distancing themselves from drunkenness and its devil-may-care deeds, discovering the dark corners of London's deserted streets. From High Holborn to Kingsway and down to Aldwych, passing insomniatic traffic lights and insensible beggars, they have gravitated to Waterloo Bridge, and all the time Skelgill fighting the realisation that he is even lonelier than on his last visit.

*

Half a day earlier they had checked into their familiar, seedy hotel, and set out in search of a cuppa. DS Jones had encouraged Skelgill to try a handy local café, in Endell Street. An elderly hippy

186

couple ran it along Bohemian lines: dimly lit and draped with eastern-style wall hangings. It had taken Skelgill some time to convince the waitress that he really did want just plain English Breakfast – and yes, milk *and* sugar. "Aye – and a couple of those large currant buns, please love."

Suitably revived they had emerged blinking into the bright afternoon sun, to explore the fan of narrow streets that radiate from Seven Dials. Skelgill had marvelled at London's ability to support shops that sold only cheese, or brushes, or beads – and was elated to stumble across a ship chandler. Less enthralling were the designer-label chain stores that have colonised Long Acre. Here DS Jones had bagged several modest bargains, although it appeared to Skelgill that the prices she paid were hardly of the basement variety, deeply slashed though they claimed to be. Inside one Italian-sounding emporium Skelgill had called her attention to a suit he had casually examined.

"Jones, look at this – back home I could get a decent motor with twelve months' tax and MOT for less!"

"It's gorgeous though, isn't it?'" had been her response. "Pure silk, I bet. You'd look good in it."

Skelgill had shaken his head incredulously.

"If anyone sold me that, I'd arrest them for daylight robbery."

DS Jones had grinned, and then led him by the cuff to view a polo shirt she had found, marked down by 80% – to reach a just-about-palatable price in Skelgill's book. In the event, he had bought two – claiming grounds of convenience – but in reality taking advantage of his companion's knowledge of what was in vogue.

The huge discount, and DS Jones's reassurance, did not entirely dispel rumblings of post-purchase dissonance. Skelgill was picturing his next visit to his local pub.

"Thee paid 'ow much?"

"They saw thee comin', lad."

"Yer turnin' into a soft southern ponce, Skelgill."

In the same store DS Jones had bought herself a belt. As they stood together at the till Skelgill, feeling mildly euphoric, had clumsily tried to pay on her behalf – in return for her good advice. It was an offer that she had graciously declined – with the somewhat less-than-convincing excuse that it was a gift for a girlfriend – but not without a little embarrassment for both parties. Afterwards, they had padded reflectively through the quiet cobbled lanes behind Long Acre, a little distant from one another.

They had been rescued from their reverie by their accidental coming upon the Lamb and Flag, one of London's most ancient and noble hostelries. An oasis of beery aromas and convivial laughter, it already played host to a sizeable post-work crowd enjoying alfresco the warm air and tepid ale. Empty pint-glasses were stacked high on windowsills and against railings, and animated groups of shirt-sleeved executives neighed and brayed, blithely sloshing bitter and smudging cigarette ash upon one another's clothes. Skelgill had needed little encouragement.

"The Milky Bars are on me."

*

The next thing Skelgill could properly remember had been an insistent voice calling, "Guv – Guv – are you alright – Guv?"

He had related this a little later to DS Jones – for it had been half a dream.

He had been out on the fells. By order of the Chief his recent solo-completion of the Bob Graham Round (a 24-hour fell-running challenge) had been disqualified (an act entirely outwith her jurisdiction, but nevertheless in dream-logic something Skelgill had unquestioningly accepted). So Skelgill had to do it again, all forty-two peaks and seventy-two miles. But unlike his real-life experience, this time there was an added problem. The landscape kept changing. On a clear day you could take a hooded Skelgill virtually anywhere in the Lakes, remove the blindfold, and he'd not only be able to tell you exactly where he was, but also name the surrounding hilltops and list their spot-heights. In his dream, however, he would toil his way to a summit, only to find an unrecognisable panorama lying before him. It *looked* like the Lakes, but it wasn't quite right. To compound the problem, he relegated his doubts to the back of his mind and went on with his run. They've changed things around, he said to himself, as though he had read in the papers about the reorganised topography that now had him crossing directly (and bizarrely – he knew) from Helvellyn to Hopegill Head. The 'New Lakes', it was to be called. Atop Scafell Pike he paused at the enlarged cairn to take a drink, but his water bottle contained strong beer. He realised he was looking *up* at Great Gable's screes, and that the Ordnance Survey had made a mistake about Scafell Pike being the highest mountain in England. He needed badly to urinate. There was nobody about so he just did it there and then in the open. Suddenly something cold touched him, at the back of one knee. He turned – it was the wet nose of a vaguely familiar chocolate Labrador, attracted no doubt by the tasty salt crystals on his skin. Just then, from behind the cairn appeared the shapely Midlands woman he had met briefly on Haystacks. She was straightening her white t-shirt as though it had been pulled up. He could see her hard nipples protruding beneath the tightly stretched cotton (he omitted this part in his explanation to DS Jones). He felt self-conscious in his skimpy running shorts and sleeveless vest. In fact, he suspected he had no shorts on at all, but dare not look directly. He stooped as if to stroke the dog, in an effort to cover up his modesty. Then, as the dog persisted in trying to lick him, in a voice of increasing urgency the woman began to repeat the word: 'Guv – Guv!' He realised it must be the dog's name. Now the woman's accent was no longer of the Midlands – in fact her voice reminded him of DS Jones. Then he woke up.

In the disoriented daze that follows an ill-timed catnap, things had then started to come back to him. After four pints of best bitter (and four bottled concoctions in DS Jones's case), they had retired to the hotel at about seven-thirty to shower and change, aiming to meet at nine to go for something to eat. Skelgill, having showered, had made the fatal mistake of lying (naked) on the bed and closing his eyes. In the heat of the room and under the equally soporific influence of the best bitter, he had fallen asleep. Thus it was DS Jones (herself half an hour late) – and not the buxom dog-owner – who was summoning him back from the Land of Nod.

Their first port of call had been a bustling pizza restaurant on Bow Street, where they passed an undemanding hour or so. During the course of two carafes of house wine, they had discussed the case – though they both recognised the futility of talking themselves into ever-decreasing circles. Conversation, therefore, tended to jump about, matters domestic, the police force, Skelgill's fishing – DS Jones's London connections. Skelgill noted that on the couple of occasions he had tried subtly to draw her out on the subject of her boyfriend, she quickly pulled in her horns, and diverted to some other vaguely related matter.

Time came to pay their bill and leave – indeed the place was emptying with surprising speed – a feature of Central London, where few diners live, and must dash like Cinderella for their carriages to the suburbs. As they wandered rather aimlessly, Skelgill had suggested they find a "nice quiet pub", but DS Jones's rather uncharacteristically racy retort had been that the only way to get a late drink in that part of town was to "mug a down-and-out".

Their hitherto futile search had them pass by the sunken entrance of a basement club, in a back street off High Holborn. The queue had snaked around a corner, and when they reached its end DS Jones had suddenly turned and leaned against the wall, posing it seemed to Skelgill like a rock chick in a pop video.

"Let's give it a try," had been her only words.

Skelgill had begun to protest, indicating the peaceable if outlandish types before them – and that he was more than a little out of place. She had shaken her head and tugged on the hem of his new shirt. While they waited in silent anticipation, he had eyed up his would-be fellow clubbers; at least a few were older than he, if more aptly dressed for the occasion. When their turn came to be vetted by the hefty doorman, Skelgill sensed he should appear both sober and unthreatening – but DS Jones simply pushed in front of him and slipped off her thin black cardigan to reveal a glittering bustier top that left little to the imagination.

It had immediately struck Skelgill that there would be no conversation hereafter. The dungeon beat was deafening, with no gaps separating tracks. They had eased between twisting torsos clad only in underwear and fake tan to reach the bar. It was packed and overwhelmed, and Skelgill ordered double when his turn came. The extra drinks would numb the shock of the bill. They found a spot by a brick pillar that afforded some protection. Skelgill could see no dance floor; people were breaking into motion all around them.

His conundrum became one of where to look. He could hardly stare at his colleague, but wherever his gaze fell there seemed to be bare flesh. DS Jones, meanwhile, seemed entirely relaxed, half closing her eyes and rhythmically shaking her head. After a while she had tapped him on the shoulder and beckoned him to bend towards her. She had suggested they dance. His response was a look of trepidation – that he had no idea how – but she simply smiled and began to move her hips in time with the beat. Stiffly, Skelgill shuffled his feet and rolled his head from side to side, certain that everyone was looking at him.

In the intense heat, and in the absence of conversation, they had soon both drained their drinks, and DS Jones had insisted upon going for refills, leaving him to keep their space beside the pillar. He could see her at the bar – she was laughing with a guy of about her age, good looking, with a stylish haircut and a tight-fitting t-shirt that showcased his physique. DS Jones already had their drinks – four bottles, their necks clasped between the knuckles of each hand. She held them aloft as she mirrored his offered dance for maybe ten or fifteen seconds. He had insisted on taking a selfie with her, to which she acquiesced. But then, to Skelgill's relief, she had gradually backed away through the writhing crowd, until she had returned to his side.

Skelgill had made short work of his next few drinks, and the tide that had been pulling at his sensibilities, urging flight, had begun to turn in favour of fight. Not literally to get into a fight, but the impulse to escape was replaced by some other primeval yearning, which he did not fully understand. But he began to relax into the vibe and the smiling mute company of his companion. At some point he had glanced at his watch and was surprised to find it was after two a.m. Despite the hour, the club seemed to be filling up, and gently gyrating, glistening bodies increasingly hemmed them in. In time, there became a choice between being separated and standing toe to toe – but DS Jones for the moment had been jostled such that she backed into Skelgill – and the contact had been too much – he had wrapped his arms around her and she had instantly turned and raised her face and pulled him down to kiss her.

33. KRISTA MOROCCO

Wednesday 9.15 a.m.

A solitary Skelgill, bleary-eyed and balanced awkwardly upon an aluminium barstool, sips absently on his beaker of unsatisfactory tea. He has taken up position in the window of a takeaway sandwich deli on a busy corner in St Martin's Lane. His view should give him sight of DS Jones's anticipated approach. Outside is another glorious morning ruined by not being on Bass Lake.

He watches the goings-on of this very different world. Porters pass with trolleys stacked with cardboard boxes. An elderly guy, scruffy, a large rucksack on his back and a laptop under one arm, hails a cab. Two young men, peroxide crew cuts, tight sleeveless vests, mirrored sunglasses, glide by, arm in arm. A dapper business-suited female gnaws at a great flapping wedge of breakfast pizza. Directly below him at a pavement table a smoker pores over a newspaper that announces, "Police Raid Cracks Drugs Gang". He can see the pictures: cops with a battering ram, and another arresting a skinny youth who seems more interested in giving the finger to the camera. Skelgill is intrigued by the idea of the press photographer being in on the act. The man rises and leaves, and immediately a shabby feral pigeon moves in to scavenge crumbs, artfully dodging the passing footfall that could prematurely end its Wednesday.

'Penny for your thoughts?'

Skelgill starts.

'Jones – how did you get here?'

'There's another entrance – over by the counter.'

'Right.' Skelgill swallows, unready for the conversation. 'Look, Jones – about last night –'

She interjects, putting a hand on his wrist.

'Guv – thanks for getting me back in one piece – I can't remember a thing after we left the restaurant – it must have been that red wine.'

'Aye –'

DS Jones steps away.

'I'll get you a top up – back in a mo.' Then she hesitates. 'Oh, Guv – message from Forensics – that blackmail letter of Elspeth Goldsmith's – the only prints they could get off it were hers and yours.'

Skelgill nods. His eyes are pensive and his stool seems to revolve with a power of its own as her athletic form wends its way around the perimeter of the café.

*

'So, who do you think might have sent it?'

Krista Morocco's ice-blue eyes switch from the letter on her desk to meet Skelgill's inquiring gaze. She is more relaxed than before, albeit there is a guardedness about the finely chiselled Scandinavian features.

'I find the whole thing impossible to believe, Inspector.'

'But, if you had to pick someone?'

'Well, I suppose – Grendon Smith would be my first thought.'

Skelgill nods thoughtfully.

'And what would he know that you wouldn't want the cops to find out?'

Krista Morocco gives a shake of her blonde locks, impeccably cut to curve below the jawline, with a parting just off centre. She reminds Skelgill of someone from the television.

'That, I should like to know, also.'

'Do you have any theories?'

'Maybe whoever sent it *thinks* I know something, when actually I don't.'

'When did you receive it?'

'It was in my tray when I arrived on Monday at about ten-thirty – I'd been at a meeting first thing.'

'Had it been opened?'

'No. It was sealed in a plain white DL envelope, typed 'Private & Confidential' on the front. There was no stamp or postmark – I'm afraid I didn't keep it.'

'How do you think it was delivered?'

'I'm not sure. Geri who sorted my mail says she doesn't remember seeing it.'

'Is it possible that Grendon Smith still has access to these offices?'

She pauses to consider, and a frown creases her smooth brow.

'As you may recall – Ivan took his keys off him when he left. But I suppose he could have had copies made before then. We work such irregular hours that everyone has their own set, and can come and go as required.'

'What about Julia Rubicon? Could she have done it?'

'The letter?'

'Aye – what did you think I meant?'

'Oh, I thought for a moment – that you were asking me about the murder.'

Skelgill opens his palms invitingly.

Krista Morocco keeps her pale eyes fixed on Skelgill.

'She's might be the jealous sort – but murder Ivan?' She shakes her head decisively.

'What about the note?'

Now she ponders for a moment, her gaze alighting on the crudely produced message.

'She might be a little crazy at times – impetuous, even – but Julia's a very intelligent young woman. Why would she do something pointless like that?'

Skelgill shrugs indifferently, as though what he is about to say is of no consequence.

'Maybe – if she thought you were the murderer?'

Perhaps the slightest tinge of red colours Krista Morocco's prominent cheekbones. She chooses to remain silent.

'How about Saturday night at Bewaldeth Hall – has anything more come back to you?'

'I've been racking my brains, Inspector.' She hesitates, and sighs. 'There's nothing tangible, but – you know – I just have this lasting impression of Ivan being really happy.'

Skelgill makes a little cough.

'And no further thoughts on the vanishing underwear?'

Now Krista Morocco's lips crease into a gentle smile.

'That, I think I would remember, Inspector.'

Skelgill turns to DS Jones and indicates with a hand that she should take over.

'Ms Morocco – we've spoken with colleagues who worked with Mr Tregilgis and Mr Goldsmith at WNKR Advertising.'

There is perhaps just the very slightest narrowing of Krista Morocco's eyes.

DS Jones continues in a matter-of-fact manner.

'When we last met – you mentioned that you'd had a brief relationship with Ivan Tregilgis around that time. Can you recall exactly when that was?'

Krista Morocco seems to deliberate before forming her reply. She glances at Skelgill, to see that he is observing her closely.

'It began on Valentine's Day. We were held up at a meeting in town – it got to about eight p.m. and Ivan suggested we went for something to eat – and I accepted.'

'Did you know he was engaged?'

Krista Morocco holds the younger woman's gaze.

'So was I, Sergeant.'

DS Jones allows herself a moment to absorb this information.

'And for how long did the relationship last?'

'A couple of months – we only met on a handful of occasions. We lived on opposite sides of London in those days.'

'And was it an intimate relationship?'

'We were very close.'

DS Jones becomes more direct.

'I meant – did you sleep together?'

Now Krista Morocco folds her hands on her lap and takes a few deep breaths. Her gaze moves unseeingly about the items upon her desk.

'There are some things that will always remain private between Ivan and me.'

She looks back at DS Jones – and perhaps there is now the tiniest hint of triumph in her eyes. For whatever is private between her and Ivan Tregilgis is entirely in her power to keep as such.

DS Jones looks ready to press for clarity, but now Skelgill intervenes.

'Krista –' His first use of her Christian name seems to cast the interview into a different mode. Though the woman might reasonably suspect some good-cop-bad-cop ploy is at play. 'You told us you loved Mr Tregilgis – can you explain that in time terms?'

She lowers her eyes. She sighs, and after a moment begins to speak, slowly as if she is finding her words as she goes.

'We fell in love a long time ago – I know that we did, both of us – and I suppose we never fell out of it.'

'Yet you got married – and still are?'

She nods slowly. She looks up, imploringly.

'I've been very lucky with Marco – he's a good man. My feelings for Ivan seemed to exist in a parallel universe.'

'And – since then?'

Krista Morocco looks intently at DS Jones – as if she has noticed something about her reaction that has surprised her. She regards the younger woman almost benevolently, and then turns back to Skelgill.

'I guess you can't stay properly in love with someone you can't have – but something special always remains.'

Skelgill folds his arms. He looks discomfited.

'It was mentioned to us that you'd said Mr Tregilgis had you on his conscience. What did that mean?'

Krista Morocco shakes her head.

'I don't remember saying that to anyone.'

Skelgill ponders for a moment.

'Which of you ended the relationship?'

'I would say that *events* ended the relationship, Inspector. Once Ivan left WNKR to set up with Dermott he was so busy – and I didn't see him for a while because our working relationship was ended. Then it was about a year later that I joined them. By then our engagements had become marriages.'

'When we spoke about this previously you described yourself as having lost out – what did you mean by that?'

'I suppose I was referring to Miriam, that's all – there's no shame in that, Inspector.'

Skelgill is not entirely sure if he agrees, but he accepts her answer.

'How did you feel about Mr Tregilgis and Ms Rubicon?'

It is clear he does not need to elaborate upon his meaning.

'I was hardly in a position to cast any stones, Inspector. I've learned that life is not perfect.' Krista Morocco smiles generously. 'And I wouldn't want to resent Ivan – if he was doing something that made him feel good.' She suddenly laughs. 'To feed us all he had to get his creative energy from somewhere!'

Skelgill raises an eyebrow.

'You're from Sweden, right?'

There seems to be a rather obvious juxtaposition between her permissiveness and his question.

'That's correct.'

'And did you marry in England?'

'Yes – Marco is British, despite the unusual surname. Although his paternal line is originally from the USA.'

'Where did you get married?'

'Just a registry office in Streatham, Inspector – nothing so exotic as Stockholm, or even Stockbridge, Georgia.'

She smiles endearingly.

Skelgill pushes back his chair and straightens his lapels, as if he is making ready to leave.

'You don't have kids – we've asked you that?'

Krista Morocco shakes her head.

'I'm still hoping for that to happen.'

Skelgill regards her thoughtfully. He gets to his feet and DS Jones begins to gather in her notes.

'Oh, there is one thing, Krista.'

Again he has used first name. But she seems unnerved. Is this the detective's classic parting shot?

'That kukri – with the fingerprints – it's been ruled out as the murder weapon.'

'Oh!' Her reaction is of unrestrained delight. She brings up her hands and presses the palms together in the manner of prayer. 'I'm so glad – Mel has been mortified ever since she told you she'd seen me fooling about with a knife. She will be so relieved.'

Skelgill cannot help but be struck by her unselfish concern for her colleague. It is almost as an afterthought that she poses what should surely be the burning question.

'Inspector – does this mean I'm no longer a suspect?'

'It certainly helps.'

34. MIRIAM TREGILGIS

Wednesday, 11.45 a.m.

'I can't believe half of that gear's legal.'

Cutting through Soho towards Cambridge Circus en route to Miriam Tregilgis's apartment, the detectives pause at Skelgill's words beside the window of a fetish accessories emporium.

'They mostly wear it for clubbing, down here, Guv.'

'Then I'm glad that wasn't the type of club you took us to.'

'I didn't take us, we stumbled upon it.'

Skelgill glances suspiciously at his colleague.

'I thought you couldn't remember anything after dinner?'

She beams mischievously.

'Me and Krista Morocco. You believe her, don't you?'

She has him. He gestures to the window.

'Truncheons and handcuffs.'

'A souvenir for the Chief?"

'Behave, Jones.'

Skelgill glowers. She is getting into her stride – he is reminded of her precocious mood last night. He turns and sets off.

'Howay, lass. Else we'll miss her.'

They have been informed that Miriam Tregilgis is unexpectedly on a tight schedule. DS Jones catches him.

'Guv – I thought you were kind to Krista Morocco.'

She says it with good intent,

'Aye, well – happen I'm going soft in my old age.'

Skelgill glances at his colleague like a dog that knows a treat is an outside possibility. But DS Jones is single-minded, and his hoped-for rebuttal is not forthcoming.

'I don't see what she has to lose by being entirely candid. It just creates suspicion.'

Skelgill looks like he disagrees.

'Or shows her confidence in her innocence. We've given her a rough ride – the underwear, the kukri – enough to make most folk clam up. She could have denied the affair with Tregilgis.'

DS Jones nods; Skelgill is right about this.

'I suppose so.'

Skelgill clears his throat.

'One thing you can perhaps answer.'

'Guv?'

'Why would she take those fancy undies to the company party?'

A little paradoxically, she comes to the defence of Krista Morocco.

'They go with nice clothes – it makes you feel nice. It doesn't have to mean anything.'

Skelgill ponders for a moment.

'Then again – she claims she didn't wear any on the night.'

'Now, that must be a Swedish thing.'

*

It is an uncharacteristically flustered Miriam Tregilgis that admits Skelgill and DS Jones to her flat a few minutes later. Beside the door in the long hallway stand a pristine fawn-coloured designer flight bag and a matching attaché case. Miriam Tregilgis sports a smart lime-green two-piece outfit.

'Do you mind awfully if I don't offer you coffee?' She sounds genuinely apologetic. 'It's just that I'm running late and there's a taxi coming at twelve.'

Her aspirated pronunciation of taxi is a reminder of her Welsh provenance.

She delves distractedly into her handbag.

'Any news, Inspector?'

The question seems to come out of the blue.

'We're still hoping you might help us on that front, Mrs Tregilgis.'

'Oh, really?'

Now she turns to a cabinet and rummages in a drawer.

'There has been an attempt at blackmail – letters sent to members of the company.'

She looks up sharply, alarm in her eyes.

'I was wondering if you've received something similar?'

She stares at him blankly.

'Nothing, Inspector – unless it has been addressed to Ivan – there's mail for him that I haven't touched.'

Skelgill looks doubtful.

'Doesn't seem very likely, madam. And no strange phone calls – anything like that?'

She shakes her head.

'Is it a clue – a lead – something to do with the identity of the killer?'

Now Skelgill draws breath.

'It's not as straightforward as that, I'm afraid.'

Miriam Tregilgis is about to speak when the entry phone buzzes stridently. She looks imploringly at Skelgill.

'Can I say I'll be two minutes?'

'Aye.'

She communicates this information via the handset and remains standing by the main door. Skelgill gestures at the luggage.

'Off to the valleys?'

A deeper hue seems to infuse her meticulously applied blusher.

'Well – not the Welsh valleys. Lausanne, actually.'

Skelgill is plainly taken off guard.

'What's that, France?'

'Switzerland.' She takes a step towards him, raising her hands in a placatory manner. 'I'm sorry I haven't let you know yet, but I was going to ring the number you gave me when I got to the airport –

when I get my details, you see?'

'I'm not sure I do, madam.'

'What it is, Inspector – the chance of the trip only came up yesterday – a friend's partner dropped out – and it's just for two nights – then I go up to Edinburgh.'

Skelgill is discomfited.

'If it's all the same, I'd prefer if you could get me your flight numbers and address just now.'

Miriam glances at the entry phone, as though it might summon her again.

'Okay – I'll try, Inspector.'

She fishes her mobile from her handbag and taps out a number. It is answered promptly.

'Hi it's me – no, everything's fine. Look, I need the flight and hotel details for the police.' She traps the phone with her shoulder and produces a leather-bound organiser and an expensive-looking pen. 'Okay – okay – got it.' Then she chuckles. 'There's lovely – see you in about forty-five minutes. Ciao.' She drops the mobile into her bag and tears out and hands a page to Skelgill.

'Thanks.' He frowns as he tries to read her slanting italic script. 'Hotel du Lac. Sounds like my sort of place.'

'It's a health spa.'

'Second thoughts, cancel that.'

And now the buzzer does sound – a longer, insistent press. Miriam Tregilgis looks appealingly at the two detectives.

'Okay – we'll help you down.'

Miriam Tregilgis taps a code into the control panel of a burglar alarm. Skelgill reaches for her flight bag.

'Whoa! It's the kitchen sink!'

Miriam Tregilgis looks amused.

'The bathroom cabinet, actually, Inspector. I prefer my own toiletries. And it lessens the temptation to buy everything they ply you with.'

Skelgill looks inquiringly at DS Jones; she seems content with this explanation. She picks up Miriam Tregilgis's attaché case.

As they begin to descend, Skelgill calls back over his shoulder.

'You said you were going to Edinburgh, madam – is that to do with the company?'

'It is, Inspector. Elspeth phoned me last night. They're organising a get-together – to rally the troops, I suppose. Apparently, we're doing a treasure hunt round the city on Saturday, then there's a barbecue on an island in the Firth of Forth in the evening.'

Skelgill looks perplexed – perhaps even a little shocked.

'How do you feel about that – so soon?'

She shakes her head – but she seems to understand his concern.

'Actually, Inspector – I'm sure Ivan would have approved – he wouldn't have wanted us all to mope about in widow's weeds.'

An image of the females in the company competing in their mourning flashes into Skelgill's mind. But now they reach the ground floor and he sees the taxi driver peering agitatedly through the wired glass. Evidently he is holding down the call button, for there is a distant buzz from above. Skelgill uncompromisingly jerks open the door, eliciting an aggressive *"Oi"* from the shaven-headed cabbie.

Skelgill stares coldly and holds out the flight bag.

'Police.'

This is all he says, but it carries conviction. The man hesitates, but takes the bag, wincing as Skelgill releases its full weight into his possession. He retreats muttering into the refuge of his cab. Skelgill turns to Miriam Tregilgis.

'I've upset your driver.'

'Oh, don't worry, Inspector – there's nothing like the prospect of a tip to bring out the best in people.'

Skelgill holds open the door of the vehicle.

'Mrs Tregilgis – just one question?'

She seems to know that a question of some import is imminent, and she steps away from the taxi.

'Aha?'

'Have you ever been pregnant?'

A shadow seems to cloud her features, and she turns away and climbs into her seat before facing him.

'I don't think I can have children, Inspector.'

35. THE DOWN-TRAIN

Wednesday, 12.30 p.m.

Half an hour after watching Miriam Tregilgis's taxi disappear into Upper St Martin's Lane, Skelgill squints through grimy glass and bright sun as Euston station recedes around a curve of track. Despite the rather depressing outlook he feels a small sense of satisfaction. In a rare sequence of good fortune there had been a tube train waiting to receive them at Leicester Square, and a Glasgow-bound express standing at the ready at the mainline terminus. Now all it requires is the opening of the buffet service.

'You seemed a bit perturbed about Miriam Tregilgis's trip, Guv?'

Skelgill yawns and stretches.

'I've got used to the idea. I can't believe she's smuggling the murder weapon out of the country.'

DS Jones smiles obediently, but she has an angle in this regard.

'I noticed she avoided using her friend's name in front of us.'

Skelgill seems unfazed.

'She sounded natural to me.'

DS Jones indicates to her mobile handset.

'I checked the flight time. It doesn't leave until after four. I think the rush could have been manufactured – to get out of our way.'

Skelgill shrugs but does not argue with her contention.

'Also – you thought her flight bag was heavy.'

'Aye it was. The cabbie nearly broke his wrist.'

'But I carried her attaché case. It felt like it was full of bricks.'

'More make up?'

'What if the Tregilgis's have got a Swiss bank account?'

Skelgill leans back in his seat and shades his eyes from the sun. He gazes at DS Jones pensively.

'Wouldn't she be bringing money *into* the country?'

'Not if someone's paid her.'

'What – she's the blackmailer?'

But now DS Jones looks like it is her superior that is wide of the mark. She takes a moment to compose her reply.

'I was thinking more along the lines of drug money, Guv. The truth is – we've not been able to interview Ivan Tregilgis – we've relied on everyone else for what a decent guy he was. And even there, you could argue. What if this business with Ron Bunce and Grendon Smith is something he were mixed up in? If Miriam Tregilgis found a pile of suspected dirty money, might not she be tempted to take the chance to launder it?'

Skelgill produces the shrew-like countenance that tells of inner discord. Though he nods and makes conciliatory hand gestures, it is plain he finds this hypothesis runs up against the buffers of some deeper instinct. But he contrives a grin and leans forward and taps on the table that separates them.

'Okay, look – keep it in the mix – let's see what develops.' He rubs his eyes – he is clearly tired after last night's inadequate sleep. 'Switzerland – always fancied a crack at the Matterhorn. Right now, though, I'd settle for a Toblerone.'

*

Skelgill returns from the buffet car laden with wrapped rolls and polystyrene cups to find DS Jones has settled down to the Daily Telegraph cryptic crossword.

'I'm getting there.' He takes a couple of lateral steps to accommodate a sudden sideways surge in the train's motion.

'Here, let me take them – yow! You must have asbestos hands.'

'Aye, well – it comes from years of manhandling a Kelly Kettle.' He slides into his seat and begins to deal out the food, two sandwiches each. 'Bacon and-tomato rolls.'

'Guv – one's fine for me.'

'Ah – you never know.'

'I know it won't go to waste.'

Skelgill smirks.

'Got to keep my creative energy up somehow.'

DS Jones raises her eyebrows and affects to busy herself with the crossword. But there is something she has to tell him.

'I just phoned Krista Morocco – about this weekend in Edinburgh.'

'Aye?'

'Well, it suddenly struck me that she hadn't mentioned it to us – but it seems she didn't know – she only got a call from Dermott Goldsmith after we'd left her.'

'What does she reckon to it?'

'Actually, she said she thought it was a good idea – that they'd all left the Lakes in a state of shock and not really said goodbye to one another. She's happy that the two teams can get back together and commiserate properly.'

Skelgill munches industriously, gazing out of the window with a rather glazed expression in his eyes. It could just be the way food has of inducing a temporary state of trance, although there is something about the slow nodding of his head that suggests more profound contemplation. DS Jones waits for him to emerge from his brown study, which is only as long as it takes him to finish his first mouthful.

'I was thinking, Guv – what with the timing of this event in Edinburgh – the deadline for response to the blackmail demand will still be live.'

Skelgill raises his bacon roll and observes her with what could be a frown of reproach. He might just be alluding to her commendably inventive mind, and the competition it faces in the shape of lunch.

She perhaps takes the hint, for she reaches for her folded newspaper.

'Guv – is there a fish called a vendace?'

'What? Aye – vendace. They're like hen's teeth. But I've had a few out of Bass Lake – returned them, mind.'

DS Jones fills in the missing letters.

'How come you know the name, but you've never heard of it?'

She glances up, her hazel eyes inquisitive.

'Oh – it's, er – just the way these clues work – *"Sell star for uncommon swimmer"* – seven letters.'

'Come again?'

Skelgill is patently baffled. DS Jones chuckles.

'I think "sell" is "vend" and "star" is "ace" – and together they make an "uncommon swimmer" – a rare fish.'

Skelgill raises his eyebrows, there is something belligerent about his expression.

'Give us another one, then.'

'Okay.' She peruses the column of clues, and selects one she has not yet crossed off. It appears, however, that she solves it even as she considers it. 'This one's right up your street, Guv. *"Untidy bins even up top"* – two words, three and five letters. Now, the code here is –'

'Nay –' Skelgill interrupts her. 'Pass it over. And the pen – I can't think without a pen.'

He sets to, immediately chewing the pen. DS Jones settles back to watch him cogitate – and in due course, lulled by his mutterings and the rocking motion of the express train, she falls asleep.

*

When DS Jones wakes just as they cross the Manchester ship canal, she sees that Skelgill is now asleep. However, in a moment he too is roused by the ringing of her mobile. They both look about blinking – for there is no sign of the handset – then Skelgill realises it has found its way to the floor beneath their table. He instinctively ducks down to retrieve it – only to find himself staring at stockingless bronzed thighs, and a smooth white triangle of silky underwear. He gropes for the phone and rises with a jolt, cracking his head off the metal rim of the table.

'Aargh ya –'

They are not alone in the carriage, and he only just restrains himself from using an anagram of a medieval Anglo-Danish king. He yields the phone to his colleague, and sits upright, vigorously rubbing his crown, feeling suitably chastised.

It appears he inadvertently answered the call when he grabbed the handset.

'Hi – yes, we're on the train. What – oh, it was the Inspector – my phone fell on the floor.'

There is now a longer pause while she listens – she makes murmurs of encouragement – it seems she is receiving an update of progress. Suddenly she laughs throatily – a little reminder for him of last night – and he wonders to whom she is talking.

When she ends the call she regards him a little warily. In fact she half-heartedly begins to tidy the wrappers and empty cups that litter their space. Then she notices the quartered Daily Telegraph.

'Guv – you finished it!'

'Creative energy – that's three bacon rolls for you.' Skelgill sits back and folds his arms. 'But what was the call about?'

Now she frowns a little.

'Don't shoot the messenger – but the Chief would like an update first thing in the morning.'

Skelgill makes a disparaging face. But then he bows to the inevitable, and folds his long fisherman's fingers before him on the table.

'Better rehearse my excuses.'

But DS Jones's expression becomes combative.

'We have learnt more, Guv. Ivan Tregilgis was popular with his colleagues and the ladies. Dermott Goldsmith wasn't. The latter was immature and probably jealous of the former. Ivan Tregilgis had a relationship with Krista Morocco at the same time as he was

210

engaged to Miriam. Somebody got pregnant. Both of these females continue to be economical with information.'

Skelgill does not look impressed. DS Jones's hazel eyes flash defiantly.

'And you're not a bad dancer.'

Caught entirely off guard, all Skelgill can do is scoff.

'Jones – that proves conclusively you can't remember anything about last night.'

However, he seems buoyed by the compliment.

'I can hardly go in swinging, though.'

DS Jones looks like she might disagree; Skelgill is impressed by her spirit. Now he speaks rather blithely.

'Happen I should have taken a leaf out of Smart's book.'

But DS Jones looks alarmed. He refers to Detective Inspector Alec Smart – a rival of Skelgill's in more ways than one, and a man who might be said to share many of the less endearing characteristics of Dermott Goldsmith. They both know that DI Smart would, on the very first morning, have had the entire Tregilgis & Goldsmith staff subjected to third-degree interrogation.

'Maybe someone would have cracked.'

But DS Jones is unwilling to accept this analysis.

'Perhaps if it were a crime of passion – but not if it were premeditated – they'd have had their excuses at the ready. I think we've done the only sensible thing – and that's to look into the possible motives.'

Skelgill frowns introspectively. It is a few moments before he speaks.

'Remember when we sat down beside Bass Lake – having breakfast?'

'I liked that, Guv.'

He glances at her in surprise – this is not the response he is aiming to elicit. He grins briefly, however.

'I felt – gut feel – that I actually had it in my grasp – something that I'd picked up.'

He shakes his head and shrugs rather dejectedly, and gazes out at the anonymous countryside, passing almost so quickly as to defy description.

DS Jones remains positive.

'Perhaps it will come in time.'

Skelgill looks at her sharply.

'Aye, it better had – before your blackmail window slams shut.'

36. TELEPHONE CALLS

Thursday, 10 a.m.

Skelgill is on the telephone at his desk, in conversation with Edinburgh-based accountant Rory Macdonald.

'So, it's still in the melting pot?'

'In a manner of speaking, Inspector – while your investigation is still active, the insurance company is keeping its head firmly buried in the sand.'

'What if the Coroner deems it unlawful killing?'

'Och – they say so – but, there would be a caveat – the question of who is charged with the crime.'

'Aye, I get your drift.'

There is a moment's polite hesitation at Rory Macdonald's end.

'I don't suppose, Inspector – you're any further?'

Skelgill inhales deliberately.

'Not that I can say – but, I wanted to ask you, sir – your man with the big magnifying glass.'

'Woman, actually.'

'Aye.'

Skelgill waits.

'Well, nothing to set alarm bells ringing – but perhaps one small oddity. Have you heard of Pictorial, Inspector?'

'Can't say I have, sir.'

'It's a local society magazine – a kind of poor man's Hello!'

'Now you mention it – there's a Goldsmith connection, I believe?'

'I'll say. Our lady auditor happens to be a subscriber. She was running a check on national insurance calculations and noticed that the editor is actually on the Tregilgis & Goldsmith payroll.'

'Who decides that sort of thing?'

'We would only take an instruction from a director. Dermott Goldsmith submits a monthly staff update to our payroll department. We process the salaries, PAYE and NICs.'

'Was that something Ivan Tregilgis got involved in?'

'Not that I'm aware of, Inspector – I think that was exclusively Dermott Goldsmith's bag.'

'Okay – well, thanks for letting me know that, sir.'

Skelgill, not known for his note-taking, jots a few untidy words on his pad. Another question for Dermott Goldsmith, perhaps.

*

'Aye, right – aye – well, thanks for that Cam – aye – maybe see you next week. Cheers.' Skelgill replaces the receiver and looks across his desk at DS Jones, who has joined him in his office. 'Cameron sends his regards.'

DS Jones nods gracefully. Then she looks at Skelgill more pointedly.

'Suits you, sir.'

Skelgill grins somewhat sheepishly.

She refers to his polo shirt, the twin of his clubbing attire.

'Aye, well – it's the weather for it.'

More honest an answer would have been expediency, a lack of laundered alternatives. But certainly the early summer heatwave does persist.

'They said on the radio it might break at the weekend.'

Skelgill scowls.

'Not before Saturday, I hope – I'm pistols at dawn with a pike.'

He has not touched a rod since the morning of the murder, and now he gazes longingly out across the landscape beyond his office window, luxuriant and vibrant in the bright heat.

'What news from DS Findlay, Guv?'

Skelgill nods.

'I'd asked him to have a word with Julia Rubicon – about Lady Goldsmith's letter.'

'Did he tell her what it said?'

'Nay – but that didn't prevent her being uncooperative.'

'Really?'

DS Jones does not sound surprised.

'Kept him waiting while she was on the phone – then just ill-tempered and obstructive.'

'And no further forward?'

Skelgill shakes his head. He looks out of the window again, more distractedly now.

'So, I'm going to give her a call – I'd be interested in your thoughts on a line of attack.'

DS Jones regards him with what might be affected intrigue.

'Well – she probably knew that Krista Morocco and Ivan Tregilgis had some history, and possibly she could have got wind of the sale of the company – reasons to think Krista Morocco and Elspeth Goldsmith were worth targeting.'

She stretches out her legs and runs her fingertips down onto her knees. Skelgill's gaze is drawn by his colleague's lithe movements. She looks up sharply, and catches his wandering eyes. He blinks and shakes his head, as though he were daydreaming. DS Jones grins artlessly.

'Or you know what they say about a woman scorned, Guv.'

*

'Why is everyone hassling me?'

'Are they?'

Silence.

'Have you had any threats made against you? It would be sensible to tell us.'

'No.'

'Look, Julia – I'm worried about you – if that's hassling I'm sorry.'

Silence.

'I don't doubt you feel isolated without Ivan to confide in. You obviously had a close working relationship with him.'

'Huh.' The dismissal is one of disdain.

'Come on, Julia – you're successful – incredibly so for your age – you're attractive – you've got everything going for you. It seems to me like you've been dragged into a situation you didn't ask for.'

'Tell me about it.'

'Well, you tell me.'

'There's nothing *to* tell.'

'Listen – think about it – next week I'm going to be up in Edinburgh – we need to do a round of more formal interviews – there must be some things you'd be happier about if they were off your chest.'

Skelgill says it as a matter of fact, rather than posing the question. There is again a silence – though more accommodating – and he makes small circles on his desk with the thumb of his left hand, as though he is picturing her winding a lock of hair anxiously between her own crimson-tipped talons.

'When you say formal – do you mean at the police station?'

'That would be one option. Or at your office if you preferred.'

'Couldn't we go out somewhere – make it look like we were having a drink – without everyone staring at me as if I'm some kind of criminal?'

'I'm not sure that's why they stare.'

Julia Rubicon makes a sharp expiration of breath that hints at an appreciation of the compliment.

'Look, it's fine by me, Julia – but folk might think you're out on a date.'

'That's not one of my problems.'

'I'm surprised to hear that.'

'I've been entirely career-focused since I arrived in Edinburgh, Inspector. When I put my mind to something, I make sure it happens.'

'Thanks for the warning.'

Now there is the semblance of a laugh, husky, from deep in her throat.

After Skelgill has replaced the receiver, he stands up and walks to his window. He separates the venetian blind with two fingers at eye level and lets out a sigh. Beyond the glass it is still sunny and cloudless. After a few moments a hawthorn fly lands on the pane, and his thoughts make the natural connection. There will be the mother of all rises on Bass Lake this evening.

But not for him. He has been roped in to play in the annual cricket match against deadly police rivals from Carlisle. He lets the slats snap shut. As he turns DS Jones enters – she reacts with alarm at the conflicting emotions written across his face.

'How did it go, Guv?'

'What's that?'

'Julia Rubicon.'

He makes a dismissive groan.

'Aye.'

Plainly something about Skelgill's reply does not satisfy her, and she glances at him questioningly. But he is no more forthcoming. She holds out a sheaf of papers.

'The report for the Chief for you to check – I was waiting for you to finish on the phone.'

Skelgill frowns at the prospect.

'When does she need it?'

'About twenty minutes ago – she's got lunch with a couple of journos.'

Skelgill glowers and takes the document to his seat. DS Jones seems reluctant to leave. She notices a folded copy of the Westmorland Gazette lying upon his desk.

'Been doing the crossword?'

'What? – er, no – I was reading the cricket scores.'

'Oh – I heard you're playing tonight.'

Skelgill shakes his head ruefully.

'Don't know why I agreed. The fish'll be jumping into the

boat.'

'Word is you're a bit of a demon bowler, Guv.'

Skelgill pretends to study the first page of the report. DS Jones offers a further prompt.

'George reckons Carlisle have been trying to find out if you're in the team. I thought I might come down and watch – I've got to do my Dad's medication tonight because my Mum's over at her sister's – but not until ten.'

Now Skelgill glances up warily.

'Don't get your hopes up – I haven't bowled since I put my back out rescuing a tourist off Striding Edge last July. Wearing flip-flops.'

'I take it you weren't the one in flip-flops?'

'Nay – but I might have to wear them tonight if I can't find some boots.'

DS Jones grins.

'Apparently there's a bit of a knees-up in The Cross Keys afterwards. According to the jungle drums the Chief's going to put in an appearance – apparently she wants the Blencathra Shield back – at all costs.'

*

'Skelgill.'

He sounds a little out of breath as he answers the call. He has been practising his delivery stride in the limited space available in his office, door firmly closed. Now he flexes his back – it feels to be okay, and his grimaces merely precautionary.

'International call, sir. Sounded like *Floyd*. He said you'd know who it is?'

'Aye, put him on.'

There is a click, and even heavier breathing from the waiting caller.

'Mr Zendik?'

'Call me Ford, Officer.' The American gets straight into his stride. 'Any further?'

Skelgill inhales audibly, by way of lowering expectations.

'Not as far as I'd like, I'm afraid, sir – though I have my suspicions, naturally.'

'Listen Officer – you asked me to let you know if Dermott contacted me – with anything out of the ordinary.'

'Go ahead.'

'He called last night – to put me in the picture, he said.'

'Is this the first time he's been in touch?'

'Yup. He knows we've got an M&A firm working for us in London – he said he'd assumed they gave us the headlines last week. Said that he'd been too messed up to call until now.'

'Ford – M&A?'

'Mergers and acquisitions, Officer.'

'Got it. Did he mention the takeover?'

'Couldn't be more thirsty. Offered me a big discount so long as he gets the top job and a cut of the profits. Said he'd privately thought Tregilgis was pushing for too much and would rather take some of the dough as payment-by-results. And he wants to put the deal back by three months while he gets things straight with the staff. Said he's got a big sympathy thing going with clients right now and could pick up some extra contracts on the back of it.'

'So he was fully informed about the details of your provisional agreement?'

'The heads of terms?'

'That's it.'

'I'd say so, Officer – he sounded pretty au fait to me.'

'Is he afraid of losing the sale, sir?'

'It's been eating him up, all right. When he called I was working late at the office. Then it hit me when I got in this morning – it must have been after three a.m. your time.'

*

Skelgill, following some minutes' contemplation over a mug of tea, dials a number from a list on his desk. He is a little surprised when the call is answered almost immediately.

'Hello?'

'Mr Goldsmith – it's Inspector Skelgill. Do you have a moment?'

'Certainly, Inspector. What can I do for you?'

Skelgill is unprepared for Dermott Goldsmith's amiable manner. He finds himself buying time with a meaningless enquiry.

'How are things going?'

'Oh – we're working at it. Everyone's pulling together. We'll get through this as a team and come out stronger on the other side.'

Skelgill grits his teeth.

'I understand you're having a company get-together this weekend?'

There is a moment's hesitation before Dermott Goldsmith replies.

'That's correct, Inspector. Elspeth and I thought it would be good for morale. Especially given the state of limbo at present. Unless you have – er –?'

'No arrest as yet, I'm afraid, sir.'

'I see. That is a shame. I was hoping that's why you had called.'

Dermott Goldsmith inhales as though he is about to add something, but then thinks the better of it. Skelgill fills the void.

'I gather Mrs Tregilgis will be joining you in Edinburgh?'

'Yes.' Now he adds, hurriedly, 'I mean, she insisted – there was no pressure, Inspector.'

'Life must go on.'

Dermott Goldsmith sounds encouraged by Skelgill's further use of a platitude.

'Just what I said, Inspector. And we've got an obligation – to the business – to one another – our jobs – our livelihoods.'

Skelgill senses that the man is still a little traumatised from the perhaps somewhat unfair interview of the previous week. Without total success, he attempts a tone that expresses solicitude.

'If your company was taken over, sir – would that mean job

losses?'

Dermott Goldsmith is quick to answer.

'Unlikely, Inspector – we run a tight ship – that's one of the reasons we're attractive to so many potential buyers – our ratios are the envy of the industry.'

'But isn't it usual – when there's a takeover – for the new owners to put their own people into the key jobs – what about your office heads, for instance?'

'Well – you can never say *never*, Inspector – but I should have thought their jobs would be safe in such circumstances. They know the clients best, after all.'

'And how are the two ladies bearing up?'

This seems to be a question to which Dermott Goldsmith has not devoted much thought.

'I, er – think they're fine – just getting on with the job.'

'I see, sir – okay. Well, that's about it for now –' Skelgill pauses a little melodramatically, as though a final question lurks in the wings. 'One of my Edinburgh colleagues mentioned you had an involvement with a magazine called Pictorial?'

But Dermott Goldsmith does not betray any discernible unease.

'Oh, we, er – we place ads with them – and they cover some of our corporate events – cocktail evenings, sponsored awards dinners, that kind of thing. Guaranteed publicity – our clients like their five minutes of fame, you know?'

'I see, sir – that must be what it was.'

*

Skelgill is ruminating upon his conversations of the past couple of hours when his phone rings once more. It must interrupt him at an especially profound moment, for he glowers at the handset, ignores it for some while, and finally – when the caller refuses to desist – barks his greeting.

'Skelgill.'

There is a sudden stiffening of his demeanour. Then an

unfamiliar change of tone.

'Yes Ma'am.'

'Sorry Ma'am – I was just finishing a call to a potential witness on my mobile, Ma'am.'

'Right Ma'am – of course, Ma'am.'

'I realise it's important, Ma'am – I'll make it my top priority.'

'I'll do my best, Ma'am.'

The caller abruptly clears, and Skelgill is left with the handset dangling and the distinct impression that there is only one thing that will find him in deeper water than if he does not soon crack the Bewaldeth Hall case, and that is defeat in the Blencathra Shield.

37. IT'S NOT CRICKET

Thursday, 10 p.m.

The late hour finds Skelgill, largely oblivious to the beery commotion around him, staring thoughtfully through a pale-amber pint of Cumbrian ale at the distorted image of the Man-of-the-Match trophy on the bar just behind it. *His* Man-of-the-Match trophy, no less.

*

Yet the game had not begun auspiciously for Skelgill, who turned up at the local sports ground fifteen minutes late – much to the consternation of his teammates. Fortunately, the opposition had won the toss and inserted Penrith in to bat, with Skelgill listed well down the order. Next he discovered he had omitted to pack a white shirt, which meant he would have to wear the pale-blue polo top in which he had arrived for work that morning, and suffer the wrath of the changing room. Meanwhile, in ponderous style his team proceeded to prop and cop their way in the face of accurate and at times hostile Carlisle bowling to the ominously modest total of 111, for the loss of five wickets – a score that would not have brought home the Blencathra Shield in the last decade. The services of Skelgill, padded up and due to go in at number eight, had thus not been required (a double relief to him, since he had also forgotten his protector). Instead, he had spent much of the innings chatting with DS Jones, whom he had spotted sitting alongside a couple of the admin staff on a bench on the far boundary. Most of the crowd – which numbered a good hundred – plus the non-batters, were thronged around the pavilion, their attentions divided between on-field events (or lack of) and the ducking of errant cricket balls emanating from a group of young lads who had raided the spare kit. Certainly there had been no such danger from the direction of the middle.

There ensued a short tea-interval, for the teams only, a sit-down affair with cucumber sandwiches, during which Skelgill was regaled with sardonic locker-room humour along the lines of:

'Ah, thou've graced us with thou presence, then.'

'Can't thee stop work for a minute, lad?'

'It's not work 'e's up to – eh, Skelly, lad?'

'He's been playin' to a gallery of one.'

'Aye – we saw thee sniffin' round Fast-track.'

'Is she a nat'rel blonde, eh Skelly?'

'Yon lad's got no chance – t' lass'll eat 'im alive.'

There was much guffawing, and solid thumping between Skelgill's shoulder blades. For the second time in the day, he was relieved that DS Jones had been well out of earshot.

*

As fate would have it, when Penrith took the field Skelgill had been promptly posted to the deep – more or less in front of DS Jones's vantage point – on the grounds that he had a 'good arm'. In the meantime, the team's regular pair of opening bowlers began to ply their trade. However, while Penrith had scratched around for runs in their innings, Carlisle experienced no such difficulties, with ten coming off the first over, and a score of thirty-five for nought being clocked up by the end of the sixth. At this rate they would win at a canter. One batter in particular – a sullen stranger suspected of being on assignment from the Leicestershire force – was especially making hay, and continued to post the ball to all corners of the ground. As tendrils of discontent began to insinuate themselves among the uneasy home crowd, rumblings about his origins began to surface. Following another clean hit for six by the East Midlander, the most vocal local wag – despite being a policeman – was unable to contain himself any longer and yelled out, "Bloody ringer!" – thus drawing angry rebuttals from the assembled Carlisle batters-in-waiting.

With the score already past seventy, in the next over things had gone from bad to worse for Penrith – and for Skelgill in particular. Fielding right on the rope at deep long leg, DS Jones almost beside him, Skelgill was halfway through an anecdote when a cry went up of, "Skelly – catch eet!" The bowler had pitched one short and the big East Midlander had gone for a hook. Skelgill initially reacted by setting off to his left, following the line of the shot, but the batsman had spliced the ball and it was instead sailing high in the direction of fine third man. Skelgill, whose cracked off-white boots had seen better days, and were now lacking half their studs, suddenly picked up the flight and abruptly changed direction, slipping on the dewy outfield as he did so. This lost him a precious second, and as he dashed frantically across it looked like he would not make it. At the last moment, however, he took off in a swallow dive and made the catch in his outstretched, but weaker right hand inches above the turf – only to land with a crunching impact that jolted the ball free of his grip. To add insult to injury it rolled over the boundary for four, and Skelgill acquired a great green smear across his expensive shirt. (Later in the pub an old lady would advise him to "soak it int' yowe's milk.")

This event, of course, was manna from heaven for the wag, now in full sarcastic flow:

"Skelgill – what *can* thee catch?"

Given the current lack of progress in the Bewaldeth case, the significance of this remark was not lost on a good many present, not least the Chief, who had silently appeared at the side of the congregation, unashamedly intending to bask in the reflected glory of the rightful outcome.

Skelgill threw the ball back angrily to the keeper and stood with his hands on his hips, shaking his head.

"Nice try, Guv."

DS Jones had encouraged him, but he was too full of self-admonishment to respond. Thankfully, as Skelgill was later able to reflect, this turned out to be his nadir.

At the end of the over the Penrith skipper, a fresh-faced DC, had trotted down from slip to speak with the disconsolate Skelgill.

"Hard luck, Sir."

His brown eyes were calm beneath a bloodstained bandage. Batting earlier, bravely without a helmet he'd taken a vicious bouncer square on the brow.

"It was a miracle you even got to that."

An embarrassed shrug from Skelgill.

'Look, Sir – we need this devil out. Will you take this over?"

He had tossed the ball to his surprised superior.

Thus Skelgill had come on to bowl. He asked the skip for a run-saving ring of fielders and meanwhile marked out his fourteen-pace approach. The East Midlander, now facing, after a single off the last ball, was five short of his half-century, and seemed to be steering Carlisle home to their fourth victory in a row.

Umpire to Skelgill: "Right-arm over?"

Skelgill to umpire: "Left-arm round."

Umpire to batsman: "Left-arm round."

The batter moved his guard across to middle and took up his stance. Skelgill's first delivery, a loosener, was overpitched, and was deservedly despatched to the boundary for four. The next would have suffered the same fate, but for a smart bit of work by the skipper at mid-off. There were rumblings in the pavilion, and the wag could be heard winding up for his next broadside.

Then came the turning point.

The first two half volleys had been meat and drink to the batsman, his eye firmly in. But Skelgill is a lot faster a bowler than his medium-pacer's run up suggests. With a fisherman's whip and timing – that can send a fly skimming a good sixty yards across the water – he is deceptively quick. His third delivery was short of a length and the East Midlander instinctively leaned back to pull –

226

but the ball was upon him and before he knew it he had spooned it back down the wicket high above Skelgill's head. Instantly, up went the panic-inducing chorus of "Catch eeeet!"

Skelgill, neck craned skywards and eyes bulging, turned from his follow-through and like a man possessed levelled the stumps, the non-striker and the umpire – but emerged triumphantly from the resulting ruck clutching the ball. As he was surrounded by jubilant teammates, he caught a glimpse of DS Jones on the boundary, hopping about and clapping excitedly.

As the applause died down for the retreating East Midlander, out for 49, the wag took the opportunity to punctuate the silence.

'Aye – 'e can catch 'em off've 'is *own* bowling!'

But the careful listener might have detected a first hint of jubilation – and perhaps, even, hope – beneath the thickly layered irony.

The incoming batter had let Skelgill's next two balls go through to the keeper, but the final delivery of the over, pitched just short on middle-and-leg had forced him to play – but it lifted barely a couple of inches and struck the back pad ankle-high.

"Owzat!"

The entire Penrith team went up in unison – it was clear even to the fielder at cover point that the man was trapped plumb leg-before-wicket – but evidently not to the Carlisle umpire adjudicating at the bowler's end.

"Not out."

Skelgill had walked back to his position in the field deep in thought.

As is often the case, the next over had brought another wicket – again not without controversy, since the batsmen, caught-behind off a snick to the keeper that was audible halfway to Brough, had refused to walk and had to be sent on his way by the Penrith umpire, in the shape of George Appleby, Desk Sergeant. Such insubordination on the part of the opposition simply served to heighten the determination of the home side and its supporters.

The wag took the opportunity to introduce a touch of

hyperbole.

"They don't like eet when they're ont' run!"

Though this met with the general approval of those around him, it was hard to ignore the facts. Carlisle needed only twenty-seven runs to win, with eight wickets still in hand. Any such gloating was severely premature.

Skelgill, however, had other ideas. On the grounds that he would get no assistance from the surly Carlisle umpire officiating at his end, he switched to bowl over the wicket at the start of his next over. Although this decision brought perplexed expressions to the faces of his teammates, they were quickly erased as he proceeded to hit the dead spot on the pitch and take out the batsmen's off-stump with an unplayable grubber.

The very next ball Skelgill repeated the feat. And then, with the crowd roaring him in – he did it again! A hat-trick. All bowled. All grubbers!

Carlisle had subsided to 85 for 5 and chaos broke out. There was a fourth wicket in Skelgill's over – this time a simple caught-and-bowled as he fooled the batter with a slow delivery – and then another run-out in the following over as Carlisle's panic-stricken lower order began to scramble for singles.

With the tension mounting and the light fading into dusk, two further wickets fell (both to Skelgill). But the score was edging ever closer to the modest Penrith total. Indeed, it stood at 101 for 9 when Carlisle's last man came out to the middle. A tall, craggy paceman, he had been responsible for the blow that had earlier cracked the Penrith skipper's skull. He looked like he was more than capable of swinging a bat, but Skelgill wasn't about to allow him that luxury. He glanced at his skipper as he walked back to his mark and gave an almost imperceptible nod. The unseen message was passed on to the fielders. Skelgill spun on his heel and sprinted in, unleashing his fastest delivery of the match. It whistled past the astonished giant's nose and had him hopping backwards like a great mantis. The next ball embedded itself in his ribcage with a satisfying thud and saw him appealing voicelessly to the umpire for protection.

A Carlisle player, yelling plaintively from the pavilion, had called for leniency.

"Come off it, lads – he's a Number Eleven."

But the wag, now in full partisan flow, was ready for him.

"Get on wi'it – if thee kernt tek eet – thee shunt dish eet out!"

The number eleven didn't have to *tek eet* much longer. Stepping fearfully away from Skelgill's third approach he was suckered and clean bowled by an arrowing yorker. A tumultuous roar went up from the boundary; grown men hugged one another (and took turns with DS Jones – who had gravitated to the centre of the excitement); small boys streamed out to the middle; and the wag surreptitiously stowed his baseball cap out of sight, having bet someone – at the point that Skelgill had come on to bowl – that he would eat it if Penrith won.

Sportingly, the Carlisle captain and his team shuffled onto the outfield to clap-in the winners, and Skelgill (doing his best to appear modest and surprised by his achievements) was given the honour of leading his side off. Even the big paceman shook his hand, wincing and admitting, "I'd 'ave done t'same mesen, marra."

Thereafter, for most participants it had been a case of frantically stuffing one's kit into one's bag, and of joining the exodus to the pub. When Skelgill finally surfaced, his sweaty exploits requiring him to take a shower, he'd found DS Jones waiting for him in the descending gloom.

"Give you a lift to The Keys?"

"I thought you had to look after your Dad tonight?"

"Time enough to buy you a drink – you were brilliant, Guv."

Skelgill had grinned ruefully.

"If I could do that on purpose I'd be playing for England."

*

Thus it is that Skelgill finds himself, innumerable pints later, perched at the bar with only his trophy for company. DS Jones duly purchased a celebratory round as promised, departing shortly after the presentations by the Chief, including the Man-of-the-Match award to a bashful Skelgill, for his haul of 7 wickets for 18 runs in 4.3 overs – a record return in the long and illustrious history of the Blencathra Shield.

But it is not upon his wizardry with the ball that he now reflects, nor the Chief's public words of congratulation. A little later – before taking her leave – she had motioned him aside to impart the disconcerting news that his time was running out; she referred to the murder of Ivan Tregilgis. She needs a result, and if – just like this evening – to bring that about requires a change of bowling (so to speak) – then so be it. DI Smart will be given a crack at the case unless there is significant progress by close of play on Monday.

Skelgill sighs and slips down off the barstool. Leaving his pint and his trophy where they stand, he casually makes his way through a door marked for the gents. The conveniences are situated across a yard at the back of the pub. But Skelgill is merely using this route to make an inconspicuous exit. A ginnel leads from the yard into the main street, and from there he can pick up a taxi.

But, just as he passes the door of the toilets, out stumbles the wag, more than a little the worse for wear.

'Skelly, marra – thou won it off your own back!'

'Aye, thanks – it's *bat*, isn't it?'

Doubly puzzling when the matchwinner is a bowler!

38. READING

Friday, 8.30 a.m.

Skelgill, en route to the office on Friday morning, becomes diverted by an 'all-cars' emergency following a bizarre incident on the northbound M6. Evidently, a hostile convoy of animal-rights protestors and ramshackle hippies' charabancs had been shadowing a travelling circus from Lancaster. As they neared Penrith these wacky races had abruptly halted owing to a sizeable and probably mutually intentional coming together of those in the van. The entire carriageway was blocked by debris, a minor pitched battle broke out between the opposing forces, and assorted exotic species of animals were reported to be roaming southbound and in adjacent fields (although this proved to be somewhat exaggerated).

By the time Skelgill reaches the scene, however, tempers have cooled, and several of the protagonists are being led away towards a fleet of brightly marked police patrol cars. Skelgill makes himself useful by circulating among the smouldering groups and unceremoniously snuffing out any remaining flickers of enmity with a few well-chosen words of Anglo-Saxon wisdom. Such pragmatism wins him the respect of the warring parties, and he finds himself enjoying strong tea and gypsy toast inside an immaculate caravan with a trio of exceedingly attractive female acrobats (although he half suspects this is a ploy to keep his prominent policeman's nose from poking where it isn't wanted).

Thankfully nobody has been seriously injured in the confrontation, which was more handbags than handguns, and the vehicles are soon safely lined up on the hard shoulder. The circus elders opt to continue their journey towards Scotland, and not press charges (and, yes, they'll go right now, thanks, and – no thanks – they won't need an escort) in return for the police sending back the new age travellers whence they came. Skelgill is later amused to hear of a twist in the tale, concerning a pair of enthusiastic constables who radioed to say they had cornered a group of escaped llamas, while simultaneously a farmer's wife was telephoning to report that strange men in black were rustling her valuable rare-breed wool-alpaca flock.

*

When, finally, he does arrive at headquarters, shortly before lunchtime, Skelgill wonders if he has imagined the whole affair. The same can be said for the bewildering events of the previous evening, were it not for two aspects. First, his aching muscles, and the stiffness in the small of his back. Second, he enters his office to find upon his desk a neat display of objects: his forsaken Man-of-the-Match trophy, a cheap gold-effect winner's medal in a flip-up black plastic display case and – touchingly – what appears to be the bruised and scuffed match ball. He phones Desk Sergeant George Appleby.

'Hey up, George.'

'Skelly, lad – didn't see you come in. Hear the clowns were out in force on the M6 this morning.'

'Aye, very good, George – and that was just our lot.'

'What can I do for you?'

'I just wanted to say thanks – I presume this cricket stuff was you?'

'No problem, lad.'

'I was a bit distracted last night.'

'I hear the Chief's given you while Monday.'

Skelgill hisses bleakly.

'How come that's got out?'

'You know how word gets around. Apparently, Alec Smart's been putting it about that it's his case, all bar the shouting.'

With a few notable exceptions, that include Angling Times, his beloved Wainwright guides, and maps of any description, reading is anathema to Skelgill. It is a handicap that he has borne for as long as he can remember, and something for which he has developed various survival strategies. Prime amongst these, in the analysis of written evidence, is to get someone else to do it.

Today, however, given the 'sword of Damocles' dangled over him by the Chief, he has determined to put his nose to the grindstone, in the possibly vain hope that something will strike him (not the sword, of course) that others may not notice. He begins with a series of reports helpfully compiled by DS Jones, prefaced in each case with a short note that highlights the most salient aspect. The first concerns the hotelier, Mrs Groteneus, and carries the emboldened legend, *"No trace of Groteneus spouse."*

According to Mrs Groteneus, her husband had left her some ten years earlier to return to his native South Africa, to Johannesburg. It appears that technically they are still married, though she has lost touch with him and claims not to have heard from him since. Nor, it seems, has anyone else, as the Jo'burg cops can find no record of such a person. Of course, the man could be somewhere else altogether, and Mrs Groteneus would be none the wiser. Skelgill flirts briefly with the idea of Mr Groteneus having never left the premises, instead living in secret in the attic, to spy upon and selectively murder guests – not such a crazy notion, as anyone who has read of H. H. Holmes would testify.

'Come off it, Skelgill.'

He turns the page with a certain finality.

"Drugs suspect." The next report features the shady Ron Bunce. It seems DS Jones's hunch is correct. While Bunce has no criminal record to speak of (although two dubious acquittals for alleged grievous bodily harm), there is an official file being kept: he is under surveillance by UK Border Force, suspected of trafficking drugs out of Africa and into Europe via the British colony of

Gibraltar. But Skelgill has already pointed out to DS Jones his difficulties with the hitman-theory, and the notion that a narcotics connection would somehow extend to Ivan Tregilgis seems improbably tenuous. Yes, there is a possible legal action – but it had not appeared to be giving Ron Bunce any sleepless nights – and in any event Ivan Tregilgis's death would not make the writ go away.

"Smith trail cold." Thus is headed the third report. Background checks into Grendon Smith have so far drawn a blank. Nobody as yet has been forthcoming from the companies suspected of involvement in his alleged 'cash-for-projects' scheme, nor has anything turned up amidst Ivan Tregilgis's admin that indicates Smith had been formally put on notice of legal action. The only fingerprints on the blackmail note received by Krista Morocco belong to her, a PC from Charing Cross, and Skelgill. A survey of staff in the London office of Tregilgis & Goldsmith has concluded that there has been no contact with Smith since his sacking. And at the present time his home telephone is disconnected for non-payment, and his mobile is diverting to voicemail.

Skelgill sits back and consults his watch. One o'clock. He stands up, extracts his wallet and car keys from his jacket, hoists up the venetian blind and promptly climbs out of the window onto a fire escape. A seasoned Skelgill watcher might find this behaviour out of character. As the newly installed saviour of the station's honour for his exploits on the cricket field, why not take the long route to the canteen to bask with ingenuous modesty in the rays of adulation that will surely be showered upon him? But today that prospect is heavily overshadowed by the prospect of staring eyes that know he is living on borrowed time in regard to the Bewaldeth case.

He drives the short distance into the centre of Penrith and parks at a supermarket. Inside he buys a sandwich, which he quickly dispatches while heading on foot to his favoured fishing tackle shop. Radios playing and occasional voices drift from open windows of the small houses that crowd the kerb. The sun is cracking the cobbles and melting the tarmac. But to Skelgill's trained weather eye a change is in the air. High up in the blue, great swirling mares' tails of cirrus are sliding in from the west: an innocuous-looking advance cavalry, but harbingers nonetheless of the legion of great grey clouds that will inevitably follow. The forecasters have got it right.

The consensus in the tackle shop is that the rain will come by midday tomorrow. The mother of all depressions is whipping itself into a frenzy over the Atlantic, in preparation for a charge at Britain: it is predicted to rout the prevailing anticyclone. Skelgill brags that he will be enjoying pie and chips and ale in his local by then; he plans to be out on Bass Lake well before dawn.

His spirits buoyed by this thought, he purchases some treble-hooks and a couple of wire traces, and even contemplates buying a mean-looking plastic plug, the type of lure that imitates an injured fish when retrieved jerkily through the water. Generally he manufactures his own plugs; indeed his two most successful models started their lives as a pool cue and a paintbrush handle respectively. The latter has played a blinder through the winter months, but has suffered a loss of form more recently – hence Skelgill's musings over a last-minute substitution. In the event, after some deliberation, he decides to stick with his tried and trusted rig.

Retracing his steps he returns to his desk by the same clandestine means he left it, only to find that without the protective blind in place his office has filled up with winged insects. Now he spends the next ten minutes variously swatting and shepherding them out, according to his prejudices about their habits or value as bait. For blowflies and clegs the outlook is not good, whereas craneflies and lacewings can have greater cause for optimism unless they behave with singular stupidity and refuse to go quietly.

Aerial distractions eliminated, Skelgill settles down for an afternoon of further reading. He purses his lips in an act of concentration. Some years back he attended an NLP training course, and had been classified as a 'visual' person. This had delighted him, confirming a phobia that had begun at school with

235

an aversion to the printed page, and which continues to this day with a dread of challenges such as he faces now. He gathers himself, pen poised – and then gets up and digs in his pocket for change for the hot drinks machine.

*

It is just after three-thirty p.m. when DI Smart's weaselly countenance insinuates itself into the narrow gap between Skelgill's door and the jamb.

'Alright, Skel?'

Skelgill looks up, his expression darkening. He does not consider DI Smart a friend, nor is he endeared by his use of the familiar. DI Smart is undeterred.

'Hear you were cock of the walk last night. Nice one.'

Skelgill shrugs.

'Didn't see you there.'

'Leave.' Smart sidles uninvited into the office and rests an elbow upon Skelgill's cabinet. 'Went for a meal in Manchester. New afro-asian fusion restaurant. First outside London.'

Skelgill, still unsmiling, gives a faint nod of disinterest.

DI Smart's eyes rove hungrily around Skelgill's office, like a shoplifter casing a new store. Skelgill has moved the cricketing paraphernalia to the cabinet, and now DI Smart picks up the cricket ball and weighs it in his hand, as if he knows what he doing. He attempts to flip it, and it falls with a clunk and rolls conveniently towards Skelgill's desk, affording him the opportunity to make further ground.

'How's the case going?'

He reaches out casually to pick up one of DS Jones's reports. Skelgill is too quick for him and slaps a proprietorial hand on the item.

'Between you and me, Smart,' (Skelgill lowers his voice to the level of the conspiratorial) 'I've cracked it. Have it all tied up by Monday morning.'

DI Smart jerks back, his sharp features seeming to pale.

236

'Right. Nice one.'

His left eye seems to develop a tic.

Skelgill stares implacably.

'Was there something?'

'Er – no. I just, er – came to say well done, cock.'

He replaces the ball beside Skelgill's trophies, and then gestures towards the pile of admin.

'I'll leave you to it. Nice one.'

He backs out of the office with a curt nod.

Skelgill gazes forlornly towards the window, to freedom and beyond. He takes a deep breath and releases it slowly. Then he turns back to the stack of papers that shackle him to his desk.

39. BACK ON BASS LAKE

Saturday, dawn

Skelgill paddles watchfully beneath a lowering ceiling of cloud that might have been hewn from Lakeland slate. Dawn is on hold, and even the birds are subdued; save for a cackling mallard that breaks ranks, somewhere in the reeds, finally getting last night's joke. Otherwise it is only the occasional resonant plop of a brown trout sipping an unlucky mayfly from the surface that punctuates the silence.

Periodically Skelgill cranes over his shoulder, trying to discern his position from the indistinct silhouette of Skiddaw in the east. After a few minutes more – now satisfied – he draws in his dripping oars and allows the boat to drift. Hand over hand, he weighs anchor, though in the windless dale he could probably manage without. Bassenthwaite Lake lies mercury-flat in its shallow basin; the air, heavy and humid, blankets the water.

Now that Skelgill is becalmed, the midges that have trailed him from the hanger at Peel Wyke move in – perhaps exacting revenge for their cousins displayed about his office walls. He pulls down his *Tilley* hat and raises his collar, grimacing as he resists the Lilliputian torture. Swiftly he hooks up a pair of slippery dead baits, and casts them out thirty degrees either side of the stern. Setting down the second of the rods, he yields to the agony – death by a thousand bites – and rubs fish scales into his hair and ears in an effort to dislodge the invisible assassins.

Indeed, he spends the next few minutes protecting himself from the no-see-ums. He fits a beekeeper's veil beneath his hat, and rummages for repellent in a tin of tackle, smearing it upon the backs of his hands. Then he casts about, trying to decide what to do next. At three-thirty a.m. it is still too dark to employ a plug to good effect – and, anyway, his spine is still stiff from bowling and he does not relish the nagging method that plugging demands. Instead he opts for his trusty perch rod, rigged at the tip with a small piece of bent-over lead (formerly a section of water pipe) and a size ten hook on a dropper eighteen inches above. As a finishing touch he adds a juicy wriggling brandling, and with a flick of his wrists he sends the whole arrangement spinning a chain's length to starboard. He waits half a minute, and then begins a slow, deliberate retrieve. Almost immediately there is a bump. Then a bump-bump. Then he strikes – and – yes! – the fish is hooked.

On many a drunken night he has argued angling's corner: the greatest feeling on earth – scoring a goal or hooking a fish? (This after certain more primal urges have been excluded by mutual agreement). Man's primitive emotions at play: the tribal battle versus the solitary hunt. Of course, such a debate leads to inevitable stalemate, with neither party sufficiently comprehending the other's perspective. But for him – more of a lone wolf than a pack dog – there is nothing to surpass the sublime split second of solitary anticipation and triumph. I did it. And I did it my way.

The perch is giving a good account of itself. A pound and a half, he would guess. He plays it unfussily, then draws it unerringly into his waiting landing net. He unhooks it carefully with pliers on a piece of old carpet, and in the waxing light admires its tiger stripes and hump-backed profile, the pike-scarred warrior that it is. He raises its jagged dorsal fin, as always, remembering his father's hissed warning upon his very first catch – words that came too late; blood was already streaming from his palm, tracking his lifeline. That small specimen was sent spinning in his agony; now he weighs the fish carefully in one hand, gripped from below, revising his estimate upward to two pounds (worth three in the pub later). Then he leans over the bow and reverently feeds the creature back into the meniscus, feeling its kick as it realises its freedom.

He wipes his hands on his jacket and taps out a satisfied drumbeat on his thighs. Maybe it's going to be his day?

But this view is soon tempered. On the very next cast he snags a sunken obstacle. It had felt like a take and instinctively he struck – driving the hook deeper. It is not an uncommon problem on Bass Lake; all manner of debris flows down the Derwent and passes through its waters bound for the sea. Patiently he hauls in the anchor, and by waggling one oar manoeuvres the boat so that he can tug from the opposite direction. But still the hook will not dislodge. It may be a matter of brute force or bust. He increases the pressure, winding down until the tip of the rod arcs into the water. Now, steadily he lifts, grimacing, teeth barred teeth. And then – it gives – not a snap, but a shift – and slowly he is able to bring up his catch – it breaks the surface with a hiss, glistening black and slimy – a long-sunken branch.

How!

The sudden revelation recalls his dream – nightmare, more like – from which he was released by his alarm barely an hour ago. He was here on the lake – playing a great fish – hanging on, rather. For he'd hooked the fabled *Mameluke* (a childhood appropriation) – a blind Ice Age monster, as old as the glacial mere itself. It dived deeper than he knew the lake to be, and threw his boat about at will. And yet, though he could win no line, suddenly the creature began to tire, and its fearsome pull became an immense dead weight. Inch by inch he reeled it in, but when it broke the surface there was no fish – but a jet-black suit of armour like those that guard the passage at Bewaldeth Hall. Foul water spouted from the helmet – and the visor fell open, as if in an anguished gasp for air. Inside, a staring skull – its jaw flapping – the rank breath of stagnant death filled the air – it was the missing husband, Groteneus!

Now he shudders, and leans to reach the branch, like he might grasp the wrist of a shipwreck survivor. The hook gleams, bereft of its worm – perhaps a crafty perch saw its opportunity – and he frees it with a sharp tug. Relieved, he releases the dead wood to find its resting place.

He lays down the rod; his momentum is stilled – and he should really re-cast the dead-baits to keep them from becoming tangled. Instead he wipes his hands on his jacket and hauls his rucksack from the bow. A mug of tea is called for.

He unfastens the top strap and parts the drawstring with both hands. But even in the dim light of dawn he can see that his flask is not there. In disbelief he delves into the bag's depths – to no avail. Of course, he has his Kelly Kettle – but he can't set a fire in a wooden-hulled boat. He pulls off his hat and veil and draws his fingers through his hair, as if he is trying to scrape the memory from some recess of his mind. He stares across the water; a fine mist, like steam is beginning to coat the surface. He nods. He remembers where he left his flask. He can picture it now – standing upon the dishwasher, where he had searched for his insulated mug.

The dishwasher.

His grey-green eyes slowly track across Bassenthwaite Lake to the distant but distinctive half-hidden gables of Bewaldeth Hall.

Five minutes later he is pulling hard for the shore.

40. FLIGHT TO EDINBURGH

Saturday, 8 a.m.

'Guv – you seem to have glitter in your hair.'

'Scales.'

'Pardon?'

'It'll be fish scales. I was on Bass Lake this morning.'

'This morning? But it's only eight now.'

'Aye, well – I made an early start.'

DS Jones stares at the road ahead. Skelgill had called her at six-thirty, giving her an hour to get ready. Now they speed down the on-slip from the Penrith junction of the M6, Skelgill accelerating into the sparse Saturday morning traffic. He has a theory, which he is not yet ready to share.

'Do you know who it is, Guv?'

It takes Skelgill a good ten seconds to answer.

'Aye, happen I do.'

'Why don't you want me to know?'

'In case I'm wrong – someone needs to remain objective.'

'So why are we going to Edinburgh at twice the limit?'

'If I'm right, Jones – someone's in danger.'

'Who?'

'I'm not sure.'

'Any evidence?'

'Gut feel.' He grips the steering wheel, his arms straight out in front. 'Mainly.'

DS Jones is silent for a minute or so.

'Okay, so am I allowed to know what we're doing?'

'Joining the party.'

'The Tregilgis & Goldsmith gathering?'

'Aye.'

She is perplexed.

'What will we do?'

'We'll cross that bridge when we reach it.' He grins wryly. 'If I'm proved right, Jones – tonight, the curry's on me. No expense spared. Full banquet, Taj Mahal.'

DS Jones sighs; she does not sound entirely convinced.

They skim above the River Esk at Metal Bridge; Skelgill, out of habit, cranes to check the tide and glean a tantalising glimpse of the distant Solway. Another minute or so and they cross the border, sweeping past Gretna, where many an ill-suited marriage has been made.

'Here it comes.'

DS Jones refers to the plump drops of rain that begin to spatter the windscreen, exploding like water bomblets. The warm front has made landfall, and is rapidly overhauling their flight to the Scottish capital.

*

'Ye brought the weather, Danny.'

No amount of rain can dampen DS Findlay's dry greeting.

'You'll be calling me a Jonah, next – and that's all we need.'

'Maybe I'd better drive, then.'

This brief conversation is conducted through car windows; accordingly Skelgill and DS Jones make a dash for DS Findlay's vehicle. They have rendezvoused at a sprawling shopping centre on the outskirts of Edinburgh. Families are already arriving for a day's entertainment. Small boys break away to stamp in puddles and be scolded ineffectually, until they dodge into the mall where they can skylark unsupervised.

'You guys nae got any waterproofs?'

'Plenty in my motor, Cam – but I'm hoping we shan't need

them.'

DS Findlay nods.

'Aye, well – we can park right outside their hotel – it's down in the New Town, Great King Street.'

DS Findlay navigates first through a new business park of burgeoning brick and glass structures, thence through housing estates of unkempt privet hedges and rendered post-war tenements and graffiti that adorn walls and installations. Parked cars are thin on the ground, and those present reflect the air of austerity that pervades the district.

DS Findlay notices his colleagues' slightly ghoulish fascination.

'All fur coat and nae knickers.'

Skelgill and DS Jones exchange an uneasy glance – their colleague cannot know that the popular aphorism about the Scots capital cuts close to the bone.

Soon they join the main Glasgow road, turning east for Edinburgh city centre. At Roseburn, a narrow urban canyon of Victorian tenements with small shops at ground level, Skelgill requests they pull over. DS Jones gazes through the rain-streaked glass – there is a nail bar, a sauna – ah, and baker's – that might be it. But Skelgill dashes back some fifty yards to a bridge, and leans over the parapet. Beneath, the Water of Leith is beginning to run swift and dark. He returns, a little wet for his trouble.

'What was it, Guv?'

'Just wanted a deek at the river.'

DS Findlay casts him a questioning glance.

'Looks like it's rising, Cam.'

'The flood plain ends at Murrayfield – after Roseburn it cuts through the gorge – it comes up quick, Danny – all these streets, rooftops – there's nowhere else fae the rain to go.'

Skelgill nods pensively.

Another five minutes and they are rumbling across the slippery cobbles of the New Town. As the downpour intensifies, the water begins literally to wash in waves down the hill towards the river at Stockbridge. The drains are simply overwhelmed by the volume, they become boiling springs that add to the flow. DS Findlay casts an arm to his left.

'Chemist who discovered chloroform lived just along there. Simpson.'

'You make it sound like you knew him, Cam.'

DS Findlay chuckles.

'And Robert Louis Stevenson used to play in these gardens as a boy.'

Skelgill grins.

'You should get a Saturday job – tour guide.'

Indeed, at this moment a tourist bus struggles past them up the hill. The open top deck is bereft of passengers, while a few huddled figures crouch in the steamy shadows beneath.

'Here we are.'

DS Findlay pulls up outside the hotel where the Tregilgis & Goldsmith staff are staying. It forms part of an imposing Georgian terrace that runs the entire length of the street – perhaps half a mile in all, mirrored by identical buildings opposite.

'Know anything about the place?'

'Cannae say I do, Danny.'

DS Jones leans forward between the seats.

'Guv – I read about it – it's owned by a celebrity chef, from Berlin – it's one of these trendy boutique hotels.'

DS Findlay switches off the engine. He has double-parked, and this is his private car – he will have to keep a sharp eye out for wardens, for there is no respite on a Saturday.

'Do they ken you're coming, Danny?'

Skelgill shakes his head.

'Didn't want to give them a head start.'

*

But head start they have got.

From reception Skelgill and DS Jones are conducted to meet the manager. His room is a minimalistic affair where two stark black leather sofas mirror each another across a low glass coffee table. He is a German-sounding man with cropped blond hair and looks barely above college age. He wears a collarless black jacket above a black t-shirt and tight jeans, and frameless spectacles in the current mode. His cobalt-blue eyes dwell over-long on DS Jones, and he seats himself opposite her rather than Skelgill.

'The Goldsmith party – they have left for their treasure hunt, Inspector.'

Skelgill looks alarmed. He consults his wristwatch. He had banked on a far more leisurely itinerary.

'When did they go?'

'I believe you have just missed the final pair.' He pulls a tiny mobile device from inside his jacket and presses a pre-set number. 'Trudi – you organised the printing of the Goldsmith admin? Ja – could you please bring a copy – for the police.'

DS Jones glances at Skelgill. It has not escaped their notice that Tregilgis has been dropped from both references made to the company name.

'Trudi' arrives almost immediately. Slim, suntanned and sporting the corporate peroxide-and-black colour scheme, she exudes Teutonic efficiency. She hands the manager a sheaf of papers; he makes a cursory check and passes them on to Skelgill. The girl informs them that these details were emailed through last night and she has printed and collated them into sets. They comprise a series of treasure hunt questions, and a separate sheet with the pairings and their starting times. They have departed at three-minute intervals, starting at ten o'clock. Trudi acted as 'neutral' starter, and to ensure fair play she has their mobile phones safely in her possession.

Skelgill peruses the running order. It begins:

10:00hrs Team 1 – Goldsmith/Rubicon

10:03hrs Team 2 – Goldsmith/Stark

10:06hrs Team 3 – Tregilgis/Morocco

And so on, continuing up to Team 10, which departed at 10:27hrs.

Skelgill's expression darkens as he stares at the combination of names before him.

*

'Get your tour-guide hat back on.'

'What's that, Danny?'

DS Findlay might have been cat-napping; he starts as Skelgill unceremoniously leaps into the car.

'They've gone – we need to find them. They can't be far.'

'What do they look like?'

'They're wearing black rain ponchos – standard issue from the hotel.'

'Which way did they go?'

'That's where you come in, Cam.'

41. THE PRETTY CROSSING

Saturday, 10.40 a.m.

'Aye – it's a treasure hunt.' DS Findlay glances over the rim of his reading glasses at his two colleagues. 'These are clues, see.'

'We know that, Cam!' Skelgill is uncharacteristically exasperated. 'We need you to decipher them.'

DS Findlay takes a second look, muttering under his breath. He pats the papers with the back of his hand.

'This is gobbledegook, Danny.'

Skelgill lets out a hiss of frustration – but DS Findlay is not to blame. He might have an encyclopaedic knowledge of Edinburgh, but he cannot be expected to understand these riddles. The three of them now pore over the first page – DS Jones leaning forward from the back seat. The rain drumming on the roof might be the sound of their brains being collectively racked. The glass is steamed up all around them, heightening the sense of helpless isolation. Skelgill wrings his hands.

'We need to get ahead of the first group – then we can intercept the lot of them.'

DS Jones points to the top of the page.

'It's supposed to last about two hours – so they're probably not even halfway yet.'

'Where's halfway?'

DS Findlay turns the page. There are twenty clues in all. He jabs a stout index finger at clue number eleven.

'What about this?'

He reads aloud:

"*At the pretty crossing below the weir, how many flags fly on the castle – my deer?*"

DS Jones is first to comment.

'Think that's a typo? Deer spelt with two e's?'

They shake their heads uncertainly. Now Skelgill pipes up.

'The *weir*, Cam – how many rivers are there in Edinburgh?'

'In town, just the Water of Leith – nearest point, five minutes' walk down to Stockbridge.'

'What about a weir?'

'Must be a couple of dozen, all along. The flour mills used to be water-powered – the weirs built up a head of water to feed into the lades that served the mills.'

'Aye, aye – okay.' Skelgill's patience is tested. 'The *"pretty crossing"*, then – what does that mean?'

DS Findlay shakes his head.

'Dinnae ken – I've never heard of it.'

'I know that, Cam – it's disguised – but it must ring some bell – come on Cam, think!'

'Well – *"crossing"* could mean bridge – the most spectacular one's the Dean Bridge. And you can probably see the castle frae there.'

'Okay – let's try that.'

They fasten seatbelts and DS Findlay sets his jaw determinedly. He employs his local knowledge to avoid the banks of traffic lights on Queen Street, and instead takes a winding, sliding route over the treacherous wet cobbles. They pass through Royal Circus, and cross the Water of Leith at India Place, giving them a glimpse of the rushing burn, stained brown by the flood. At Dean Bridge, Telford's great sandstone viaduct that soars twelve stories above the water, DS Findlay bumps the car halfway up onto the high kerb. DS Jones volunteers to perform a reconnaissance.

'Under your seat – there's a brolly.'

She heeds DS Findlay's offer – it proves to be a sturdy golf umbrella with a tartan pattern. She peers over the parapet, and looks all around. Then she jogs a little way beyond the city end of the bridge, before returning to the car.

'I can't see anything – no sign of them beside the river – and nothing to fit with the clue – you can't see the castle – even from beyond the bridge.'

DS Findlay's brows become knitted.

'There's another bridge – much older.' He gestures in an upstream direction. 'Down a wee lane – Bell's Brae – just past the end here. You might call it pretty.'

Skelgill nods his assent.

DS Findlay's next couple of manoeuvres are technically illegal, and earn him reproachful honks from affronted motorists.

'Aye – up yer erse.'

Skelgill grins, glad to see his colleague getting into the spirit of battle. Once roused, Cameron Findlay is a man you want in your team. They bump down a steep and narrow causeway into the Dean Village, the historic community improbably crammed into the gorge. The next bridge, low and rugged, is of an altogether more rudimentary construction, and only wide enough for one vehicle to pass. They halt just short of it.

'Thing is, Danny – there's no way of seeing the castle frae down here.'

'What if it's not *the* castle?'

This suggestion comes from DS Jones.

DS Findlay shakes his head doubtfully.

'But there isnae another castle – we've only got the one.'

Skelgill is looking at the buildings around them – more akin to the Old Town, their stones appear hand-hewn and irregular. The planked door of a seventeenth century portal swings open, and a young woman wearing a short fur coat and leather trousers makes a high-heeled dash for a silver 4X4 parked nearby.

'What's on your mind, Danny?'

Skelgill grimaces.

'High bridges – deep waters – I don't like it, Cam.'

DS Findlay nods.

'Aye – we get the odd jumper.' He shakes his head. 'Mainly off the Dean Bridge.'

Skelgill claps his palms together.

'Okay – they're not here. Where's the next bridge?'

'Next one's a wee footbridge – just by the old ford. Couple of hundred yards – you'll see it if you get out here and look upstream. The ford was the drovers' way to market before there were any bridges – you can see the cobbles disappearing intae the burn and coming back out the other side.'

'Cameron.' DS Jones's voice sounds a note of optimism. 'What if crossing means ford?'

'Aye – could be, I suppose.'

DS Jones persists, her crossword-solving skills coming to the fore.

'Is there a pretty ford – a *scenic* ford – a *beautiful* ford – a *belle* ford?'

'Och, aye – there's *Belford* – that's the name of the next main bridge.' He realises his colleagues are looking at him wide-eyed. 'Aye – and now you mention it – it's got these carved stone coats of arms with the castle on them. And there's a weir just beyond it.'

Skelgill is already tearing off his seatbelt and shouldering open the door of the car.

'How do I get there?'

'Aye – well – ye can go along beside the river – or we can just drive round to the top – the road crosses by the old Dragonara – the hotel.'

'I remember it – I did a gig there, once.'

Skelgill slams shut the door, and DS Findlay has to lower the electric window to complete the conversation; Skelgill is itching to run.

'D'ye want the brolly, Danny?'

Skelgill shakes his head.

'I'm faster wet. Streamlined. I'll meet you there – if you see any of their crowd, round them up – keep them safe.'

And Skelgill sprints away.

It takes Skelgill a minute to get his bearings. It is many years since he hiked the length of the river, from its source in the Pentland Hills to its mouth at the Port of Leith. From Dean Path the riverside walkway is accessed either via the footbridge to which DS Findlay referred, or a small detour around an old Victorian school, now converted into apartments. Following his nose he takes the latter course, and finds himself sliding down to the water's edge where the ancient cobbled ford submerges.

As he swings right to pass under the footbridge, he realises that the river has burst its banks – but he plunges in and wades until the ground rises. Starting to jog again, he reaches a roaring weir, ten feet high, its thunderous roar drowning out his footsteps as he runs up the angled pontoon that forms the walkway at this point. Trapped by the backwash beneath the fall bob luminescent tennis balls, punctured footballs, and empty cans of Irn Bru. Clumps of discoloured foam occasionally break away and sail downstream. He tops the weir and accelerates – here the footpath is almost level, a thin ribbon of slick earth that winds beneath the straining ivy-clad trees that inhabit the deep gorge.

He rounds a bend and comes upon a woman in a Mackintosh walking some breed of doodle. The woman steps back to let him pass, but the unfortunate dog needs a haircut and its rain-soaked ringlets obscure its vision. Skelgill has to hurdle it – he mumbles an apology but does not break stride. To his left, what looks like a good ironing board sails past, and an unopened charity bag featuring a picture of a guy in a wheelchair, wearing a climbing helmet and being precariously raised up a rock face.

And now he comes upon Belford Bridge. Though only half the height of the Dean Bridge, it towers a good sixty feet above him – high enough for its parapet to seem indistinct through the sheeting rain and the mist thrown up by the succession of weirs. Indeed, he can hear the roar of the next waterfall, obscured from sight by the great pier on his nearside bank. He slows to a walk, wiping with both hands the rain and perspiration from his eyes and forehead. Overhead, sure enough, one on either side of the centre, there is a stone crest – an heraldic representation of a castle, flanked by the figure of a woman and an animal of uncertain genus – the deer, it must be. On each of the three turrets of the castle flies a pendant. How many flags? Answer: three. He has found the site of the clue.

But of a living soul there is no sign.

To his right a steep flight of uneven steps held in place by cut lengths of railway sleeper leads to the road. Up there, standing opposite, is the hotel – though he knows there is also a river-level access beyond the bridge – the establishment has a kind of pub attached – an old converted granary, in fact – where *Against The Grain* were once booed off stage.

He is in two minds – ahead the walkway forms a raised shelf that runs around the pier of the bridge. If only to gain some respite from the downpour, he moves onto the platform beneath the soaring arch. His shirt is plastered to him like a second skin. The noise of the next weir intensifies, yet as he watches, a familiar Lakeland bird – a dipper, the water ousel – arrows unerringly upstream, its metallic call penetrating the wall of white-water noise.

Perhaps it is this birdcall that sharpens his senses, for suddenly he stiffens. There is another sound – shrill, irregular, and plaintive. What was it he said to Rory Macdonald – a damsel in distress?

*

And perhaps curiously – given the circumstances – Skelgill tiptoes to the end of the studded metal section of walkway and rounds the sharp angle of the pier. But: nobody – nothing, in fact. Immediately on his right, set back about fifteen feet, is the rear of the hotel, its basement level that comes right down to the river, the area between planted out with low ornamental shrubs. From here the building rises seven floors, the upper ones overlooking the bridge itself and Belford Road. Skelgill walks on a few paces, his eyes narrowed as he listens.

Then suddenly he swings about – the cry for help – for that is what it is – comes from behind and above him! Where the wall of the hotel meets that of the bridge, a narrow chimney has been formed, by accident or design. Open at the front, it is faced with stone on its other three sides. It is the sort of feature that a rock climber would die for.

On which rather foreboding note, near its top – perhaps seven or eight feet below the parapet of the bridge – hangs a figure who is clearly not a rock climber. Indeed, it is Julia Rubicon.

Though she is clad in the anonymous long black plastic rain cape supplied by the hotel, one look at the great mass of tangled hair tells Skelgill her identity. And then – again – comes the cry in confirmation. Her eyes are screwed tightly shut – as though she cannot bear to look upon her predicament – and her crimson nails are clinging for all their worth onto a jutting stone above her head. Her feet have the tiniest of footholds, off which they keep slipping, one as soon as she replaces the other. As a startled Skelgill takes in the situation, he wonders by what miracle she has not yet fallen.

'Julia!' He bellows with all of the air his drained lungs can muster. 'I'm coming for you – hold on, lass!'

Rock climbing has never been Skelgill's bag. A little cliquey for his liking – and illogical to be looking *in* at the mountain when the view is *out* – he has nonetheless acquired the basic skills as part of his mountain rescue training. So, it is with no hesitation that he springs to the foot of the chimney and begins to ascend.

'Hold on, lass – thirty seconds is all it takes.'

These words, spoken rather than shouted, seem to be more of an instruction to himself than to the terrified girl, and indeed he must be wary of panicking her. Flakes of stone and mortar shower down upon him – no helmet, of course – each time her foothold is lost. The chimney is relatively straightforward a climb, though generations of pigeons have left deposits, forcing him to take greater care than he would wish at each move.

Sensing his approach, Julia Rubicon seems to become more agitated. Perhaps an end in sight allows her instincts to wane – her

254

consciousness recognises her extreme fatigue. While without Skelgill's approach she might have clung on for many minutes more, now there are only seconds of stamina in reserve. Her cries become moans, her tone helpless, as if the inevitable is upon her.

Skelgill is just a few feet below – and in no mood to hang about, acutely aware that a plummeting Julia Rubicon will take him with her. The last section of the chimney widens out, toughening the ascent – and he realises he will not be able to get alongside her. Instead, he climbs as close as he can manage, and makes a bridge, lurching back across the chimney, so that he is braced directly beneath her. It is a strong stance, but not one from which he can easily escape.

The soles of her training shoes are within touching distance – and it is at this moment that he is thankful she does not wear the provocative stiletto heels of their last encounter.

'Okay, lass – now let go.'

Skelgill says this softly, trying to convey a sense of calm. But Julian Rubicon and calm are on opposite continents, and her whimpers intensify and become mingled with hysterical pleas for salvation. Skelgill must now wonder what he can do. He needs the girl to let go of her handhold – she will slide down, her feet guided by his grip, and they will both be secure. But she cannot let go. She cannot take the leap of faith. Then her nails give way.

In a blur of black her body drops – Skelgill is unprepared for the unscheduled fall – but with all his strength he braces through his feet, legs and hips, and at the same time wraps his arms around her. By good fortune her feet pass on either side of his thighs – soaked and slippery as she is, she would have been impossible to hold on to. He shudders with the impact – but his bridge holds firm – and they remain – two bodies, fifty feet up, jammed in the crevice, she straddling his hips, her cape and skirt rucked around her waist, her upper body pressed against him, her breasts against his rib cage, her hair splayed across his face. There could be worse ways to go.

And now she begins to cry. Great heaving sobs rack her body,

255

she wraps her arms tightly round Skelgill's neck, tears and saliva and mucous smear her face as she blubbers and splutters and tosses her mane of hair in a growing delirium, kissing him, sucking at his mouth and neck and eyes and ears, and all the time trying to utter some words that he cannot discern.

Skelgill wrenches his head to one side. The job is only half done. Taking a deep breath he cries out at the top of his lungs.

'Cameron!'

It must take all of five seconds for the startled face of DS Findlay to appear over the parapet. And not too many more than that for him to disappear, and reappear.

A length of vehicle towrope snakes down the stonework and Skelgill grabs its loose end. He ties a bowline around Julia Rubicon's waist and yells again. The rope tightens and the girl, reluctant at first to let go of him, begins to rise – she is not so heavy, and it appears that DS Findlay alone is able to haul her weight. Skelgill watches anxiously as she flails about, scrambling at the slippery stone walls, and finally toppling over the wall in a jumble of limbs and the flash of scarlet underwear.

As he relaxes to the extent that he may, he hears her voice – more lucid now – and he understands what she was trying to tell him.

'She let go of me... she let go of me... she let go of me...'

Skelgill waits patiently for the rope to reappear. His back is giving him hell, but the stance is solid and he opts to bear the pain rather than risk a slip. He glances below – it is curious how fifty feet up always looks like a hundred feet down. And then a movement catches his eye. Some distance off, padding along the walkway having presumably gained access via the car park adjacent to the hotel, is the unmistakable figure of Elspeth Goldsmith.

Skelgill watches as she creeps cautiously, checking that no one is behind her, nor watching her from any window. She approaches until she is almost beneath him, scanning the ground where the building and the bridge make an angle, and foraging into the waist-high bushes. Not finding whatever it is she seeks she pauses and puts her hands on her hips. Then she looks up.

It is just for an instant that Skelgill sees the sly hunter's face – before the expression changes – yes, first, just fleetingly to that of the harried prey – and then quickly to a face of confused astonishment, as affected as he could ever imagine.

There is a silent standoff as the two regard one another.

And then a second movement attracts Skelgill's attention. Coming towards them at a jog, having taken the same route as Elspeth Goldsmith, is DS Jones. She notices the woman first and slows to a walk – but then she stops dead in her tracks when she spots Skelgill, incongruously wedged near the top of the chimney. His hair is plastered wildly across his brow; algal slime and guano coat his shirt and trousers, water drips from his craggy features. He raises an arm – and, like some menacing Tolkienesque necromancer about to call down a lightning strike, he points a crooked finger at Elspeth Goldsmith. Then, calmly, under the circumstances, he utters the words he has longed to hear himself say.

'Arrest her.'

*

When Skelgill hops down from the parapet and unties the rope from around his waist, he turns to find Julia Rubicon slumped nearby. Though bedraggled and undoubtedly in shock, she has recovered some degree of composure, and her eyes warm to his presence. As DS Findlay indicates he will go to assist DS Jones with her captive, Skelgill lowers himself down beside the shivering girl. She is huddled beneath a tartan rug from DS Findlay's car. Skelgill casts about – at the moment there are no pedestrians, the rain has seen to that – but they must look like a pair of unkempt beggars, hopeful that affluent hotel guests might spare them a few coppers.

He watches DS Findlay stride purposefully down the access road to the rear of the hotel – he has his phone pressed to his ear and no doubt is summoning back-up. Left alone, Skelgill turns to face Julia Rubicon. And now, for the second time in as many minutes, she pitches across and hugs him, burying her head against his shoulder.

'She let go of me – she said she'd hold on while I leaned out and counted the flags on the crest – and then she let go.'

Skelgill is nodding.

'I know what happened.' His tone is soothing, in a grim kind of way. 'You're safe now, lass.'

There is a silence. Despite the rain she seems content to rest in his protective care. Skelgill inhales – and then he speaks quietly, a statement rather than a question.

'You took Krista Morocco's underwear and hid it in Ivan Tregilgis's bed.'

She pulls her head away – a look of anguish in her eyes. Her words come in short gasps.

'I'm so sorry – I'm so sorry – I never meant Miriam to kill Ivan – I just wanted her to know Ivan had a lover – so that I could be with him – oh, no – the last time I saw him – we fought – I'll never be able to say sorry – never.'

She buries her head once more, now it seems in shame at what she has done. But Skelgill lifts her gently away from him, so that she is forced to meet his eyes.

'Julia – Miriam didn't kill Ivan. What you did – it was just a coincidence – it had no bearing whatsoever on his death.' Skelgill reaches out and brushes hair from her face. 'And – take it from me – I reckon he loved you.'

*

During the next few minutes there is a pronounced change of scene. When one moment there is just Skelgill and Julia Rubicon in their little bubble, the next it seems half of Edinburgh converges upon Belford Bridge. Emergency vehicles arrive with their usual disregard for the eardrums. DS Jones and DS Findlay appear from behind the hotel, a protesting Elspeth Goldsmith chattering twenty to the dozen between them. (Skelgill catches a fragment to the effect of, "I warned Julia not to lean out, but she wouldn't listen.") The sound of sirens brings porters and guests spilling from the hotel lobby, and – from the direction of the town centre – along the pavement wanders a bedraggled and distracted Dermott Goldsmith and his treasure hunt partner, Melanie Stark, her eyes on stalks.

Skelgill also notes DS Jones's expression of alarm at the sight of him with an arm wrapped around Julia Rubicon – but a pair of paramedics intervene to assist the casualty into a waiting ambulance. And DS Jones becomes occupied by her own charge, as the volume of Elspeth Goldsmith's complaints increases appreciably when she realises she is being fed into a waiting police car. Seeing his wife manhandled in this manner, Dermott Goldsmith strides up to confront Skelgill.

'Inspector – what the deuce do you think you are doing?'

Skelgill returns Dermott Goldsmith's bluster with a glare of mountainous proportions.

'What I'm doing, Mr Goldsmith, is arresting your wife.'

'What!' Dermott Goldsmith's face turns white. 'This is outrageous. I'm calling our lawyer at once.'

'I suggest you do, Mr Goldsmith – as a common thief and liar, I can tell you you're going to need one.'

Skelgill turns his back on the ugly little man. He walks – with the semblance of a limp – to where DS Jones stands beside the car that holds Elspeth Goldsmith.

'Jones – go with her – watch her like a hawk.'

DS Jones nods.

'Guv – what's the charge?'

Skelgill looks a little surprised by the question.

'Attempted murder of Julia Rubicon. Murder of Ivan Tregilgis.'

*

When Skelgill and DS Findlay arrive at police headquarters about ten minutes later, they are barely inside the building before a commotion attracts their attention. The noise seems to be coming from the ladies' toilets. From the clatter it could be rival hockey teams having a bit of a shindig. Just then a constable comes running from the nearby desk to say that their colleague went in with the suspect, who had asked to use the facilities.

Abandoning protocol the two males throw caution to the wind. They burst into the ladies' to find DS Jones and Elspeth Goldsmith wrestling violently on the tiled floor. The latter's underwear hangs around one ankle, while the former appears to be trying to prise open her adversary's mouth. Elspeth Goldsmith snorts and squeals through flared nostrils, heaving her bulk in an effort to throw off the lighter woman. But what DS Jones lacks in pounds she makes up for in spirit, and – evidently losing patience with the catfight – she lands a cracking short right to Elspeth Goldsmith's nose. This seems to do the trick, for there is a sufficient hiatus for the young sergeant to cry out.

'Guv – in her mouth – there's a note!'

Understanding, Skelgill intervenes, prising open Elspeth Goldsmith's jaws and – indeed – extracting a thick wad of slightly soggy paper.

Now DS Findlay joins the fray, and between them they subdue Elspeth Goldsmith until reinforcements arrive with handcuffs and take her away, spitting feathers and screaming obscenities.

Skelgill carefully unpicks the note.

DS Jones stands at his shoulder, her chest heaving from her exertions.

'I realised she was going to flush it down the loo – then when I stopped her, she tried to swallow it.'

'Bingo.'

Skelgill holds out the creased paper for his colleagues to see.

'What is it, man?'

DS Findlay does not have his reading glasses.

'What it is, Cam – is a suicide note – purportedly from Julia

Rubicon – confessing to Ivan Tregilgis's murder.'

DS Findlay purses his lips.

DS Jones shakes her head. When she speaks, there is perhaps even the tiniest hint of admiration in her tone.

'How neat is that, Guv?'

Skelgill nods slowly.

'She was on her way to plant it when you caught up with her, behind the hotel – except there was nobody there.'

DS Findlay chuckles.

'Aye – no body there.'

42. ROSEBURN

Saturday, 5 p.m.

Heads turn as DS Jones enters the bar. Indeed, the boisterous hubbub of conviviality drops perceptibly, such that Skelgill and DS Findlay look up from their pints. Skelgill rises and strides across to meet and – rather proprietorially, it might be judged – chaperone his female colleague to their alcove.

Cameron Findlay rises, now.

'Emma – what'll it be?'

'Water of Leith?'

The man is about to move away – then he does a double-take and grins at Skelgill.

'She's sharp as a tack, Danny – you've met your match, I tell ye.'

Skelgill grins self-consciously.

DS Findlay reverts to DS Jones.

'Did I mishear, young lady – or was that "water of life"?'

DS Jones smiles engagingly.

'Actually – would you mind if I had a gin and tonic?' She gestures to the men's pint glasses, branded with a saltire. 'Or is that too conspicuously English?'

'Nae worries – you Geordies dinnae count.' And with a laugh he scuttles away to the bar.

DS Jones looks at Skelgill. She blinks a couple of times, and makes the kind of face that speaks of the day they have had. Their rendezvous has finally come to fruition; each of them having taken on different tasks since the culmination of events at the "pretty crossing".

'Guv – by the way. HQ have been on. Apparently Bewaldeth Hall have reported all their knives are missing.'

262

Skelgill regards her as if he thinks she is joking.

'Didn't you wonder what was rattling in the back of my motor?'

She looks at him a little wide-eyed.

'Oh. I see. Wow.' She looks up and smiles gratefully as DS Findlay returns with her drink. 'Your car usually rattles quite a bit, Guv.'

Cameron Findlay interjects.

'I cannae believe you get that through its MOT, Danny.'

Skelgill takes a sup of his beer.

'Sails through every time.'

DS Findlay looks unconvinced, but he has a more pressing query, having eavesdropped from his place at the bar.

'So what's this I hear about a knife? It's about time you let your tour guide in on the story. Are we talking the knife that solved the crime?'

'Dishwasher, actually.'

Skelgill looks from one to the other of his colleagues; he might almost be trying to keep a straight face, were it not for the gravity of the subject.

'This morning – on Bass Lake – I realised I'd left my flask on the dishwasher. Cut a long story short, I'd been thinking about Bewaldeth Hall,' (here he opts to omit the dream about the missing husband) 'and it was around about the same time we were called over there.'

He looks pointedly at DS Jones.

'Remember – you got me out of the kitchen – with the mad Dutch woman?' DS Jones nods. 'She brought tea – the crockery was hot – straight out of the dishwasher. Actually, I'd already noticed it was on.'

His colleagues are listening with a mixture of intrigue and bewilderment written across their faces.

'The dishwasher was on at half-four in the morning. The kitchen staff left at eleven. The longest cycle – and I checked – is two hours and twenty minutes. This is what's been mithering me all along, if only I could have seen it. Add it to Elspeth

Goldsmith's behaviour. Put two and two together, to make –'

DS Jones's eyes have narrowed.

'A knife, Guv.'

Skelgill nods slowly

'The knife that killed Ivan Tregilgis.' Skelgill takes another draught of ale. 'When Elspeth Goldsmith went into the kitchen, it wasn't to feed her face – it was to return the murder weapon – she put the dishwasher back on it hottest cycle.'

'The cheesecake was just her excuse?'

'Aye – if anyone spotted her – who would be surprised? After what we saw of her, we wouldn't have been surprised! Melanie Stark didn't bat an eyelid when she brought her a plate of pudding at three-fifteen in the morning. Next thing, Miriam discovers the murder – and Elspeth shoots along to make sure she gets plenty more of Ivan Tregilgis's blood on her person by supposedly comforting Miriam.'

DS Findlay is shaking his head.

'How come we didnae get the knife?'

Now Skelgill rubs a knuckle pensively against his chin.

'Maybe in another few days we would have.' He glances at DS Jones and raises what might be an eyebrow of relief – the prospect that DI Smart might have overseen such a discovery. 'But there's a kukri goes missing and next thing it's found hidden in a cistern. By the time we realised it wasn't the weapon used on Ivan Tregilgis, we think the killer's taken the opportunity to dispose of it. Meanwhile, nothing reported missing from the kitchen – all the knives present, correct and sterilised.'

DS Jones is shaking her head.

'What a brass neck Elspeth Goldsmith has.'

DS Findlay is curious to know more.

'What about the murder itself – how did she do it?'

Skelgill inhales, and looks around, blinking.

'I doubt it took a minute. All she had to do was wander into the kitchen – pick a knife from the dishwasher – go out through the storeroom – and into Tregilgis's room through the French door. Assuming it was her that had the master key – she'd have been able to unlock it earlier in the evening. That way, she completely avoided the corridor and any risk of being seen entering or leaving Room 10. She was wearing a black dress, tights and shoes – they wouldn't have shown any blood. She returned by the same route – locked the storeroom – and put the knife back in the dishwasher and re-set it. She comes out under the cover of a couple of plates of cheesecake and joins Melanie Stark at the bar. Then waits for the hue and cry to go up.'

DS Jones is nodding.

'Do you think the kukri was planned or a spur of the moment decision?'

Skelgill shrugs.

'Dunno – she'd obviously done a recce on the place – she organises all their events – but it might only have occurred to her when she noticed Krista Morocco messing with it – except she picked the wrong one. Though it certainly put us off the scent.'

'The underwear, too.'

'Aye – and that *was* a red herring.' He shakes his head. 'You were right about Julia Rubicon, Jones. Remember you said she was hiding something? As though she was expecting the questions about it? It was her, alright.'

DS Findlay interjects.

'Why do you think the lassie kept quiet?'

Skelgill has not yet relayed his conversation with Julia Rubicon, while they lay recovering on Belford Bridge, nor a further discussion after she was released from medical care. Now he looks at his colleagues in turn.

'Because she thought she'd caused Miriam to kill Ivan Tregilgis – when it was just her cack-handed attempt to get them to break up. On top of which she was terrified that we'd find out she was in Room 10 and try to pin the murder on her.'

'Danny, so why was Elspeth Goldsmith trying to bump her off?'

Skelgill frowns.

'Combination of factors, I reckon, Cam. First, word of the underwear incident must have reached Elspeth. So, she began to worry that someone might have seen her on the terrace, entering or leaving Room 10. Then Julia Rubicon started acting all withdrawn – and next thing Elspeth receives a blackmail demand – in the mail brought to the office *by* Julia Rubicon. She thinks time is running out for her – so she convinces Dermott Goldsmith that they should hold a second reunion – she sets up the treasure hunt, pretends the hotel have designed the questionnaire – and hatches a plot to make it look like Julia has committed suicide – confessing posthumously to Ivan Tregilgis's murder.'

'Aye, well Danny – ye came up on a whim – but ye saved the life of that lassie, Julia Rubicon.'

Skelgill is reluctant to agree.

'Cam – I reckon self-preservation saved the life of Julia Rubicon. How she hung on in that chimney I'll never know. We just tidied up the loose ends. Or you did – with your rope – without that I reckon we'd have been in trouble.'

DS Findlay grins ruefully.

'I've had it in the boot for a guid ten years – can ye believe that's the first time I've used it.'

Skelgill's thoughts do not need much prompting to return to those moments surrounding the rescue. And, afterwards, when he and Julia Rubicon had passed their medical checks, and were sitting together in an ante room at the Western General. They had both been given a shower and supplied with a hospital dressing gown, although Skelgill had opted to squeeze back into his damp and distressed outfit. Julia Rubicon proved able to converse in surprisingly calm terms – although he had wondered if it was shock that had rendered her surprisingly careless with the rather inadequate garment. That was until, as he had been about to depart, she had offered beguilingly to enlighten him further – if he happened to be staying in Edinburgh tonight?

It must be plain to his colleagues that his mind has drifted.

'Guv – who could have sent the notes?'

He comes out of his reverie to see DS Jones is looking at him intently.

He starts a little, and then makes a dismissive gesture with one hand.

'Don't be surprised if that remains a mystery.'

He is no more forthcoming, but DS Jones wants to press the question.

'I still think Grendon Smith is the most likely candidate.'

Skelgill smiles sardonically.

'Thankfully, that nasty piece of work – and Mr Bunce – we can leave to our friends in the Met.'

DS Jones nods, a little reluctantly it must seem to her colleagues. She inhales to speak, but then hesitates as though she is having second thoughts. Skelgill regards her inquisitively.

'What is it, lass?'

'Krista Morocco – she was waiting to speak to me when I went back to the hotel after seeing Elspeth Goldsmith safely into custody. To be honest I promised her that what she said need not come out – but I think you'll agree, that's fine. She told me she had a miscarriage – that Ivan Tregilgis was the father. This explains the "baby" story we heard about. Apparently, he was all for breaking off his engagement to Miriam. When she lost the baby, she insisted he went through with the wedding. She's never told anyone, to avoid hurting Miriam or her husband.'

Skelgill is listening reflectively.

'Bit ironic that they were paired up for the treasure hunt. Although it did make me think that Elspeth Goldsmith had changed horses.'

DS Jones looks puzzled.

'What do you mean, Guv?'

Skelgill looks first at DS Jones and then at Cameron Findlay, who obliges him with a nod over his pint glass to show he is paying attention.

'She set up Miriam Tregilgis in the first place. Miriam had money to gain, motives against her husband that would come out, and the circumstantial evidence against her was red hot. But Elspeth spotted Krista Morocco with the kukri and realised she could muddy the waters. Then the blackmail note came along and she decided she could kill two birds with one stone. When I saw the pairings for the treasure hunt, I figured it was Julia Rubicon that was in danger.'

DS Findlay has shifted in his seat, waiting patiently during Skelgill's explanation, but now he joins the conversation.

'Talk o' muddying the waters – while you pair were doing your stuff, I had a word with our cold case manager. She wants to re-open the files on the death of Elspeth Goldsmith's wee stepsister. And those of both the MacClarty parents. We might be wanting her back when you've finished with her.'

They all laugh at his black humour, though the prospect is alarming. DS Findlay adds a postscript.

'You had the motive down as greed. But maybe she's just a plain old psychopath.'

Skelgill shrugs.

'Aye – you're probably right, Cam. But there was a catalyst. I reckon she was jealous of Ivan Tregilgis – if only on her husband's behalf. Greed? Lust for power? Putting Ivan Tregilgis out of the way before the sale could go through was worth a lot of money. And I bet she had her eye on a big job for herself. She was crawling all over the company. She must have known Ivan Tregilgis was heading for New York – so it was imperative she acted quickly.'

DS Findlay has another query.

'But you dinnae think they were in cahoots?'

Skelgill shakes his head.

'The Goldsmiths? Nay – I don't. But I don't doubt that Dermott Goldsmith took the document from the briefcase after Ivan Tregilgis was dead. Whether that was to cover his tracks or because he quickly realised there was a more favourable deal to be done, who knows. I expect he'll spill the beans when we threaten him with a charge of accessory to murder.'

For a few moments they sit in brooding silence.

DS Findlay has finished his pint, and gestures to Skelgill's almost-empty glass.

'Same again, Danny? Emma?'

Skelgill raises a palm; it is a gesture of restraint.

'Much as I love your local ale, Cam – I'd better call it a day.' He glances sideways at DS Jones. 'I've got a dinner appointment at nine – I need to keep a clear head.'

There is a flicker of disquiet in DS Jones's hazel eyes. But DS Findlay grins knowingly.

'Aye? And where's that, Danny?'

Skelgill glances away; he sees his self-conscious reflection in a large wall mirror that advertises fine ales. He looks himself in the eye.

'Taj Mahal, Penrith.'

***

Next in the series...

MURDER IN A CLASS OF ITS OWN

When a long-serving master at one of England's most prestigious public schools drowns in Bassenthwaite Lake, Detective Inspector Skelgill is summoned to .... his apparent suicide.

It soon becomes clear that senior members of staff are not all that they seem. As the school closes ranks, Skelgill realises he is pitted against a sinister power struggle for control of its highly lucrative operation.

A second violent death threatens to throw the police off the scent, and the sudden mysterious disappearance of a VIP pupil sows panic in their ranks. In a race against time Skelgill is faced by the unthinkable consequences of a third tragedy on his watch.

'Murder in School' by Bruce Beckham is available from Amazon

FREE BOOKS, NEW RELEASES, THE BEAUTIFUL LAKES ... AND MOUNTAINS OF CAKES

Sign up for Bruce Beckham's author newsletter

Thank you for getting this far!

If you have enjoyed your encounter with DI Skelgill there's a growing series of whodunits set in England's rugged and beautiful Lake District to get your teeth into.

My newsletter often features one of the back catalogue to download for free, along with details of new releases and special offers.

No Skelgill mystery would be complete without a café stop or two, and each month there's a traditional Cumbrian recipe – tried and tested by yours truly (aka *Bruce Bake 'em*).

To sign up, this is the link:

https://mailchi.mp/acd032704a3f/newsletter-sign-up

Your email address will be safely stored in the USA by Mailchimp, and will be used for no other purpose. You can unsubscribe at any time simply by clicking the link at the foot of the newsletter.

Thank you, again – best wishes and happy reading!

Bruce Beckham

Made in the USA
Middletown, DE
10 August 2023